THE VIOLET LIGHT HOUSE

A SPIRITUAL SAGA

Karajah Yashar

Orlando, FL

Acknowledgments

First and foremost, I give all praises to the Most High, for the experiences that shaped me, and for the lessons that continue to unfold along this journey. This story would not exist without His guidance and mercy. Through every trial and every revelation, I have come to understand that the Most High is never finished working on us. Our role is to humble ourselves, surrender to the refining process, and trust His perfect timing.

To the 12 Tribes of the Nation of Israel, whose heritage, struggle, and spiritual awakening continue to inspire the deeper themes within this story.

To Melodie- thank you for seeing something in me that I hadn't yet seen in myself. I was so focused on non-fiction, on delivering information, that I never considered fiction as a way to share this message.

Big thanks to the leadership at Deeper Fellowship. Your lessons and teachings continue to renew and revive!

To my mother, Dorothy- you have always been my biggest supporter. From the beginning, you took it upon yourself to be my unofficial editor, reading, offering feedback, and pouring into this book just as you have always poured into your children, Your dedication means the world to me.

Finally, to every person I've crossed paths with—whether in the church, the conscious community, or anywhere in between—you have each left an imprint on my heart. Your stories, your wisdom, and your presence have inspired and influenced this work in ways you may never know.

Thank you all. This book is as much yours as it is mine.

Table of Contents

Chapter 1

A New Reality

Jayden's family told him to pray. So he did. Morning to night, night to morning, he prayed with everything in him. He didn't just pray—he believed. He believed in a God who listened, a God who saw, a God who would not ignore the cries of a desperate son. At church, hands stretched toward heaven, voices rose in unison, pleading for a miracle. "Have faith," they told him. "God will heal her."

But the more Jayden prayed, the sicker his mother became. He pressed his forehead against clasped hands, whispering the same words over and over. "God is love. He wouldn't do this to me. He wouldn't take my mother away like this." The weight of it all—hope and fear wrestling inside him—pressed against his chest until he could barely breathe.

Then one day, a flicker of light in the darkness. The doctors said her vitals had improved, that maybe—just maybe—she had a chance. And that was all Jayden needed. A chance. A sliver of hope. If he just kept praying, just held on a little longer, God would see this through. At church, the pastor spoke of healing, of prayers answered, of divine mercy swooping in at the last moment. Jayden clung to those stories like a lifeline. Every afternoon, he sat by his mother's hospital bed, whispering reassurances. "They're all praying for you, Mama. You're gonna make it."

Until everything turned.

It was a Tuesday. The kind of Tuesday that started like any other, but would be the one to rip his world apart. Jayden was at school when the call came. His name echoed over the intercom. His older sister Trinity was waiting for him in the office. And before she even spoke, before her lips could form the words, Jayden knew. The knowing started deep in his stomach, curling and twisting like something alive.

By the time they reached the hospital, it was 1:28 p.m. His mother's eyes were open, but she was barely there. He sat beside her, his sisters on either side, their silence saying what words never could. They stayed until night wrapped around the city like a heavy cloak. At 10:48 p.m., his Aunt Patrice came to take him and his younger sister home. His older sister stayed behind.

That night, Jayden didn't sleep. His mind spun, questions circling like vultures. Was God fair? Did God care? Was God even real? Had his pastor, his family, his entire church been feeding him nothing but illusions? He lay in bed, watching the black of night dissolve into the slow, creeping light of morning. Then, at 6:34 a.m., the sound came. A phone ringing. A cry slicing through the quiet like a blade. He didn't need to hear the words. He already knew.

His mother was gone.

The months that followed were a blur of anger, confusion, and a hollow ache that never left. He went to church a few times, but the walls felt smaller, the voices emptier. People tried to comfort him, but their words only dug the wound deeper. "She's with God now," they said. "It's all part of His plan."

What kind of plan was this? What kind of love let a boy lose his mother and left him drowning in grief? Why had they all told him she would be healed? Were they all liars?

Little by little, he stopped going to church. Stopped praying. Stopped trying to make sense of something that made no sense at all. Instead, he went searching for answers. Answers no one in that congregation seemed to have.

And for the first time in his life, Jayden didn't know if he believed anymore.

Jayden sat in front of his screen, his fingers moving fast, his mind moving faster. He had questions—more than he could count—and for the first time, he wasn't looking for answers in a Bible or waiting for a pastor to hand them to him. He was searching on his own. And what he found made his eyes stretch wide.

The internet opened doors he never knew existed, worlds his church had never spoken of. Healing. That's where it started. He typed in words, looking for something—anything—that could have saved his mother. But one search led to another, and before long, he was tumbling down a rabbit hole of knowledge, past religion, past scripture, past the faith he had once clung to. Reiki. Crystals. Meditation. Shamans. Psychic healing. Astral projection. Magic.

Magic.

Jayden sat back in his chair, shaking his head. How had he lived 18 years and never heard of any of this? Why had no one told him? He felt betrayed—by his church, by his family, by the faith that had left him empty-handed when he needed it most. His mother had believed. She had prayed until her last breath. And for what? Nothing changed. Nothing got better. Prayer had failed, but maybe—just maybe—something else could have saved her.

Resentment built slow and steady, curling around his heart like a fist. He stopped going to church, then stopped speaking about church, then stopped speaking to anyone who still believed in it. When he looked at those people, all he saw was ignorance. He blamed the church for his mother's death, blamed the Bible for its lies, blamed Christianity for the way it had kept him in the dark for so long.

He was done with it.

And if he had been blind before, he was seeing now.

For the next five years, Jayden dove headfirst into his search for higher consciousness. He devoured books, streamed lectures, stayed up late watching video after video—each one tearing down the faith of his childhood brick by brick. The Bible? A man-made book full of contradictions. Christianity? A myth forced onto people, especially Black and Indigenous people like him. Every revelation left him more astounded, more angry. He felt like a fool. A puppet. His entire upbringing—his mother's faith, his family's prayers— felt like a joke he was just now getting.

And with every new discovery, he pulled further away.

His family noticed. They called, they texted, they asked questions he didn't feel like answering. They were still trapped in their beliefs, still stuck in a cycle Jayden had outgrown. He wasn't religious anymore—he was enlightened. He didn't believe in some father-figure in the sky dictating his life. He believed in the universe. What was real. What he could see.

Even Jesus, the man he once sang about in Sunday school, was nothing more than a question mark now. Either he had never existed, or he had simply been a man—an enlightened yogi who meditated his way into "Christ consciousness."

Jayden wasn't alone in his thinking.

In college, he met someone who got it—someone who saw Christianity the way he did. His name was Pharoah, a former Christian just like him, and the two clicked instantly. They spent hours together, their minds buzzing, their lungs full of weed smoke, their words laced with the same frustration. How could their families still be so blind? How could they not see what was so obvious? The more they learned, the harder it became to relate to the people they had once loved. They weren't just different now—they were awake.

And then came Jayden's 23rd birthday.

Pharoah leaned in close, a sly smile playing on his lips. "I got something for you," he said. "A conscious event. A whole room full of people like us."

Jayden had no idea that night would change everything.

Chapter 2

The Conscious Tribe

The event pulsed with life, the steady pounding of drums syncing with the rhythm of Jayden's heartbeat. The full moon gleamed through the high windows of the community center, casting a glow over the circle of bodies swaying to the beat. It wasn't just an event—it was an experience. A calling.

At the center of it all stood Inner-G, a man who radiated presence. Dressed in flowing linen, his locks piled high, he moved with the ease of someone who knew he was the main attraction. A self-proclaimed ascended master of Qi Gong and energy healing, Inner-G carried himself like he had the secrets of the universe tucked inside his pocket. He began the night with a libation to the ancestors, pouring water into an earthen vessel, chanting out words Jayden didn't recognize but felt deep in his chest. Then, for 45 minutes, Inner-G spoke—no, commanded.

He wove a tale of energy, healing, and the power within. Nobody had to be sick, he said. Illness wasn't real—it was a symptom of imbalance, a failure to align with the universal frequency. He spoke of people he had healed, bodies he had realigned—cancer, diabetes, things doctors could never fix but he could. Jayden leaned in, hungry for every word.

If only he had known this five years ago. If only his mother had met Inner-G instead of wasting away in a sterile hospital bed.

As the drum circle continued, Jayden wandered through the vendor tables, eyes wide at the treasures before him—raw crystals shimmering under soft candlelight, books that promised ancient wisdom, incense curling in slow-moving tendrils. He was touching a chunk of rose quartz when a voice, rich and warm like honey, pulled his attention away.

"You feelin' the energy of that crystal?"

He turned, and there she was.

Phoenix.

She didn't look like any woman he had ever met. A long, flowing dress that caught the light just right, ankh earrings that swung when she moved, a headwrap that crowned her like royalty. But it wasn't just how she looked—it was how she spoke. With authority, with certainty, like she had lived a thousand lives and held the knowledge of each one inside her. She spoke of universal frequencies, planetary alignments, sound healing, African spirituality—things Jayden had never heard in church, things that made his mind race and his heart flutter.

By the time their conversation ended, they had exchanged Instagram handles and phone numbers. And as if the night couldn't get any better, Phoenix introduced him to Inner-G.

Before Jayden could even speak, Inner-G tilted his head, studied him for a beat, then asked, "You a Leo?"

Jayden's mouth fell open. His birthday was August 10. He didn't need any more proof—Inner-G was the real deal. A true ascended master.

As they talked, Inner-G unraveled everything Jayden thought he knew. He broke down the human body, dismissed Western medicine with a wave of his hand, spoke of energy work and the cosmos in a way that felt like scripture. Jayden listened, rapt, feeling as if he had been walking blind his whole life and was just now beginning to see.

At the end of the night, Inner-G invited Jayden and Pharoah to a conscious hang out house called the Violet Light House to continue the conversation. They didn't hesitate.

By 9:30, the event had ended, but Jayden and Pharoah were still buzzing, high off the energy of the night. As they walked to the car, Pharoah couldn't stop talking about a beautiful yoga teacher he met named Starlight, while Jayden replayed every moment with Phoenix in his head. They had been searching for years—searching for people who thought like them, who saw what they saw. Tonight, they had found them.

A quick stop at Wawa, a 35-minute drive, and soon they were pulling up to the Violet Light House. A small crowd from the event lingered outside, talking, laughing, passing a blunt between them.

Inside, the air was thick with the scent of incense and something else—something herbal, earthy. Inner-G stood in the kitchen, deep in conversation with two men. Jayden scanned the room, but Phoenix wasn't there yet. Still, everything felt right. He and Pharoah sank into the couch, rolling up, taking it all in.

They had found their people.

They had found their tribe.

Around 11:30 p.m., as the night stretched its arms and settled into something slow and easy, Jayden exhaled a steady stream of smoke and leaned back into the couch, his mind still buzzing from the night's energy. And then, just like that, she walked in.

Phoenix.

Jayden felt his chest tighten, his pulse quicken in a way that had nothing to do with the weed. She moved like she belonged everywhere she went, her presence taking up space without even trying. Beside her, another woman trailed—a friend, maybe a sister in spirit—but Jayden only had eyes for Phoenix.

Pharoah caught the shift in the air, grinned, and clapped Jayden on the shoulder. "I see somebody you wanna talk to," he teased, then made himself scarce, giving Jayden the opening he didn't know he was waiting for.

Phoenix slid onto the couch next to him, her scent—a mix of sage, coconut oil, and something floral—wrapping around him like a spell. They started talking, their words falling into each other like they had been doing this for years. Astrology, energy, destiny. She was a Sagittarius, she said, and she swore up and down that Sagittarians and Leos had a cosmic pull toward each other. Jayden, caught in the gravity of her presence, didn't doubt it for a second.

Time slipped away from them. Two and a half hours passed like two and a half minutes. Pharoah eventually wandered back, stretching and yawning, signaling it was time to go. Jayden stood, reluctant, feeling the night slipping through his fingers. He pulled Phoenix into a hug—warm, lingering, a silent promise of something more.

As he and Pharoah walked to the car, Jayden felt like he was floating. The air outside was thick, humming with the echoes of the drum circle, the vibration of something bigger than himself. He knew one thing for sure—this was the best night of his life.

After his mother passed, Jayden and his younger sister had no choice but to pack up their grief and move into his Aunt Patrice's house. Patrice and her husband, Bernard, ran their home with the kind of discipline that came from deep faith. Four bedrooms, two kids—sixteen-year-old Isaiah and twelve-year-old Saraiah—and a whole lot of church.

Faith was the foundation of their household, and for a long time, Jayden had tried to stand on it, too. But now, he thought he saw it for what it was—an illusion, a bedtime story people told themselves to feel safe.

His cousin Isaiah had always looked up to him, but lately, Jayden noticed a shift. Isaiah was starting to listen to him, really listen, questioning things Jayden had long since discarded. Christianity. The Bible. The power of prayer. And that didn't sit right with Patrice and Bernard.

The arguments started small—little comments Jayden would drop, offhand remarks about how Christianity was a scam, how praying did nothing, how their mother's God had been silent when she needed Him most. Patrice, always patient, would sigh and shake her head.

"Keep praying, Jayden," she'd say. "God is good."

But Jayden didn't see any goodness in a God who let his mother suffer. And as much as he loved his aunt, he couldn't understand how she couldn't see it too. How she could still believe after all they had lost.

For Patrice, watching Jayden slip away from faith felt like watching a house she once lived in burn to the ground. She had known him as a boy—sweet, kindhearted, eager to impress the youth pastors with his grasp of scripture. Now, he was a skeptic with a sharp tongue, a college dropout who smelled like weed more often than not. And worse, he was pulling Isaiah along with him.

She prayed for him every night, prayed that the boy she once knew would find his way back. But every time she tried to reach him, he just shook his head.

"I don't need the brainwashing," he'd say, his voice cold, final.

Jayden had found work loading trucks at a warehouse five miles from Patrice's house. It was the kind of job that kept his body busy but left his mind free to wander. He had his 'smoke buddies' at work, but mostly, he stayed to himself or kicked it with Pharoah.

At the warehouse, he had a reputation. The conspiracy theorist. The one who knew about the Illuminati, the toxins in food, the real history behind the Bible. He didn't trust doctors, didn't believe the news, and didn't understand how people could still be so blind.

The Christians at work? Brainwashed. The non-Christians? Lost, drifting, not believing in anything.

Jayden knew better.

He was awake.

The week after the full moon drum circle, Jayden moved through work like a ghost. Conversations buzzed around him, but he wasn't listening. His coworkers' voices seemed thinner now, their words weightless, like leaves blowing past. What was there to say to people still asleep, people who thought life was just clocking in and clocking out, never questioning anything? He had met his people now—real people. And he had met Phoenix.

She was all he wanted to talk to, all he wanted to hear. They spent hours on the phone, her voice drifting into his late at night, her words stretching across the miles between them. They were supposed to meet up, but their schedules kept missing each other, teasing him, pulling him in deeper before he even got to see her again.

One night, between conversations about energy and consciousness, she let something slip. She and Inner-G used to be together.

Jayden paused, rolled the thought around in his mind.

"They still cool, though," she said lightly. "We all family."

And that wasn't all. She had a daughter, three years old, with one of the drummers from the event.

Jayden sat with that too.

But Phoenix didn't seem weighed down by it. She told him about her life like she was telling him about past lives, things that mattered but didn't define her. She was 25, two years older than him. Grew up Christian, but her mother wasn't strict about it—let her find her own way. Her father? Barely there. They spoke sometimes, but only when necessary.

Jayden understood that.

His own father had been a shadow his whole life, moving in and out of prison like a man who couldn't find the right door. Never married Jayden's mother, just lived with her long enough to leave memories that faded at the edges. Jayden remembered flashes—a deep voice, the smell of smoke and liquor, the weight of arms that only held him for a moment before letting go.

His mother had finally let go, too, after his father got locked up for selling coke. That was the last straw. She left, found God, quit smoking. Kept drinking, but just enough to take the edge off. And his father? He kept slipping, getting locked up for this, locked up for that, never long enough to change, just long enough to disappear. Then, at sixteen, Jayden got a call—his father had finally gotten his life together. A real job. A wife. A whole new existence on the other side of the country. And after his mother passed, he'd had the nerve to ask Jayden and his sisters to come live with him.

Jayden had refused before the words even finished leaving his father's mouth.

His little sister chose their aunt. His older sister got her own place.

And that was that.

But now, Phoenix was here. And Jayden felt something different, something real. He'd had relationships before, if you could even call them that. A few short-lived situations, a few nights that didn't mean much by morning. But none of those women had fed his mind, none of them had a vision beyond what was right in front of them. Phoenix was different. She read books that made her think. She questioned everything. She ate like food was medicine, like the body was sacred.

Jayden was changing, too. He had stopped eating red meat, started paying attention to what he put in his body. He thought about all the sickness in his family, the things that could've been avoided if they had just eaten better, taken care of themselves.

At night, he and Phoenix talked until the hours blurred. Sometimes until 2, 3 in the morning. Her voice was the last thing he heard before sleep pulled him under.

One week after they met, Jayden and Phoenix finally made plans. A Sunday morning yoga session in the park. She had been going every week for two years, said it was like church but better.

Jayden had never done yoga before, but he had read about it. Studied it online. It made sense to him— discipline, breath, control over the body. A way to connect with something bigger without bowing to it.

Sunday morning, he left the house early, picked up a yoga mat at the store, then grabbed a muffin and some juice. By the time he got to the park, Phoenix was already there, standing in the sun, laughing with a few of her friends.

She turned when she saw him, smiling.

"Jayden," she said, like she had been waiting on him all along.

She introduced him to her friends, then the session began.

Jayden didn't know exactly what to expect.

But he knew one thing—he was exactly where he was supposed to be.

Jayden hadn't expected yoga to be this hard. He'd watched a few sessions on YouTube, seen people folding into poses like their bodies were made of water, but standing on one leg in a park, legs shaking, arms burning, he felt like he was at war with gravity. And losing.

He was in shape—he hooped a few times a week, hit the gym when he could. But yoga? Yoga was something different. It demanded patience, control, balance. He wobbled, fell out of poses, stretched too far and regretted it. Every now and then, he stole glances at Phoenix, who moved like she had been born for this, her body flowing from one pose to the next, no hesitation, no struggle.

He hoped he didn't look stupid.

When it was finally over, his muscles ached in places he didn't even know existed. But when Phoenix asked how he liked it, he didn't tell her the truth.

"That was amazing," he said, stretching his arms like he hadn't been suffering inside. "I needed that."

Afterward, he and Phoenix sat in the grass with her friends—two men, two women. They talked about clean eating, fasting, zodiac signs, all things Jayden was still learning about but acted like he had known forever. Phoenix spoke like she carried wisdom in her bones, and Jayden hung on every word.

By the time the conversation wrapped up, he and Phoenix were making plans to grab lunch at a vegetarian spot a mile away. He couldn't have asked for a better day.

Over lunch, Phoenix got deep.

"Marriage," she said, twirling her fork through her quinoa, "was created for men. It was never about love. It was about control."

Jayden chewed slowly, thinking. He didn't know if he agreed, but he wasn't about to challenge her.

"I believe in twin flames, though," she continued. "Soulmates. Two people who are meant to live and grow together. But all that traditional stuff?" She shook her head. "Not for me."

Jayden had mixed feelings. His aunt and uncle had a solid marriage, one of the few he respected. But he had seen enough toxic ones to know love didn't guarantee anything. His best friend from middle school—his parents' divorce had torn him up.

Maybe Phoenix was right. Maybe all those breakups and bitter endings happened because people didn't check their zodiac compatibility first. He found himself nodding, trying to sound like he had thought about these things before. But deep down, he felt like a student, and she was the teacher, opening up a whole new world.

When lunch was over, Phoenix had to pick up her daughter. They hugged, said they had a great time, and went their separate ways.

But Jayden carried her words with him.

Chapter 3

The Transition

That whole next week, home didn't feel like home anymore.

He never had much of a relationship with his Uncle Bernard, but his Aunt Patrice had always been different. They didn't see eye to eye, but at least she listened. Still, Jayden found himself pulling away. His little sister? Lost cause—still caught up in church. His cousin Isaiah? He was cool. He could be saved. Jayden felt like he could school him, show him the real truth. But more and more, Jayden was realizing his real family wasn't in that house—it was out there, with Phoenix, with the conscious community, with people who saw the world the way he did.

Pharoah felt the same way. They spent most nights smoking, talking about how asleep everybody else was, how they were the only ones awake.

Then, on a Thursday night, everything shifted.

Jayden came home from work, tired, ready to lock himself in his room. But as he walked down the hall, he heard voices—his aunt and uncle arguing.

And his name came up.

Jayden froze.

Isaiah had been caught smoking, and Uncle Bernard wasn't having it. Said Jayden was a bad influence, said he didn't want him around his son anymore.

Aunt Patrice? She agreed.

Not about cutting him off completely, but she said something about prayer, about love bringing him back to the right path.

Jayden's stomach twisted.

It was one thing for his uncle to judge him—he expected that. But his aunt? The one person he thought understood him at least a little? She was standing on the other side too.

That night, he lay in bed, staring at the ceiling, the words circling his mind like vultures. He thought about his mother. How much he missed her. How much he hated this house.

By morning, he had nothing left to say to his Aunt Patrice. He barely looked at her. Kept his answers short, cold. She noticed.

"You okay?" she asked.

Jayden stirred his cereal, shrugged. "Christians are judgmental."

Patrice sighed. "I'm here for you, Jayden. If you ever need anything."

Then she grabbed her bag and left for work.

Jayden wasn't going anywhere. He called out sick, lay in bed, his mind racing.

Then he texted Phoenix.

Jayden: You free? Need to talk.

Phoenix: My daughter's sick, but if you don't mind germs, come over.

Jayden didn't hesitate. Got dressed, grabbed his keys, got the address.

Phoenix lived 25 minutes away.

As he drove, he felt that familiar mix of nerves and excitement. First time seeing her place. First time meeting her daughter. What would her roommates be like? Would they be as cool as she was?

But mostly, he just wanted to vent. Wanted to tell Phoenix every bitter thing sitting on his chest about his aunt, his uncle, their judgment, their small-mindedness.

When he pulled into her driveway, the first thing he noticed was the Buddha statue by the walkway, a few worn chairs outside, an ashtray full of half-smoked blunts. It wasn't just a house—it was a vibe.

He didn't even have to knock. Phoenix must've heard his car because she opened the door before he reached it.

She smiled, pulled him into a hug.

As soon as he stepped inside, Jayden took it all in. The smell of incense, the walls covered in posters—mystical images, quotes from all kinds of religions. Meditation bowls, drums, a guitar in the corner. Crystals glimmering on an altar. Pipes, ashtrays, smoke lingering in the air. African masks staring down at him from the walls.

The place was messy, but it felt alive.

Jayden exhaled.

Yeah.

This was where he was supposed to be.

When Jayden followed Phoenix into the kitchen, he noticed a little girl perched on a stool, head bent over an iPad, eyes fixed on the screen like the rest of the world didn't exist. She didn't even glance up when they entered.

"Who's that, Mommy?" she asked, still absorbed in her show.

Phoenix smiled and ran her fingers through the girl's thick curls. "That's Baba Jayden."

Jayden blinked. Baba? The word carried weight in the Pan-African community—meant for elders, wise men. At twenty-three, he felt neither. But if Phoenix saw him that way, maybe—just maybe—he could grow into it. The thought settled on him like a warm cloak, unfamiliar but welcome.

He knelt beside the little girl. "What's your name?"

For the first time, she looked up at him. Her father's face stared back—the same deep-set eyes, the same sharp cheekbones. Jayden had seen the man playing the drums at the Full Moon circle. He hadn't known he had a daughter.

"Serenity," she answered softly.

Jayden smiled. "That's a beautiful name."

Phoenix kissed the top of her daughter's head. "Go ahead and keep watching your show, baby, but lay down for a bit, okay?"

Serenity nodded, already turning back to her screen. Jayden followed Phoenix to the living room, where they sank into the couch, the air thick with incense and something unspoken.

Jayden wasted no time unloading his frustrations about his aunt and uncle, the way they talked about him behind closed doors, their suffocating judgment. Phoenix listened, nodding in all the right places, chiming in with her own battles against what she called 'religious conditioning.' Her voice was a balm to his wounds, her words echoing thoughts he hadn't yet found the courage to say aloud.

"The age of Aquarius is shifting everything," she said, passing him the pipe. "People are waking up. You are waking up."

Jayden inhaled deeply, letting the smoke curl in his lungs before exhaling. He could feel it—the shift, the change in himself. He'd arrived at her door angry, but now, his body hummed with something different. Something lighter. The night stretched on with conversation and music, a cocoon of peace wrapped around them.

He didn't leave until 10:30 pm, just as Phoenix's roommates—Afrika and Chronic—walked through the door. They greeted him with casual familiarity, like they'd known him forever. Jayden said his goodbyes, stepping back into the night, back toward a house that no longer felt like home.

Days blurred into weeks. Jayden spent more and more time at Phoenix's, only stopping by his aunt and uncle's to grab a forgotten hoodie, a pair of sneakers, or his headphones. Each time, Patrice tried to engage him, tried to pull him back into conversation, but Jayden kept his words clipped, his visits brief.

"I'm fine."

"Everything's good."

That was all he'd give her.

She saw the changes in him—his distant eyes, his unkempt clothes, the way he carried himself like he was walking through fog. But what could she do? She prayed, hoping he'd find his way back.

Jayden, on the other hand, felt like he was finally walking in the right direction.

Three months after that first visit, he packed up what little he had left at his aunt's house and officially moved in with Phoenix. His 'old self' would have hesitated, held onto the belief that a man and woman shouldn't live together before marriage. But Phoenix made it make sense—marriage was a construct, outdated. Cohabitation wasn't a sin; it was just life. So he let go of that last thread of his past and stepped fully into his new world.

At first, it felt like freedom. Late nights of deep conversation, music vibrating through the walls, smoke curling in the air. No more rules. No more judgment. But the exhaustion set in quickly. Working thirty-six hours a week at the warehouse on four hours of sleep, his body heavy, his mind clouded. His days off blurred into endless wake-and-bake sessions, sunrises slipping past unnoticed.

By the time he saw Patrice again, even she could tell. The sharpness in his eyes had dulled, his once bright future seemed dimmer. He had dreams once—big dreams. A business degree, a nonprofit to help the community. Now, those dreams felt like they belonged to another person.

But Jayden didn't see it that way. He was learning more now than he ever had in church. While his sisters found solace in scripture and prayer, he was uncovering 'real' truth—ancient civilizations, astrology, reincarnation, government conspiracies. His new circle scoffed at Christianity, called it a tool of oppression. And Jayden drank it all in, letting it fill the spaces in him that used to belong to faith.

Every Saturday, Jayden went to Black Pyramid Bookstore, flipping through pages of books on metaphysics and energy healing. Inner-G led the discussions, his voice dripping with knowledge, his presence commanding. Jayden hung on every word, even when they clashed with the convictions he once held dear. Polygamy, sacred sexuality—ideas that would have repelled him before now made sense, wrapped in layers of history and spiritual rhetoric.

The old Jayden would have bristled at the idea of Inner-G sleeping with multiple women, Phoenix included. But the new Jayden? He understood. This was enlightenment. This was evolution.

His transformation was nearly complete.

Nearly.

Since his mother's death, Jayden wrestled with God like a man fighting his own shadow. He no longer believed in the 'Christian' God—at least not the way his aunt did, with her faith stitched so neatly into the fabric of her life. But the question of God still loomed, stubborn and unanswered. If there was no God, then what explained the order of the universe, the way the sun rose each morning, the way the tide knew when to pull back? But if there was a God, why did the world bleed? Why did babies starve? Why did his mother, a woman who had loved fiercely and prayed without ceasing, die too soon?

A few weeks at Inner-G's book club began to shape his thoughts into something solid. Inner-G didn't speak of one God, but many—gods of the sea, gods of the wind, gods of destruction, gods who took and gods who gave. The God of the Bible? Inner-G dismissed him with a wave of his hand, calling him a "spook God," a fiction invented to control people. And Jayden, hungry for answers, found himself nodding along. Maybe there was no benevolent God watching over the world. Maybe there was only chaos and death, and gods who ruled over those forces. At least that made sense. At least that explained why his mother had been taken from him.

At work, Jayden was slipping. Once, he'd been the kind of employee supervisors used as an example— punctual, sharp, ambitious. Now, he was late more often than not, his body sluggish from late nights and hazy mornings. He called out when he felt like it, rolled his eyes when his boss told him to pick up the pace. He used to joke around with his coworkers, but now he barely spoke to them. He saw them as blind, unawakened, still chained to the system. And when his supervisor wrote him up after a heated argument,

Jayden felt nothing but disgust. They were all just puppets. The job cut his hours, shifted his schedule, pushed him to the side. He didn't fight it. He had bigger things to think about.

Money got tight fast. Rent was $300 every two weeks. His car payment was $400 a month. His weed budget? That was creeping up to $100 a week, then $150, then more. When his car started acting up—stuttering at stoplights, making a sound like a dying animal—he took it to a mechanic and nearly choked on the estimate. $800. He thought about asking his aunt but shut that idea down quick. She'd only use it as an excuse to lecture him. Phoenix had the money, but he didn't want to ask her either. She offered. He refused. Instead, he scrapped the car for $400 and told himself it was a win—no more car note, no more insurance. Phoenix could just drive him to work. She agreed, though Jayden could tell she wasn't thrilled. To keep her sweet, he made sure to buy her weed every time he re-upped, sometimes spending as much as $250 a week just to keep their stash full.

Without a car, seeing Pharoah became a hassle. Pharoah had no ride of his own, no real home base. He bounced between his mom's house, his cousin's couch, his girlfriend's apartment, and, when all else failed, Phoenix's living room. Pharoah didn't believe in jobs. He believed in being a king, in being above the grind. He sold weed but smoked most of his own profits, always broke, always talking about how one day, he'd be rich without ever punching a clock. Jayden started borrowing Phoenix's car to pick him up, but that wore thin quick. Three months in, Phoenix was done playing chauffeur.

And that was when everything cracked wide open.

They had fought before—over the toilet seat, dirty dishes, philosophical debates that stretched late into the night—but this was different. This was war. When Phoenix told him she wasn't driving him to work anymore, Jayden saw it as betrayal. How could she claim to be his partner and not have his back? Phoenix, unfazed, hit back harder. Called him a bum, a spiritual baby, a leech. The words landed sharp, cutting away the illusion he had built for himself. He had no car. No savings. No backup plan. He was living under Phoenix's roof, riding in Phoenix's car, eating food Phoenix bought. Where was the king in that?

For the next two weeks, they fought like it was their new full-time job. Jayden spent more nights sleeping on the couch than in their bed. Pharoah started crashing on the other couch, offering quiet, knowing nods whenever Jayden ranted about Phoenix's lack of loyalty. Then, one night, Phoenix ended it. "I'm done," she said, voice flat. "I want you out."

Jayden, pride wounded, shrugged like he didn't care. Told her he didn't need an unsupportive woman dragging him down anyway. But the truth was, he had nowhere to go. And that truth sat heavy in his chest as he sat in the living room, seething, with Pharoah beside him, nodding along in agreement, though they both knew he didn't have any answers either.

The next morning, Jayden woke up with a weight on his chest. It wasn't just the blunt he smoked before bed, or the one he knew he was about to roll—it was the knowing. The knowing that by the end of the day, he wouldn't have a place to call home. His job had already warned him about his absences, but he didn't see the point of showing up today. He had no way to get there, and besides, what did a job even matter when his whole life was crumbling?

He grabbed his phone and called the warehouse early, before anyone could answer, leaving a message on the machine. He wanted to avoid the judgment, the disappointment. That done, he sat back, rolled his standard blunt, and meditated on his next move. His first thought was his aunt and uncle's house, but he dismissed it just as fast. That house carried too much weight, too much history. He hadn't been there in months, barely even spoke to his aunt. He imagined the heaviness of their silence, the unspoken I told you so in their eyes. Nah, he couldn't go back there.

Then, he thought about Inner-G. A man of wisdom, of enlightenment. If anyone would understand, it was him. Maybe even guide him to the next step in his journey. He shot a text: *You free?* Inner-G's reply came quick—*Call me after 3.*

The hours stretched long. Pharoah left early, escaping to the comfort of a less dramatic couch at his cousin's place. The house was silent, except for the occasional shuffle of Phoenix moving in and out of the kitchen, tending to her daughter. They never spoke, never even looked at each other. Jayden felt like a ghost, just waiting for 3:00 to come so he could find out if he had a place to land.

When the time came, Jayden dialed. He gave Inner-G his version of events—how Phoenix had flipped on him, how she was unsupportive, unreasonable. Inner-G listened, letting out the occasional "Women be trippin'" in agreement. By the end of the call, Inner-G gave him the okay. "You can stay for a week," he said. "After that, I got family coming in."

Relief flooded Jayden, but he knew a week wasn't much time. He'd figure something out. He packed a book bag and a tote with clothes, ordered an Uber, and when it arrived, he called out to Phoenix, "I'll be back for the rest of my stuff. Thanks for everything."

As he stepped toward the door, he caught sight of Serenity in the corner, her big eyes watching him. Something about the way she looked at him made his stomach knot up. He forced a smile, waved. "Bye, princess. You be good."

Then he was gone.

Chapter 4

Next Moves

Jayden had never been to Inner-G's house before. He'd usually meet him at the bookstore, at events, or at Phoenix's place. He knew he had his own spot—a two-bedroom house—but not much else. As the Uber pulled up, Jayden noticed the red, black, and green flag in the window, the ankh sticker on the glass. Symbols of consciousness, of power.

He knocked, and it took Inner-G a long minute to answer. When the door finally opened, the smell hit him first—incense, weed, fragrant oils, fresh-pressed vegetable juice. The air was thick with something intangible, something mystical.

Inside, the walls were adorned with posters—Malcolm X, the Black Panthers, images of African gods and warriors. There were altars, statues, bottles of oils and handmade jewelry, the same kind Inner-G sold at events. It was like stepping into another world, a world where Jayden felt small, but also like he belonged.

Inner-G wasted no time. "I wish I could keep you longer," he said, "but I got family coming."

Jayden nodded. "I appreciate this, man."

"You don't owe me nothing," Inner-G said, waving off Jayden's offer of money. "Just soak up the knowledge."

And that's exactly what Jayden did.

Their conversation turned to the topic Jayden had been eager to discuss: multiple wives. Inner-G leaned back, eyes gleaming as he spoke. "We kings, man. We ain't supposed to be working for the man, living under these systems. And we damn sure ain't supposed to be tied down to just one woman."

Inner-G had three children by three different women. Two he saw often, sent a little money here and there. The third—he hadn't spoken to the mother or the child in years. The relationship had ended ugly, and that was that. No ties, no looking back.

Christianity came up, and with it, a sneer. "That slave religion," Inner-G scoffed. "My family deep in it. But I don't talk to them no more. My real family's at Black Pyramid."

Jayden nodded, feeling a swell of agreement. He thought about his own family, how he had cut them off.

"Same, man. I get more love from the conscious community than my own blood."

As Inner-G spoke of African kings and their harems, Jayden closed his eyes, letting the vision take over. He saw himself—a mighty ruler, surrounded by five beautiful women who hung on his every word. Women who raised his children, who honored his presence, who made his world a kingdom.

A slow smile stretched across Inner-G's face. "Yes, my mighty brother," he murmured. "You are King J."

The words sank into Jayden's bones. From that moment on, he wasn't Jayden anymore. He introduced himself differently, made sure his circle knew—he was King J now.

The week flew by in a haze of weed smoke and deep conversations—African civilizations, astrology, ancient healing methods. But as the days dwindled, reality crept in. On the fifth day, Jayden sat back, realizing he had no next step.

His mind flickered back to his aunt and uncle—quickly dismissed. Then, Phoenix—no way. He missed her, but she refused to submit, refused to honor his vision. He needed real queens, not someone who would argue him down.

His circle of friends? No stable living situations. Pharoah was bouncing from couch to couch, Omni was still with his mom, Universe had moved in with his girl.

That left one person—his sister, Trinity.

She was solid. Married, stable. Even if she was lost in Christianity, he respected her. She had a spare room, too.

Jayden picked up his phone and dialed.

Trinity answered with a sneer in her voice. "You must want something."

Jayden chuckled. "Come on now. I can't check in on my big sis?"

"Uh-huh," she said. "What's up?"

He told her his version—how his girl kicked him out, how she made him lose his job.

Trinity wasn't buying it. "Jayden, you been slacking," she said, no sympathy in her tone.

Still, he pushed forward. "I just need a place to stay. Just for a little while, until I get back on my feet."

Silence. Long enough to make his stomach twist.

"I need to talk to my husband," she finally said. "I'll call you back."

Jayden let out a slow breath. "Thanks, sis."

They hung up. Now, all he could do was wait.

That night, at 7:45, his phone rang. Trinity's name glowed on the screen. Jayden stared at it for a second, then swiped to answer.

Trinity didn't waste time getting to the point. She loved her brother, but love came with boundaries. "Jayden, John and I talked, and you can stay, but there are conditions." Her voice was firm but not unkind. She laid them out like a mother laying down house rules for a teenager. No smoking weed in or around the house. No company. Curfew at 11:30. And two months—no longer.

Jayden nodded along, grateful for the lifeline but already calculating workarounds. The curfew? Annoying, but manageable. He'd just have to shift his late-night habits. The no-smoking rule? A joke. He could take his ritual to the park up the street or crack a window. He wasn't about to let their rules cramp his lifestyle. Still, he kept those thoughts to himself. "I got you, sis. I appreciate it," he said, meaning half of it.

The next afternoon, Jayden packed his few belongings—what was left after walking away from Phoenix's place without most of his things. A bookbag, a duffle, a garbage bag full of clothes. He and Inner-G shared one last blunt, the smoke curling between them like a sacred offering. "Man, I'm about to level up," Jayden said, exhaling, eyes half-closed. "Gonna get deep into healing work. Reiki, herbal medicine—the whole thing."

Inner-G nodded in approval, his gold ankh chain glinting against his chest. "That's what's up, King J. Manifest that greatness."

By 3:35, Jayden had an Uber on the way. He wanted to arrive before John got home, before the energy in the house shifted into something else. At 4:15, he stood at his sister's door, greeted by the scent of grilled cheese and baby powder, by the warmth of a home that felt foreign. Trinity answered, Shaniyah on her hip, her smile cautious but genuine. She hugged him, led him upstairs to the guest room.

Immediately, Jayden felt the difference. The room was too neat, too structured—like a hotel room designed for someone else's comfort. The bed, dressed in soft pastels, had an unnecessary amount of pillows. Family photos lined the walls, the air smelled like lavender and responsibility. He sat on the bed, feeling a heaviness settle in his chest. Before he knew it, he had dozed off.

When he woke, it was 6:30, and the smell of dinner called him downstairs. He hadn't planned to join them—felt too groggy, too out of place—but he couldn't start off looking ungrateful. Trinity knocked softly. "Come eat with us."

Downstairs, John was already at the table, his posture easy but upright, the kind of presence that made people sit up straighter. He stood when Jayden walked in, extending a hand. His grip was firm, warm. Not what Jayden expected. He thought there'd be tension, resentment even, for taking up space in his home. Instead, there was something close to respect. It put Jayden off balance.

They sat. Trinity brought the babies to the table. Then John bowed his head and prayed.

Jayden pressed his lips together. He knew the drill—grew up with it—but it felt foreign now, outdated. "In Jesus' name," John closed, and Jayden's whole body tensed. He wanted to laugh, to shake his head at the absurdity. These people with their false religion. He was divine, too. Maybe they should've ended it with "In King J's name." The thought amused him.

When they all said "Amen," Jayden, feeling defiant, said, "Ashe."

John's jaw tightened just slightly. The way a person tenses before responding, before deciding if the moment calls for patience or confrontation. Trinity, more focused on the faint scent of marijuana clinging to Jayden's clothes, didn't react. John held back, choosing small talk instead.

"How you been, man?" His voice was easy, but Jayden could tell he was watching, listening for something deeper.

Jayden wanted to launch into a rant about Phoenix, about her being crazy and ungrateful, but he reined it in. "We had some problems," he said, voice even. "She wasn't who I thought she was." He threw in a casual "crazy" for good measure.

Trinity and John exchanged a look. They had met Phoenix twice. They thought she was... different, but kind enough.

John, still holding onto the Ashe moment, took his shot. "What does that mean, exactly?"

Jayden smirked, enjoying the pushback. "It's an affirmation. One of our ancestral truths, before... well, before the white man erased everything and gave us their God."

John's expression didn't shift, but there was a flicker of something behind his eyes. He wanted to respond, Jayden could tell. But before he could, Trinity gave her husband a warning glance. Let it go. Not tonight.

So John let it sit, nodded. "We'll have to talk more about that." Then, back to his dinner.

That night, Jayden felt restless. No weed, no Phoenix, no Inner-G, no movement. He felt trapped. The walls, the rules, the prayers—it was suffocating. He needed something to ground him, to remind him of who he was.

He went for a walk to the park, rolling his blunt in the dark, inhaling deep. And as the smoke swirled in the air, an idea came to him. He would summon his mother.

He had heard Phoenix and Inner-G talk about calling on ancestors. He never tried it himself, but now felt like the time. When he got back, he rearranged the nightstand, removing his sister's framed family photos and replacing them with a small shrine. A statue of the sun god. A statue of the god of the afterlife. A photo of his mother. A dish of water, candles, incense. He lit the incense and whispered the chants from the book Inner-G had given him.

He closed his eyes, let his mother's face fill his mind. He imagined her speaking, guiding him, reassuring him. The energy in the room shifted, or maybe it was just the weed, but he felt something.

Then came the knock.

"Jayden?" Trinity's voice was hesitant. The door cracked open, and her face shifted from curiosity to concern. "What's that smell?" Her eyes scanned the nightstand. The candles, the statues, the photo.

Jayden could tell she wanted to say more. She wanted to ask what, exactly, he was doing. But she kept her voice measured. "Can you put the incense out?"

Jayden clenched his jaw but complied, exhaling sharply as he pinched the flame between his fingers. Trinity lingered for a moment, as if debating whether to say something else, then turned and left.

Downstairs, she went straight to John. "We need to talk to him," she said.

John, already simmering from the Ashe moment, nodded. "Yeah. We do."

It was late, so Trinity returned to Jayden's room, this time keeping her voice cool and neutral. "John and I want to sit down with you tomorrow. Just talk."

Jayden didn't need to ask what about. He already knew.

"Alright," he said, leaning back against the pillows.

When she left, Jayden grabbed his phone, dialed Pharoah. As soon as Pharoah picked up, Jayden let out a laugh. "Man, my sister and her Christian husband think I'm a problem."

Pharoah laughed too. "They just brainwashed, bro."

Jayden smirked. "Lost in the sauce."

The next day, Jayden stayed in his room on his phone, letting the hours slip past in a blur of videos, music, and games. Around two in the afternoon, he stepped out for a quick walk to the gas station to grab some food, but otherwise, he kept to himself. He exchanged a few words with his sister in the morning on his way to the bathroom, but that was it. John was at work and wouldn't be home until later, which suited Jayden just fine. He wasn't in the mood for small talk or, worse, the kind of serious conversation he knew was coming.

At six-thirty, Trinity knocked on his door, inviting him to dinner. Not wanting to seem rude, Jayden accepted. Downstairs, he gave John a casual fist bump, though his stomach knotted at the thought of what the evening would bring.

Dinner was light, easy—small talk about videos they'd seen, random thoughts, inside jokes. It almost felt normal. But as the plates were cleared, Trinity casually mentioned putting the kids to bed around eight-thirty and asked if he and John would be available to talk afterward. No one had to say what kind of talk it would be. They all knew. Jayden agreed, resigned.

By eight-forty, the three of them gathered in the living room. Trinity started, her voice warm, steady. She talked about how much she loved having Jayden there, how family mattered. Jayden nodded, thanked her again for the hospitality. Then John spoke up, asking if they could pray before the conversation began.

Jayden's body tensed. "Nah, man," he said, shaking his head. "Prayer is fake." He leaned forward, voice gaining edge. "I don't believe in some spook God. If anything, we should be calling on our ancestors."

John didn't flinch. "The Bible says, 'Do not turn to mediums or necromancers; do not seek them out—'"

"Oh, so now you quoting your brainwash book?" Jayden shot back, crossing his arms.

Trinity sighed. "Both of you—let's just listen to each other, okay?" She looked between them, waiting until they both gave small nods. Then she turned to Jayden. "Can you explain what you were doing when I walked in on you?"

Jayden took a breath, then explained—how he had been summoning their mother, how ancestor veneration was part of his African roots, older than the religion they clung to. He spoke for five minutes, maybe more. When he finished, he felt lighter, like, for once, they had actually heard him.

Trinity's eyes softened. "Jayden," she said gently, "our family has been through a lot." She talked about losing their mother, how devastating it had been, how she understood his longing. But their mother, she insisted, was at peace, wrapped in God's love. "God, our Creator, is who we should go to." She shared how she had found comfort in the Holy Spirit, how it steadied her when she felt like she would fall apart. "I remember the joy in you," she said softly. "I don't see it anymore."

Jayden gave a small, half-hearted smile, but something in him stirred.

John picked up from there, talking about the Garden of Eden, about the two trees—Life and Knowledge. "I get it," he said. "You've been learning things, seeing the world differently. But look at the fruit. The people in your circle—are they living righteous lives?"

Jayden bristled at first, ready to fire back, but the question settled in his chest. He thought about Phoenix. He had loved her, or thought he had, but after they broke up, he saw her differently. The way she dismissed chastity, the way she mocked him when he questioned her choices. He remembered the nightmares she had, the anxiety that clung to her like smoke. Then his mind shifted to his other friends—couch surfing, broke, drifting. He glanced at his sister. There was a steadiness in her that he didn't see in Phoenix, in any of the women in his circle. And John—John was solid, clear-headed, confident. Jayden wanted to dismiss it, but the truth pressed against him.

Still, he wasn't going down easy. He cleared his throat. "The Bible is fairy tales," he said, his voice steady. He talked about his spiritual journey, his connection to his ancestors. He made sure to sound respectful—told them he was happy their religion worked for them, but it wasn't his path. "If y'all respect my journey, I'll respect yours."

Trinity and John exchanged a look. Jayden knew that look. They had more to say.

Trinity spoke first. "I respect you, Jayden, but there are things I can't allow in my home." Her voice was calm but firm. "Certain rituals open doors to things I don't want around my family." Jayden scoffed but didn't interrupt. "You can believe what you want, but I need you to respect our house."

Jayden exhaled, slow. He didn't have anywhere else to go. "Fine," he muttered.

The tension eased a little. The conversation shifted—John started talking about work, cracking a joke that made them all laugh. Soon, the night wound down, and they all went to bed.

The next morning, Jayden took down the demigod statues and returned his sister's family photos. As he did, his mind worked over everything John had said. The fruits. The stability. The way his own people—his so-called conscious circle—seemed to be struggling. He told himself it was the system holding them back. But still, the thought nagged at him.

He flopped onto his bed, scrolling through job postings. His money was drying up. He needed work. He filled out an application for a forklift position, then noticed a photo album peeking out from the closet. He knew that album. He had seen it before.

He picked it up, flipping through pages. Pictures of his mother. She looked happy, but now, he could see the illness in her eyes. Pictures of his sisters, of himself. He stared at his own face, the younger version of him. He saw something there—light, joy, confidence. He remembered how he used to feel, full of purpose, full of something bigger than himself. When had that changed?

A lump formed in his throat. Then, before he could stop it, tears spilled over. He hadn't cried like this since the funeral. Some of it was for his mother, but some of it— some of it was for himself. The boy he used to be.

He lay down, exhausted from the crying, and drifted into sleep. And then came the dream.

He was climbing a pole. Pharaoh was at the bottom, egging him on, telling him to go higher. But as Jayden climbed, the pole started to shake. His grip slipped. Pharaoh just laughed. Then Jayden fell. Faster and faster. He thought Pharaoh would catch him, but Pharaoh was gone.

He woke up sweating.

Chapter 5

An Old Friend

Something about Jayden's dream unsettled him. Why did he feel like he was rising, yet more unstable than ever? Why did it feel like the higher he climbed, the closer he got to crashing?

After the nap and all of the crying, Jaden felt a cleansed feeling. For the first time in a long time, he didn't feel like smoking. His mind drifted to Caleb, an old friend from school and church. Someone who actually had his life together. Caleb lived nearby. Maybe, Jayden thought, he'd give him a call.

Jayden hadn't spoken to Caleb much lately. They used to be inseparable, but as Jayden's spiritual journey began to shift, so did his circle of friends. The connection with Caleb had been strained, like the slow unraveling of a thread that once held tight. They still crossed paths from time to time, running into each other at random spots, but Jayden couldn't shake the feeling that they were no longer in sync. Caleb had moved on—he'd graduated with a degree in Social Work, was deeply involved in the church, and had settled into a career as a school counselor. The last time they spoke, Caleb was engaged to his college girlfriend, their future laid out in front of them like an open road. Jayden's own life had taken a very different turn, and Caleb, for reasons of his own, didn't reach out as often either.

Once, Caleb had looked up to Jayden. Back in school and at church, Jayden had been the one everyone turned to—the honor roll student, the prodigy of their youth group with an uncanny ability to unravel the most complex scriptures. Caleb had relied on him, sought his counsel, trusted him. But after Jayden's mom died, things had shifted. The first signs came when Jayden began smoking weed, then came his changing views on God, and the moral compass that seemed to lose its true north. When he started talking about demigods and tantric rituals, Caleb knew then that his friend was no longer walking the same path.

On this day, Jayden made his way to the nearest gas station, grabbed some snacks, and walked to the park. As he sat on the worn bench, the weight of his thoughts hung heavy. He dialed Caleb's number. When Caleb answered, there was a pause, a slight surprise in his voice, as though hearing from Jayden after all this time didn't quite make sense. "Is everything alright?" Caleb asked, genuine concern laced in his words.

Jayden chuckled softly, the sound carrying a hint of irony. "Yeah, everything's cool. Just checking in with my boy."

The conversation drifted into small talk, the kind that fills the silence between old friends who haven't seen each other in a while. Caleb was married now, had been for four months, and was about to become a father. Jayden felt a pang of joy for him, but it was quickly followed by a quiet sadness. He hadn't been invited to the wedding. A dull ache settled in his chest as Caleb shared his news, the life Jayden wasn't a part of. Jayden felt smaller in that moment, like his own struggles—his recent breakup, the job he'd lost, his broken-down car—were just loud echoes in a room full of joy and promise. Hearing Caleb's success felt like a mirror held up to his own uncertainty. He used to be the one Caleb looked to for answers, the one others leaned on. Now, it felt like Caleb had left him in the dust.

But as much as Jayden felt ashamed, a quiet pride stirred within him for everything Caleb had accomplished. He wanted the best for his friend, even if that meant standing on the outside looking in.

When the conversation began to wind down, Jayden found himself hesitating before speaking up. "We should hang out sometime," he said, his voice soft but hopeful.

There was a pause on the other end, a slight hesitation. But then Caleb agreed, his tone warmer now, a bit more open. "Yeah, it'd be great to kick it like old times."

They made plans on the spot to meet at Lake View Park that weekend. And just like that, despite the distance between them, they had carved out a moment to reconnect.

At 10:15 Saturday morning, Caleb pulled up to Jayden's sister's house in a black truck, engine purring like it had something to prove. From his bedroom window, Jayden spotted the ride and squinted. That wasn't the old, beat-up bucket Caleb used to drive, the one that rattled and wheezed like an asthmatic. Jayden pushed aside the curtain, glancing again to make sure it was him. It was. He slid his pipe and lighter into his pocket, then grabbed his hoodie before heading out.

When he climbed into the passenger seat, Caleb gave him a nod, then a fist bump. No words, just that brief connection that said, *yeah, we still cool.* The truck smelled like fresh leather and new beginnings. The dashboard gleamed, the floor mats crisp and spotless. Jayden glanced around, almost embarrassed. He couldn't remember the last time he'd sat in a car that didn't have blunt papers, food wrappers, or somebody's old gym clothes cluttering the floor. Phoenix's car? Man, that thing looked like a crime scene. His old car wasn't much better.

Music played low in the background, a smooth hip-hop beat with a steady groove. But it wasn't the kind of rap Jayden expected—no talk of money, women, or the streets. These rappers were spitting about God, salvation, righteousness. *Christian rap?* Jayden listened for a second. It didn't sound half bad. Different, sure, but not corny like he assumed that kind of music would be.

The drive to Lake View Park took about thirty minutes, and in that time, they caught up—surface level stuff at first. Caleb talked about counseling kids at the school, the ones slipping through the cracks, the ones nobody wanted to deal with. Jayden shook his head, talking about his last job and how they did him dirty. It felt good, in a way, like slipping into an old rhythm.

The park was already alive when they arrived, the morning sun spilling golden light over the shimmering lake. Kids laughed on the playground, couples walked hand in hand, joggers moved in rhythm along the fitness trail. Trees stood tall and strong, their leaves catching the breeze, and benches dotted the landscape, waiting for stories to be told.

They found a spot under a tree near the lake, a picnic table half in the shade. Jayden stretched out his legs and let out a breath, glancing at Caleb. "Man, it's good to see you," he admitted.

"Yeah," Caleb nodded, "good to see you too."

Jayden leaned forward, resting his arms on the table. "Life's been wild, though. You wouldn't believe some of the things I've been getting into." And with that, he launched into the details—Full Moon drum circles, Money Manifestation rituals, vegan festivals, spiritual retreats that promised enlightenment and power.

Caleb listened, his face giving away nothing. Jayden knew him well enough to tell he wasn't sold on it, but he still let him talk. When Jayden finally paused, Caleb took a breath, then tilted his head slightly.

"So why haven't you come to any of the church events?" The question landed between them, heavy but not aggressive.

Jayden chuckled under his breath. He knew this was coming. They both did. They had walked different roads for a while now, and this moment—this conversation— was inevitable.

He sat up straighter, rolling his shoulders back. "Man, let me tell you something. We come from a people that had civilizations long before Christianity even existed. African empires, polytheism, demigods, knowledge that was stripped away when they forced religion on us through colonization. I'm not knocking what you believe, but I'm on a different journey now."

Caleb listened, nodding here and there, but Jayden could see it in his eyes—he was waiting. Holding his words like a man loading a slingshot, ready to fire.

After Jayden finished, Caleb leaned in slightly, his voice even, steady. "Where was the Bible written?"

Jayden scoffed. "Man, you know the deal. King James changed that book. Europeans twisted it, forced it on people—"

"You didn't answer my question," Caleb cut in, not harsh, but firm. "Where was it written?"

Jayden opened his mouth, but Caleb didn't wait. "Africa. The Bible was written on the continent of Africa. Egypt, Ethiopia, Cush—these are all African nations mentioned in the Bible, and even Israel itself is right there on continental Africa, bordering Egypt. The Bible is an African book."

Jayden exhaled sharply, shaking his head, but Caleb wasn't done.

"Who wrote it?"

Again, Jayden went into what he'd learned—King James, the Council of Nicaea, how Jewish elites ran banks and controlled the media.

Caleb let him talk, then shook his head. "Wrong answer, bro." His voice was calm, but it carried weight. "The ancient Israelites were Black, just like the other nations around them. Those European converts to Judaism? No blood relation to the original Israelites. The Council of Nicaea? They didn't remove books from the Bible. It was about Christianizing Roman doctrines and adopting Pagan Easter instead of celebrating the Lord's Passover as Christ and His disciples did. Most people today honor pagan rituals instead of Yahweh's feasts. And King James? He didn't *write* the Bible, he commissioned an English translation of it. From Hebrew and Greek—the original languages.

Jayden leaned back slightly, chewing on the words. Some of it sounded familiar, but some of it... man, he had never heard it put that way before.

Caleb pressed on. "In 70 AD, after Rome destroyed Jerusalem, our people fled. You know where they went? Deeper into Africa. They lived among African nations until centuries later, when the slave trade happened. Our people—Israelites—were sold into slavery by Africans to Europeans and sent to the Americas. You want proof?" Caleb's eyes locked onto Jayden's. "Read Deuteronomy 28:15-68. Look into the Igbo of Nigeria, the Ashanti of Ghana and Togo. The proof is all there."

Jayden wanted to brush it off, to hit him with another rebuttal, something from the conscious community he'd been around. But the confidence in Caleb's voice, the way he wasn't rattled, wasn't flinching—it made Jayden pause.

Instead, he shifted tactics. "Man, you know Christianity was forced on Black people," he shot back, his voice tinged with frustration. "Africans had their own gods, their own systems. Voodoo, medicine men—now all that's demonized by this Eurocentric Christianity."

Caleb let out a breath, nodding like he'd had this conversation before. "Yeah, I used to think that too," he said. "Until I really studied. Not all spirits are good, Jayden. Not all of them are from God. A lot of these African spiritual practices open doors—but not to the Holy Spirit. And divination? That's just trying to manipulate God's plan. Ancestor worship? You're putting trust in created beings, instead of the Creator." He sat back slightly, then added, "Jesus—Yeshua—is the only mediator between us and the Most High. Nobody comes to the Father but through Him."

Jayden stared at him, lips pressed together. He had expected to run circles around Caleb, to overwhelm him with everything he'd learned. But Caleb had come prepared. This wasn't the same younger friend who used to hang on his every word. This was a man who had done his own digging, who had answers Jayden hadn't even considered.

And for the first time, Jayden asked a question—not to argue, not to debate, but because he wanted to know.

"You really think we're the true Israelites?" His voice was quieter now, measured.

Caleb didn't hesitate. "I *know* we are."

Jayden rubbed his chin. "And the proof?"

Caleb met his gaze. "It's all there, bro. You just gotta look. Did you know that over eighty-five percent of males taken from West Africa during the slave trade were circumcised in the flesh? It was, and still is, common across much of the region in places like Nigeria, Ghana, Senegal, Mali, Guinea, and Sierra Leone. Now the million-dollar question, why did the males get circumcised?"

"Read the Bible", Caleb continued. "Scripture says 'This is my covenant which ye shall keep, between me and you and thy seed after thee, Every male child among you shall be circumcised.' That's Deuteronomy 17:10. Hosea 4:6 speaks of a time when 'My people are destroyed for lack of knowledge... seeing thou hast forgotten the law of thy God.' The Father knew there would be a time when Israel would forget its heritage.

"And then there are the prophecies" Caleb continued. "Deuteronomy 28:15-68 describes what would happen to Israel if we turned from the commandments of the Most High. Verse 48 says 'he shall put a yoke of iron upon thy neck'. It goes even deeper. Verse 68 says we would be taken by ships into Egypt, which is today's America, and sold as bondmen and bondwomen. It's all in the Bible"

Jayden sat speechless. He then retreated to a more familiar place as his hands moved on autopilot. Pocket, pipe, pack. He didn't hesitate—didn't even think. This was what he and his people did. Caleb, on the other hand, sat stiff. His jaw tightened as he watched his old friend settle in like this was just another day.

Jayden flicked his lighter, then paused. He caught Caleb's expression—wide-eyed, uneasy. Jayden smirked. "Oh yeah, Christians don't do this type of thing. I forgot."

Caleb exhaled, choosing his words carefully. "Why do you smoke?"

Jayden leaned back, inhaling deeply before answering. "It's natural. God put it here for us—to open our minds, expand our creativity, elevate our spirits."

Caleb had experimented a few times in college, but paranoia wasn't his thing. He shook his head. "God gave us the Holy Spirit for that. That smoke? It blocks Yahweh's signal, opening you up to something else, other spirits."

Jayden waved him off with a lazy hand. "Okay, man." He took a slow drag, eyes drifting toward the lake, his body sinking deeper into the picnic bench.

Caleb watched him, watched the way the smoke dulled his sharp edges. This wasn't the Jayden he used to know—the one who used to be so clear, so quick, so alive. Now, his clothes looked worn, his eyes heavy with shadows. Caleb thought about Jayden's sister who he ran into a few weeks back, how she'd said the same thing. Where had his friend gone?

For a while, silence sat between them. Caleb scrolled through his phone, Jayden stared at the water.

Then, the conversation turned.

"Tell me about that girl you were dating. What happened with that?" Caleb asked.

Jayden perked up. Talking about his "crazy" ex was always easy. He launched into it—how she betrayed him, didn't respect him, didn't appreciate everything he did. "I put gas in her car, made sure she always had something to smoke, and she still took me for granted."

Caleb listened, but his mind worked differently. He didn't understand why Jayden was depending on a woman for rides, why either of them was throwing so much money at weed. He didn't say any of that, though. He knew Jayden wouldn't take it well. Instead, he said, "You need a good, godly woman."

Jayden scoffed. He knew exactly what Caleb meant—a Christian woman. That wasn't for him. He needed someone who was awake, someone who saw beyond the system. "She was enlightened," he said. "She knew a lot about a lot. I need a woman who thinks for herself, not someone just going along with the program."

Caleb didn't argue. He just nodded. "By their fruits, you'll know them."

That phrase hit different. Jayden had been hearing it a lot lately. He glanced at Caleb, really looked at him. His clean-cut appearance, his steady demeanor, the way he carried himself with ease. Then his mind flickered to Pharaoh—crashing on couches, bouncing from woman to woman, broke. Caleb had stability, but Jayden convinced himself that was only because his life was simple. Enlightenment came with struggle. The system wasn't designed for thinkers.

Caleb shifted the conversation again, talking about fatherhood, about his wife, Tamia. About her patience, her kindness, the way she embodied the Fruits of the Spirit.

Jayden's mind wandered to Phoenix, to the way she spoke about sexual freedom. He felt something tighten in his chest—envy, maybe—but he pushed it away. He wasn't Caleb. He wasn't built for that kind of life. He was King J. He'd have a harem of women who followed his lead. The thought settled him, eased the unease creeping in.

"I'm happy for you, man," Jayden said. "Can't wait to meet the baby."

They talked for two more hours, agreeing to stay in touch. That night, Jayden lay in bed, staring at the ceiling. His mind replayed their conversation. Caleb had a job, a wife, a family. He was steady, grounded. Back in the day, Jayden had been the one with all the answers. Now, he could tell—Caleb didn't see him that way anymore. He respected him, sure, but he wasn't looking up to him. Maybe he even looked down on him.

Jayden wouldn't let it stay that way. No, one day Caleb would admire him again. When he had money, power, women. When he had the life he was meant for. He just needed a plan.

And then it hit him—business. Entrepreneurship. His own thing. No boss, no system, no begging for a job. He'd build his own empire.

Lion Heart Healing.

Yeah. That was it. That was the vision. He had the knowledge, the experience. People would come from all over. He'd be respected. He'd be *somebody*.

Lying in the dark, Jayden felt something he hadn't felt in a long time...Hope.

Chapter 6

Lion Heart Healing

Jayden woke up the next morning charged with a new energy. Today was the beginning of everything. He could see it so clearly—his family, Caleb, even Phoenix, the one who called him a bum. They would all have to eat their words. When he became a world-renowned healer, when his name was spoken with reverence, she'd be the one begging to be in his presence. Maybe even to be one of his wives.

First things first—branding. He grabbed his phone and went online to design his business cards. The name had to be bold, undeniable. At the top, in thick, commanding letters, he typed: LION HEART HEALING. Below that, an image—a lion, cross-legged, meditating, bathed in the glow of the sun and moon. Then his name, or rather, the name he gave himself: King J. And beneath that, his title, his declaration: CEO – Master Healer. He added his phone number and stared at the screen, a slow grin spreading across his face. This was it. His path to greatness. He clicked "order" and felt a surge of pride.

The excitement buzzed in him so strong, he had to tell someone. He could hear his sister, Trinity, washing dishes in the kitchen. She'd be the perfect first person—his first supporter, the one who'd see that her brother was a go-getter. An entrepreneur. A boss.

Jayden strode into the kitchen. "What's up, Trinity?"

She turned, hands still wet from the sink. "Hey, Jayden. How's it going?"

He barely let her finish before launching into it—his new business, his title, his mission to heal people from cancer, AIDS, diabetes, all of it. He spoke with the confidence of a man who had already made it. He expected Trinity to light up, to beam with pride.

Instead, her brow furrowed. "So... what kind of certification do you need for this?"

Jayden scoffed. Here we go. "Certifications? That's just the system's way of controlling people. You don't need a certificate to be good at something."

Trinity folded her arms. "Okay, but how are you getting clients? And how's this supposed to make money?"

He sighed, already annoyed. "Word of mouth. Once people see how powerful my healing is, they'll come to me. I don't need a regular job. That's just a distraction."

She shook her head. "Jayden, you need to be serious. You have to find your own place in less than two months."

"I know that." He clenched his jaw, feeling the heat rise in him. "I got it handled." And with that, he ended the conversation.

Still irritated, Jayden stepped outside for some air. He pulled a blunt from his pocket, lit it, and took a slow drag. He needed to talk to someone who *got* it. Someone who saw the vision. He dialed Pharaoh.

The moment Pharaoh picked up, Jayden launched into it—Lion Heart Healing, his title, his plans. Pharaoh, self-proclaimed entrepreneur himself, ate it up.

"Bro," he said, voice thick with admiration. "You about to make things happen, my king!"

That's what Jayden needed to hear. He thought about Trinity's doubt, the way she just couldn't *see*. Maybe he shouldn't have told her. Maybe she was too blind to understand. This only confirmed what he already knew—he needed to stick with *his* people. The conscious community. The ones vibrating on his level.

By the time he hung up, all the hesitation Trinity had put in him was gone. Jayden was locked in.

It had been a few weeks since he lost his job. His last paycheck had come in, but that wouldn't last forever. He needed to move fast. He started walking—destination: the public library. There, he sat down and mapped out his pricing.

- $50 for a half-hour health consultation

- $70 for a Reiki healing session

- $100 for initial treatments for cancer, asthma, or any other ailments

- Continued charges until full healing

He did the math. If he got 15 clients a week, he could make $1,000 easy—way more than any job could offer him. Satisfied, he turned to social media. Instagram, TikTok, Facebook, Twitter. It was time to let the world know about Lion Heart Healing. He had thousands of followers—turning 15 into paying clients would be *nothing*.

He posted for hours, building his empire one click at a time. By the time he finished, he was drained. Between the social media grind, the walking, the weed, and the sheer high of his own ambition, exhaustion hit him hard. He needed a nap.

When he woke up three hours later, the first thing he did was check his phone. He expected his inbox to be flooded. Thirty, maybe fifty messages. Instead—four likes. Two inbox messages.

He swallowed down the sting of disappointment and opened the first message.

@LightLady67826: *Hey! Just learning about Reiki. Do you teach classes?*

Jayden's spirits lifted. He quickly messaged back, listing his prices and offering to set up a call.

The second message? @MarketingMan347. A spammer asking if he needed help marketing his business.

Jayden rolled his eyes.

Then, @LightLady67826 replied. *Oh, I thought it was free. I'm a student, so I can't afford it.*

His fingers hovered over the keyboard. He explained the immense benefits of Reiki, but she never responded.

Jayden leaned back, staring at the ceiling. This wasn't how he imagined his first day of marketing. But he shook it off. Patience. Every great leader started somewhere. This was just the beginning.

Tomorrow, the real work would begin.

That evening, Jayden knew he needed a shot of motivation, something to push back the doubt creeping into his mind. He clicked through YouTube, searching for the right voice, the right message. One after another, the self-help gurus filled the screen, their voices booming with certainty. *Don't give up on your dreams. Stay true to your purpose. Push through the discouragement—success is on the other side.*

Jayden leaned in, soaking it up like a parched man at a well. This was what he needed to hear. This was *truth*. The struggle, the slow start, the silence from potential clients—it was all part of the journey. He wasn't failing; he was just in the early stages of greatness.

Then he found *him*: Milton Money Maker. Sharp suit, gold watch, smooth delivery—Milton spoke like a man who *knew* the road to success because he had walked it. Jayden devoured five of his videos back-to-back, nodding along, feeling the fire return to his gut. By the end of the night, he had ordered Milton's book, convinced it would hold the missing key to his breakthrough.

Success wasn't about immediate results. It was about consistency, about belief, about grinding even when no one was watching. So Jayden made a decision. Tomorrow, he would post again. And the next day. And the next. He wouldn't stop until the world knew his name. Until they came knocking at *his* door, looking for healing.

Jayden lay back, staring at the ceiling, the glow of his phone still illuminating the room. *They'll see,* he told himself. *They'll all see.*

The next morning, Jayden woke up with a name already on his tongue—Inner-G. He didn't need empty hype. He needed real guidance, someone who could do more than just applaud from the sidelines. Pharaoh had given him that surface-level enthusiasm, but Inner-G? Inner-G was the real deal. A decade in the game, five years teaching, and a legend in the conscious community. If anyone could help him take *Lion Heart Healing* from a dream to a movement, it was him.

He grabbed his phone and dialed, heart thudding against his ribs. Second ring, Inner-G picked up.

"Peace, King J."

That greeting always hit different, but today? Today, it felt *earned*. He was making king moves, stepping into his destiny.

Jayden launched into his plans, words tumbling out fast—*Lion Heart Healing, natural remedies, spiritual awakening, energy work*. He could hear Inner-G nodding through the phone, slipping in a "That's what's up" here, a "That's dope" there. But Jayden knew Inner-G wasn't just filling space. He was *listening*.

Then, Inner-G spoke. His voice, smooth but firm. "I'm proud of you, brother. You've come a long way." He let that sit for a second, let it soak in before shifting, his tone sharpening like a blade. "But listen—if you're serious, you gotta tap in for real. It's time to use the power of manifestation."

Jayden had heard talk of manifestation before—*think positive, attract positive.* That surface-level law-of-attraction stuff. But the way Inner-G said it? It had weight. There was something deeper, something locked behind a door Jayden hadn't yet opened. And Inner-G held the key.

"Manifestation is about frequency," Inner-G continued. "You gotta align your energy, your mind, your breath, your whole being. This ain't just hoping for success, King. It's *commanding* it."

Jayden sat up straighter. This was it. This was the knowledge he needed. The kind of teaching that turned ordinary men into masters.

"I'll initiate you into the science," Inner-G said. "Come through tomorrow."

Jayden didn't hesitate. "I'll be there."

He hung up, his mind already racing ahead. Tomorrow, he wasn't just stepping into mentorship. He was stepping into power.

Jayden woke up the next day with purpose in his bones. Inner-G had told him to come by anytime after three, and he wasn't about to waste a second. First, more posts. Then, more research. Then, at exactly 3:00 p.m., an Uber straight to Inner-G's place. He needed to be on time. He needed to be ready.

He spent the next hour flooding his social media with Lion Heart Healing. Videos. Quotes. Testimonials he hadn't actually received yet but knew were coming. Then he dove into the science of manifesting. He read how it was more than wishful thinking—it was psychology, neuroscience, and spirit all rolled into one. You didn't just dream about something. You aligned your thoughts, your emotions, your whole body with it. You *became* it.

At 2:45, Jayden ordered the Uber. By 3:05, he was in the backseat, vibrating with anticipation. By 3:40, the car rolled into Inner-G's driveway.

Inner-G answered the door, his arms wide like he'd been expecting Jayden all his life. "There he is! The big boss! CEO and Founder of Lion Heart Healing!"

Jayden grinned. It felt real. Not just a dream anymore. He *was* this.

Inner-G led him into the living room, where crystals lined the coffee table like sacred relics. He picked one up, turning it between his fingers. "You see this crystal?"

Jayden nodded.

"This is the first step to manifesting." Inner-G leaned in, his voice steady, certain. "Not the crystal itself, but what it represents. Clarity. The beginning of manifestation is a crystal-clear vision of your goal and mission. If you don't see it, how can it ever be real?"

Jayden flipped open his notebook, his pen scratching across the page.

"Next," Inner-G tapped Jayden's chest, "is emotional alignment. Emotion is the fuel. You have to *feel* success, abundance, healing—*before* it happens. The subconscious listens to feelings, not words."

Jayden soaked in every word. Inner-G had this power about him, like he breathed manifestation.

Then, out of nowhere, Inner-G sat back, shook his head, and said, "Man, I don't think this healing thing is for you."

Jayden's heart slammed into his ribs. "Wait, what?"

He barely had time to process before Inner-G burst into laughter.

"Brother, you just failed step three—Belief and Subconscious Reprogramming." Inner-G leaned in, eyes locked on Jayden's. "Doubt kills manifestation. If you don't *truly* believe you can have it, your subconscious will block it. You gotta reprogram that mess—affirmations, visualization, deep meditation. And don't let *anybody* shake your belief. Not even me."

Jayden exhaled, shaking his head, half in frustration, half in admiration.

Inner-G grinned. "Now put the pen down. Time to do some real work."

He lit candles, set incense to smolder, and pulled out a crystal bowl. The first strike of the bowl sent a deep hum through the air, like the sound could reach down and rearrange Jayden's very cells. Three more strikes, then a low, rhythmic chant in a language Jayden didn't understand.

His whole body shivered. This was real. This was deep.

"Close your eyes," Inner-G murmured. "See it. See yourself as a world healer. See people coming from everywhere, seeking *you.*"

Jayden did as he was told. And for the first time, he didn't just see it. He *felt* it. The energy, the power, the certainty of success thrumming through his veins.

This was it. This was the method.

The first three steps and the meditation stretched on for about two and a half hours. By the time they were done, Jayden felt like his mind had been turned inside out and put back together. Inner-G cracked his knuckles, stretched, and said, "We good for today. I'll hit you with the next steps tomorrow." Then, like it was second nature, he reached for the blunt papers and started rolling.

Jayden leaned back, exhaling. His brain was still spinning from everything Inner-G had dropped on him, but the moment that first cloud of smoke curled through the air, he let himself sink into it. They passed the blunt back and forth while watching a documentary about healing in the Black community. Every now and then, Jayden would glance over at Inner-G, admiration flickering in his eyes. *That's that guy.*

The documentary wrapped up an hour later, and Jayden could feel the weight of the day pressing down on him. His body wasn't tired, but his mind—his mind felt like it had been running full speed for hours. It wasn't even eight yet, but between the mental work and the weed, his eyelids started getting heavy.

Inner-G started breaking down the documentary, analyzing every piece, but Jayden was only half there. He nodded when he was supposed to, added a "That's real" here and there, but deep down, he was ready to go. They talked for another forty-five minutes before Jayden finally stretched, slapped his knees, and said, "Aight, brother, I'm about to dip."

Inner-G nodded knowingly. "Peace, King."

Jayden ordered the Uber, and when it pulled up, they dapped up at the door. Then he slid into the backseat and took off into the night, heading back to his sister's house.

As the city lights blurred past the window, Jayden's mind stayed locked on everything he'd learned. *Ain't nothing stopping me now.* He could feel it in his bones—his time was coming. He was about to manifest his greatness.

The Uber pulled up to his sister's house, but instead of going inside, Jayden turned and walked toward the gas station. He needed a pack of blunts before calling it a night.

The moment he stepped inside, he noticed her.

She stood at the counter, holding a pack of blunt wraps, tilting her head like she was trying to decide. Medium-length locs, a Bob Marley tee, jeans hugging her just right. Jayden gave her a quick once-over. *Yeah, she fine.*

Chapter 7

Energy Alignment

The woman at the counter must've felt his eyes on her because she turned, smiling.

"I see you about to get it in," Jayden teased.

She chuckled, holding up a pack. "You ever tried these?"

Jayden glanced at them, shook his head. "Nah, but I got a brand I swear by."

"Yeah? Put me on."

He pointed to his go-to, and she handed her pack back to the clerk. "Lemme get those instead."

Jayden nodded, impressed. She knew how to take advice. Then, out of nowhere, she leaned in slightly and asked, "You know anybody I can get some from?"

Jayden grinned. "Got a solid connect. But if you need something now, I got you."

She smiled. "Bet."

They exchanged names—Sonia. It fit her. Smooth, easy, rolled off the tongue like a song.

After Jayden paid for his blunts, they stepped outside together. The air had cooled a little, the night settling in soft.

"If you wanna smoke now, I'm down," he offered.

Sonia didn't even hesitate. "Let's do it."

They walked to her car, climbed inside, and Jayden got to rolling.

"What's your sign?" he asked as he broke down the weed.

"Pisces," she said, watching him with an amused expression.

Jayden chuckled. "Oh, so you emotional."

She laughed, shaking her head. "Well, I *am* a water sign."

The conversation flowed easy from there. Sonia told him she'd been in town for a year, originally from the coast, living with her family while studying psychology. Jayden liked that—she had goals, a vision.

"Love to see you doing something positive," he said. Then he leaned back, chest swelling a little. "I'm on my grind too. Founder and CEO of Lion Heart Healing." He let the words sit for a second, then dove into everything—manifestation, the training, how nothing was gonna stop him.

Sonia listened, eyes shining. She was three years younger, but she had this look like she *saw* him, really saw him. "That's dope," she said. "I respect the passion."

They swapped numbers before Jayden slid out of the car, heading back to his sister's house. But his feet barely touched the pavement.

He was floating.

He felt like something was divine about this, like she had walked straight out of the universe and into his path for a reason.

Like she was heaven's angel, sent just for him.

The next day, Jayden showed up at Inner-G's house right at four, rested and ready. Today felt different—like something big was about to shift. He could feel it in his bones.

Inner-G was in the kitchen, stirring a pot of something that smelled rich and earthy. "Sit back, relax," he called out. "Bout to put you on some real vital energy today."

Jayden nodded, pulled out his pipe, and took a couple of slow drags before slipping his headphones in. The music washed over him, settling him into the moment. Thirty minutes later, Inner-G stepped out of the kitchen, balancing two steaming bowls in his hands.

"I'm hooking you up, King," he said, grinning as he handed Jayden a bowl.

Jayden hadn't planned on eating, but the thought of real food—something made with care, not a quick grab from the gas station—made his stomach growl in anticipation. "Man, I appreciate this," he said, meaning it.

While they ate, Inner-G broke down the plan for the day. "By the time you walk outta here," he promised, "your frequency gon' be on a whole other level."

Jayden was ready. He wiped his hands, pulled out his notebook, and braced himself for the knowledge that was about to drop.

"Step four: Frequency and Energy Alignment. You see this?" Inner-G said, holding up his phone "I can hit up a brother in Ghana right now, no delay. Why? 'Cause we on the same frequency." He locked eyes with Jayden. "Same thing with your mission. You gotta align your energy with intention."

Jayden nodded, scribbling down notes as Inner-G explained how everything—success, wealth, love—

vibrates at a certain frequency. If you wanted it, you had to *become* it. Surround yourself with the right people, the right environments, the right thoughts.

Jayden's mind flickered to his sister and her dismissive words about his dream. That energy? That doubt? He couldn't afford it. He was starting to realize—he couldn't truly manifest while staying in a place that didn't believe in his vision.

Inner-G reached into his pocket, pulled out a five-dollar bill, and handed it to Jayden.

Jayden took it, slightly confused.

Then, quick as lightning, Inner-G snatched it back. "You ungrateful," he said, sneering.

Jayden blinked. "Huh?"

"I just gave you a five, and you ain't say thank you."

Jayden let out a small chuckle, still not quite sure where this was going.

"That five represents step five: Gratitude as a Magnet," Inner-G said, flipping the bill between his fingers. "Picture this—you hand a friend five dollars. He just takes it, don't say nothing, walks off. You gon' wanna give him more?"

Jayden shook his head.

"Exactly." Inner-G leaned in. "Now, imagine he thanks you, tells you how much he appreciates it, says he's gonna put it to good use. You'd feel good about giving him more, right?"

Jayden nodded.

"That's how the universe works, my brother. Gratitude raises your vibration. The more you appreciate what you got, the more you attract. And not just what you *have*—you gotta feel grateful in advance for what's coming." Inner-G handed the five-dollar bill back.

This time, Jayden took it with both hands. "Thank you," he said, meaning it.

"That's yours. Always remember step five."

Inner-G leaned back, studying Jayden. "Tell me—what you been doing to build your business?"

Jayden sat up a little straighter. "I been posting on social media the past couple days."

Inner-G nodded but didn't look impressed. "That's good, but there's more to it than that." He folded his arms. "Step six—Inspired Action."

Jayden flipped the page in his notebook, ready.

"Brother," Inner-G said, tapping his chest, "your *every breath* has to be Lion Heart Healing. Manifestation ain't about sitting around waiting. It ain't even about just posting online. You gotta *move* toward it. Every step, no matter how small, tells the universe you serious."

Jayden wrote fast, absorbing every word.

Then Inner-G threw him off guard. "You been applying for jobs?"

Jayden hesitated. "Yeah... a couple the other day."

Inner-G shook his head. "See? Right there. That's doubt creeping in. That's you telling the universe, 'I don't really believe my plan A is gon' work, so I need a plan B.'"

Jayden stared at the page, his mind racing.

"If you truly believe in your vision, you gotta *commit* to it," Inner-G continued. "Your every move, every action has to be intentional. That's how you step into your highest reality."

Jayden sat with that for a moment. He knew exactly where that doubt had come from—his sister's words, her skepticism. It had seeped into him without him even realizing.

But now? Now he saw it.

And he wasn't about to let anything—or anyone— shake his focus again.

Jayden looked up at Inner-G, his jaw set.

"Yeah," he thought to himself. "This brother is the truth."

Inner-G leaned back in his chair, hands clasped behind his head, eyes fixed on Jayden. "So," he said, "what's the response been like so far?"

Jayden's voice dipped, the way it did when he was trying to keep his disappointment from showing. "Not too good," he admitted. "I got two messages. One from a spammer. The other from some girl wanting free classes."

Inner-G laughed. "Bro, pick your head up. You thought you was about to be an instant millionaire?"

Jayden let out a chuckle, shaking his head. The way Inner-G said it, like he was pointing out the obvious, made him feel a little foolish for expecting overnight success.

Inner-G leaned forward, rubbing his hands together. "Listen. The next step? Detachment from the outcome. You gotta trust the process. Desperation?" He shook his head. "That's resistance. It blocks what's already making its way to you. When you let go of the how and the when, you allow divine timing to unfold."

Jayden sat with that, thinking back to the letdown he felt after posting for hours and getting almost nothing in return. He could see now—he had been clenching too tight, trying to force results instead of letting them flow.

Inner-G continued, his voice smooth, rhythmic. "A seed don't just hit the dirt and pop up a tree overnight. First, it goes deep, spreads its roots, gets grounded. Then—*then*—it starts to rise. Slowly, steadily, until one day, it's bearing fruit."

Jayden nodded slowly. Yeah. He could see it.

"I see what you mean," he murmured, letting the words sink in.

But as Inner-G kept talking, Jayden's mind started drifting—Sonia. He planned to text her that evening. Just the thought of hearing from her sent a little buzz through him. He had been at Inner-G's house for three hours, soaking up all the wisdom, but now, his body felt restless, ready to move.

"Bro," Jayden said, stretching his arms. "You blew my mind today. I appreciate all this."

Inner-G nodded, eyes warm. "Each one, teach one, King."

Jayden stood, signaling it was time for him to go. Inner-G let him know he had something going on the next day but told Jayden to come back in two days for the final lessons. Jayden agreed, dapped him up, and stepped outside to his waiting Uber.

On the ride back, his thoughts bounced between the manifestation steps and Sonia. Then, like puzzle pieces clicking together, a new idea formed—what if he used these steps to manifest *her*? A great relationship, a deep connection. Why not? Jayden felt untouchable, like he was moving through the world as King J, unstoppable.

When he got back to his sister's house, he spotted his brother-in-law, John, cleaning out the garage.

"What's up, Jayden?" John called out.

Jayden walked over, dapped him up. "Chillin'. What about you?"

John shrugged. "Same old. What you been up to?"

Jayden hesitated. Had his sister already filled John in on his business plans? Was this just small talk, or was John fishing for a reason to doubt him the way she had?

Jayden thought back to what Inner-G had said about surrounding himself with positive energy. He decided to just put it out there. If John was negative, he'd cut the conversation short and keep it moving.

"Man, I got big things happening," Jayden said, lifting his chin. "Just started my own business—Lion Heart Healing."

John raised an eyebrow. "Oh yeah? Tell me about it."

Jayden studied John's face. He didn't seem like he was coming from a place of judgment. Jayden started talking, explaining his mission, his vision. As he spoke, he watched John's body language, trying to gauge his reaction. John nodded along, seeming genuinely interested.

Then John asked, "So, you going to school for that?"

And just like that, Jayden's excitement deflated.

His jaw tightened. "I was born for this. I don't need a school to tell me that."

John held up his hands, like he hadn't meant to step on any toes. "I hear you. Just saying, having some kind of certification might give you more credibility."

Jayden was already halfway out of the conversation. "I appreciate that, man. Imma let you get back to what you were doing."

He dapped John up again and went inside.

The second he hit his room, he flopped onto his bed, pulling out his phone. His thoughts were on Sonia now, nowhere else. He wanted to know more about her. Was she even single? He figured she was—she had smoked with him, after all.

He scrolled to her number and, without hesitation, texted: *What's up, Queen?*

Then he stared at the screen, waiting. A minute passed. Then two. No reply.

She's probably busy, he told himself. She'll text back.

To distract himself, he started scrolling social media, half-checking his business page, but mostly just killing time. An hour went by, and then—

Message alert.

His heart jumped.

Hey King J.

He exhaled, his chest lightening. It felt just as good as he thought it would, hearing from her.

They started texting, conversation flowing easy. They talked about music—both into hip-hop and reggae (Jayden hyped up his reggae knowledge a little more than was true). They talked about food—neither ate pork, though Jayden still messed with shrimp while Sonia didn't. Sonia was an intern at her school's psychology research department and worked at a department store.

After two hours of back and forth, she texted, *I gotta go, but you can call me tomorrow.*

Jayden grinned. *Bet. Good talkin' to you, Queen. We'll talk tomorrow.*

Good night, King.

Jayden set his phone down, smiling to himself.

The next day, he had only two things on his mind—Lion Heart Healing and Sonia.

Pharoah called around 11 a.m., but Jayden let it ring. He'd call back tomorrow. Right now, he was in his zone, and nothing was about to disrupt it.

But then, like an unwelcome guest, a new thought crept in—his savings were running low. Between Ubers and food, money was drying up fast. And if he wanted to take Sonia out, he needed cash.

For a moment, anxiety tightened in his chest. But then he shook it off. He had a plan. He'd hit social media hard today, push Lion Heart Healing, bring in some clients. Even a little income would keep him afloat.

He grabbed his phone and started posting, grinding for the next hour, letting the world know exactly what he had to offer.

Then, just like that, his mind flipped back to Sonia. Where would he take her? He scrolled through ideas, nothing feeling right—until it hit him.

Black Pyramid Bookstore.

She had never been. This was his chance to introduce her to something new. She had mentioned growing up in the church but being curious about Rastafarian culture. Her dad was Rasta, but he lived in the Bahamas, so she only knew bits and pieces.

This? This was perfect. He could bring her into his world, let her see the knowledge he had been soaking up.

The day faded into evening. 7:45 p.m.

Jayden picked up his phone, took a deep breath, and called her.

Butterflies.

The good kind.

"Hello?" Sonia's voice floated through the receiver, smooth, unhurried.

"Hey, what's up, Queen? How's your evening going?" Jayden tried to sound laid-back, but his pulse betrayed him, thudding in his ears.

Sonia exhaled, a soft chuckle threading through her words. "Busy, as always. Classes, my internship, papers—never-ending."

Jayden sighed in solidarity. "I feel you. I been on my grind too." He left out the part where that grind only lasted an hour, the part where he spent the rest of the day picturing his future like it was already carved in stone.

Sonia liked that about him, his independence, his drive. "It's amazing that you have your own business," she said, a note of admiration in her voice. "That takes a lot of guts."

Jayden didn't mention the empty bank account. He didn't say he was still waiting for that first real client. Instead, he leaned into the moment, his pride swelling. "I'm a king, not a pawn," he said.

They talked for hours—astrology, goals, music, family. Jayden told her about his mother passing, but he brushed past it quickly, steering the conversation back to her. She had two older sisters from her dad's side, a younger brother from her mom's second marriage. "My stepdad is too strict," she admitted. "But my dad? He's cool. We talk every now and then."

By the time Jayden invited her to Black Pyramid Bookstore, the night had settled around him like a warm embrace.

"I'd love that," Sonia said.

They made plans for the weekend, and before she hung up, she told him, "This was good. Talking to you."

"Same here." His voice was softer now. He could've stayed on the phone all night, but she had an early morning. They exchanged goodnights, and when the call ended, Jayden lay back, grinning at the ceiling.

He swore heaven had just touched down on earth.

Chapter 8

The Consultation

The next day, Jayden woke up feeling like the universe had him on a direct path to greatness. Sonia. His business. His final manifestation lessons with Inner-G. Everything was lining up.

He grabbed his phone, checked his social media. Three messages. His heart jumped. Maybe his hard work was finally paying off.

The first message? A letdown. Some random user asking if he offered yoga.

"Yoga?" Jayden muttered. "What part of my post said anything about yoga?"

He shook his head, typed a quick "No, sorry," and moved on.

The second message? Spam. Another scammer promising thousands of clients. Jayden let out a frustrated sigh.

But the third message—this one had potential. @HealthyKitty458 was asking about his prices.

Finally. Somebody who understood that life wasn't free.

He sent over his rates. Within minutes, she replied, asking about his location. Jayden didn't have an official space, but he could use the meeting room at the public library. It was close, private, and free. He set up a consultation for the next evening. Gina—that was her name—wanted help healing her asthma.

Just like that, Jayden had his first client.

By the time he pulled up to Inner-G's spot, he was bursting with good news. "Lion Heart Healing is officially open for business!" he declared, dapping Inner-G up.

Inner-G grinned, nodding as he listened to Jayden's excitement. They settled onto the couch, Jayden rolling a blunt, a small gesture of thanks for all Inner-G had taught him.

"Alright," Inner-G said, leaning back. "What's your mission statement?"

Jayden didn't hesitate. "To heal people of their afflictions using natural methods."

Inner-G nodded. "Good. And how many clients you aiming for?"

Jayden had his answer ready. "Fifteen."

Inner-G gave him a look, shaking his head. "See, you not thinking big enough."

Jayden frowned. "What you mean?"

"You picturing average, you get less than average." Inner-G leaned forward, his eyes sharp with conviction. "Picture thousands of people flocking to Lion Heart Healing. Picture a staff. Picture yourself running the whole operation while other people handle the work."

Jayden let that sink in. "Yeah," he said slowly, a vision forming in his mind. "I can see that."

Inner-G pointed to his notebook. "Write this down:

I AM a Healer.
People Need to Heal.
People Need to Come to Me to Heal.
I am a Master.
I AM a Healer.
My Business will Be a Success.
The World Needs My Services.
I AM a Healer.

"Repeat it seven times. Say it seven times in the morning, seven times in the afternoon, seven times before bed."

Jayden nodded. Simple, but powerful.

"Now," Inner-G continued, "you need to make changes for step nine—Environment and Community."

Jayden's stomach twisted. He already knew what was coming.

"You become what you're around. Stay in negativity, doubt, fear—you manifest more of the same. Surround yourself with people on the same vibration."

Jayden exhaled. "I hear you, but I ain't got the money to move out my sister's place."

Inner-G didn't blink. "You can do whatever you manifest."

Jayden didn't argue, but doubt lingered.

Then Inner-G dropped something unexpected. "Violet Light House."

Jayden's brow lifted. He'd been there—people hung out there, smoked, talked consciousness. But live there?

"I already ran it by the squad," Inner-G said. "They cool with you moving in. You won't have to pay rent for two months. Just help out at events, run vending with me."

Jayden sat back, taking it in. He hadn't even been thinking about moving, but the universe had other plans.

"You in?" Inner-G asked.

Jayden grinned. "Man, I'm already packed."

Inner-G clapped him on the back. "Then you just passed step nine."

Inner-G leaned back, arms folded, a quiet smile playing at the corners of his lips. "You made it, man. Nine steps down." He let the moment settle before adding, "But before we get into step ten, I want you to watch something."

Jayden nodded as Inner-G queued up a short documentary about the founders of Cobra Pose, a multimillion-dollar yoga empire owned by a Black couple from the coast. Jayden knew the brand—everybody did—but he'd never given much thought to the people behind it. Now, watching them on screen, he was struck by their discipline, their grind, the way they spoke about failure like it was an old friend they had to shake hands with before they could claim success.

Twenty-five minutes later, the screen faded to black. Inner-G hit pause and turned to Jayden. "That," he said, "is step ten: Consistent Practice and Patience. Manifestation isn't a one-time thing, King J. It's daily. You gotta journal, meditate, do breathwork—whatever keeps you aligned. Stay the course, and the results will come."

Jayden exhaled, looking down at three days' worth of notes scrawled across his notebook pages. Then he met Inner-G's gaze and grinned. "This is it, man. I'm ready to take over the world."

He gave Inner-G a pound, his chest swelling with conviction. This thing was real. He could feel it. Less than a month in his sister's house, and now he was already planning his move out—without ever clocking in for somebody's nine-to-five. He had proven her wrong. Christianity, with all its rules and begging prayers, felt small to him now. He didn't need some invisible God. Shoot, he was a god.

That evening, when he walked into the house, he found Trinity and John sitting at the dining room table, Bibles open between them. Usually, he'd nod, keep it moving, head straight to his room. But tonight, something in him wanted to join them. No, not just join—he wanted to enlighten them.

"Hey," he said, pulling out a chair. "Y'all mind if I sit in?"

Trinity and John exchanged a look. John raised an eyebrow. "Sure, man. We'd be happy to have you."

They were in Matthew 5. John started reading. "Blessed are the poor in spirit, for theirs is the kingdom of heaven. Blessed are those who mourn, for they shall be comforted—"

"That's a lie," Jayden muttered under his breath.

Trinity's head snapped up. John kept reading. "Blessed are the meek, for they shall inherit the earth."

"The weak ain't getting nothing," Jayden said, louder this time.

John closed his Bible. "Did you come to participate or debate?"

Jayden leaned back in his chair, arms crossed. "I'm here to make sure the truth is known."

Trinity let out a slow breath. John met Jayden's stare, calm but firm. "Brother, meekness isn't weakness. It's strength under control. It's humility, discipline. If everybody's out here loud, prideful, and selfish, the world burns."

Jayden smirked. "Or maybe we all just manifest our own greatness."

John shook his head. "You can do great things. But if you don't abide in Christ, it won't bear fruit."

Jayden rolled his eyes. "Ain't no Christ in what I'm doing. Only me, manifesting my divine greatness."

Silence settled over the table. This wasn't going how he'd imagined. He had come to drop wisdom, to open their minds, but instead, he just felt like an intruder in their study. Still, he had one last card to play.

"So," he said, watching their faces, "I'm moving out. Within a week."

Trinity and John glanced at each other. This time, she spoke first. "You're moving out? Without a job? Is there something we don't know?"

Jayden sat up, squared his shoulders. "Yeah, there is. It's called the Science of Manifestation. I don't need a job to make things happen. Y'all don't even realize how the universe works. We manifest things through our own divine selves."

He let the words hang in the air, waiting for them to land. He expected shock, maybe admiration. Instead, Trinity just studied him, then nodded slowly. "Well, I wish you well."

Jayden blinked. That was it? No argument? No disbelief? He hesitated, then pushed back from the table, standing tall. "Alright, I'ma let y'all get back to your Bible. Sorry to interrupt. I got some great things to go manifest."

As he walked to his room, he could feel their eyes on him. He didn't look back. Let them wonder. Let them doubt. Soon enough, they'd see.

The next morning, Jayden woke up with his chest light and his spirit high. Today was the day—Lion Heart Healing was officially in business. He stretched, grinning at the thought, then snatched his phone off the nightstand. He had almost forgotten—he owed Pharaoh a call.

Pharaoh picked up on the second ring. "Peace, King."

"Peace." Jayden wasted no time diving in, running down all the latest—Sonia, the Science of Manifestation lessons, his upcoming consultation with Gina.

"You the man, King J. You really doin' it," Pharaoh said, but there was something off in his voice. A slight drag, like an anchor holding back the full weight of his excitement.

Jayden caught it right away. "You good, bro?"

"Man, I ain't tryna rain on your positive energy, your manifesting greatness," Pharaoh hedged.

"Nah, come on, what's up?" Jayden pressed. If something was bothering his boy, he needed to know.

Pharaoh sighed, then finally let it out. "Man, these women be trippin'."

Jayden exhaled, half laughing. "That's what's got you down?"

"Nah, but for real. My girl found out I been talkin' to somebody else, and now she actin' brand new. Went through my phone, locked me out of my own spot. It's crazy, J. If we was in Africa, they wouldn't be trippin' like this. They'd be sister wives, workin' together instead of against me."

Jayden nodded, half-listening, half-thinking about Sonia.

"I'm just sayin', King," Pharaoh continued, "you gotta make sure this new chick you talkin' to ain't influenced by Western values. You need a woman who's fully submissive."

Jayden thought about Sonia's easy laugh, the way she took his advice on which blunts to buy without question. That was a good sign, right? He wanted to believe she was different. "Yeah, I hear you," he said.

"I hope so, brother."

They talked for another hour, but by the time they hung up, Jayden felt off. Waking up, he'd felt unstoppable, like he was sitting on top of the world. But now, doubt slithered in. Was Sonia really the right one? Would she bring drama into his life like Pharaoh's girl? The last thing he needed was negativity blocking his manifestation.

Jayden shook the thoughts off. No—he had to stay focused. His consultation with Gina was happening today, and that's what mattered. He wasn't getting paid for it, not yet, but that didn't mean it wasn't valuable. He knew how to play the game—offer a taste, just enough to hook them, then reel them in when they needed more.

He spent the afternoon prepping, going over holistic remedies, meditation techniques, and detox methods. He had to make sure he came off as the expert. The key was confidence—he might not have a certification, but he had knowledge.

To pump himself up, he played a video from his favorite influencer, Milton Money Maker.

"You gotta cast sun on the shadow of people's doubts," Milton preached. "There will always be haters, always be skeptics, but they can't block the light. Shadows disappear when the sun shines bright."

Jayden loved that. It was poetic, but real. He repeated the mantra in his head as he packed up his materials. I'm gonna shine so bright, she won't cast a shadow of doubt on my services.

By the time he left the house, he was ready.

The library felt colder than he expected, the fluorescent lights buzzing faintly overhead. Jayden walked straight to the counter, his heart giving a small jump when the librarian checked the reservation.

"Room's available," she said.

Jayden exhaled. See? The universe got me.

He sat at a nearby table, flipping through his notes. All things can be healed through herbs and meditation. Holistic health covers areas Western medicine can't fix.

At exactly 6:45, his phone buzzed.

I'm here.

Gina.

Jayden stood, straightened his hoodie, and walked to the front. As soon as he saw her, he had to check himself.

She wasn't what he imagined.

No profile picture meant he'd filled in the blanks himself. He'd pictured someone young, slim, pretty, a little lost—maybe looking for a man to guide her into health and healing. Instead, Gina was older than him, heavyset, glasses perched on her nose, and standing with the type of posture that said she was all business.

Jayden swallowed his surprise. It don't matter. This ain't about looks. It's about business.

They walked to the meeting room, Gina settling into her seat like she was about to conduct an interview.

Her first question hit like a gut punch.

"So, what exactly is your certification in?"

Jayden hadn't prepared for that. He had rehearsed every other part of the conversation, but not this.

"Well," he started slowly, "my practices go back thousands of years, way before Western certifications even existed. I've dedicated years to studying holistic healing."

Gina nodded, unimpressed. "So, you're not certified." It wasn't a question. "You say you've spent years studying—have you actually practiced herbal medicine before? Do you have testimonials?"

Jayden shifted in his seat. "Yeah, I've helped plenty of people, they can attest to that"

Jayden knew he had helped plenty of people—family, friends, anyone who needed it. He'd given them garlic, ginger, sea moss, lemons—real, natural healing. But would Gina see it that way? Would she respect his knowledge, or was she just another skeptic, blind to the truth?

Gina's face remained unreadable. "What's your experience with asthma?"

Jayden had Googled holistic asthma treatments earlier. He had theories. But actual experience? None.

"Well," he began, sitting up straighter, "asthma, like all illnesses, can be healed through diet and herbs."

Gina's expression didn't change.

He reached into his folder, pulling out a printed diagram. "See, I researched the causes of asthma. It's all connected to—"

"How does chronic inflammation contribute to airway obstruction?" Gina cut in. "And what markers indicate worsening disease progression?"

Jayden's mind blanked.

Damn.

He had no idea what she was asking. He could stall. Buy time. Google it under the table.

"Great question," he said smoothly. "Once we start the services, I'll give you all the information you need." He flashed a confident smile, his tone calm and assured, as if he'd just dodged a bullet.

Gina raised an eyebrow.

"Can you at least explain the involvement of eosinophils, mast cells, and cytokines in my specific type of asthma?" she pressed. "I need to know if these services are right for me."

His mind raced, struggling to come up with another response, while the sweat slowly started to form on his brow. The calm confidence he'd been projecting was beginning to crack. Jayden held onto his script. "Yes, all that will be covered in our treatment."

Twelve minutes in, Gina checked her watch. "Thanks for your time. I'll let you know if I'm interested."

Jayden blinked. That's it? She didn't even use her full 30 minutes.

They shook hands, and he walked her to the door. "If you know anyone else looking for holistic healing, send them my way."

"Okay, thanks." She was already halfway to her car.

Jayden stood there, watching her go, heat creeping up the back of his neck. He told himself she wasn't serious about healing. That she was too stuck in the Western way of thinking to see the truth.

But deep down, he knew.

He was caught fully off guard.

Jayden walked home, his mind looping through that 12-minute consultation like a scratched-up record. Those weren't the questions he'd prepared for. That wasn't the woman he expected. How did he let himself get caught so off guard? He had studied—at least, he thought he had—but she came at him with words and concepts that sounded like a whole different language. Had him stammering. Had him second-guessing. That wasn't supposed to happen.

He straightened his shoulders, inhaled deep. Next time would be different. Next time, he'd be ready. If there was one thing Milton Money Maker drilled into his head, it was that the tough don't fold—they get bold. And Jayden? He was about to get bolder than ever.

He was two blocks from home when he heard a car horn blast behind him. Turning, he saw his brother-in-law, John, leaning out the driver's side window.

"Hop in, man. Looks like you're headed my way," John called.

Jayden hesitated. He wasn't in the mood for small talk, didn't feel like dissecting that mess of a consultation, but a ride was a ride. He slid into the passenger seat, nodding a silent thanks.

"So? How'd that consultation go?" John asked as he pulled off.

Jayden exhaled through his nose. He'd forgotten he even told John about it. Now that he thought about it, he told everybody—his sister, Inner-G, Pharoah, Sonia. Back when he was riding high, convinced this was his moment. Now? Now he wished he hadn't said a word.

"It was cool," Jayden muttered. "She ain't made a decision yet."

John nodded. "Well, I'm pulling for you, man."

Jayden forced a tight smile, staring out the window. He already knew the truth—Gina wasn't interested. But he wasn't ready to say it out loud. Not to John, not to anyone. Maybe—just maybe—the universe would shift things in his favor. Maybe Gina would think it over and see the value in what he was offering.

As soon as they got to the house, Jayden went straight to his phone. A professional follow-up message couldn't hurt, right? He pulled up her name—@HealthyKitty458. Typed it in once. Then again. The name wasn't coming up.

His fingers froze over the screen.

She blocked him.

Chapter 9

Setting a Budget

Jayden sat back, blinking at the phone like it had betrayed him.

Blocked.

A tightness crept into his chest, anger twisting with something he didn't want to name. So that was it? Another brainwashed woman, too caught up in the Western way of thinking to recognize real healing? He shook his head, exhaling sharp through his teeth.

His phone buzzed. Inner-G.

Jayden let it ring.

For the first time, he didn't pick up Inner-G's call.

He already knew what Inner-G wanted—to hear about how the consultation went, to hype him up like he always did. But Jayden wasn't in the mood for hyping. Not tonight.

Instead, he opened his browser and pulled up the latest Milton Money Maker video. He needed something, some kind of energy shift, and Milton always came through.

The video title caught his eye: *Be Like Grease—Slide Through Every Problem.*

Jayden leaned in.

Milton was saying that grease never gets stuck. It slips through cracks, moves past obstacles, keeps flowing no matter what. And that's exactly what Jayden needed to do. Gina the asthmatic tried to stick it to him, but he wasn't about to get stuck. He'd grease up and slide right through.

By the end of the video, Jayden sat up straighter.

He wasn't stuck. He wasn't defeated.

He was just getting started.

The next morning, Jayden sat up in bed, phone in hand, mind spinning with fresh determination. His business posts needed a revamp. This time, he'd make it clear— Lion Heart Healing wasn't certified by man, it was certified by the universe. That way, there'd be no more confusion, no more Gina situations. People needed to know upfront what they were getting.

Satisfied with that, he shot off a text to Sonia. Morning, queen. What you doing?

It was 9:30 AM. He figured she'd be up, but whether she was free was another story. He and Sonia had plans tomorrow, and Jayden felt that low, simmering excitement creeping in. Five minutes later, she texted back.

Hey King J, I'm in class, can talk after 11.

Sounds good, I'll hit you then, he typed back, tossing his phone onto the bed.

Jayden exhaled, then hesitated before tapping open his banking app. He had money—some money—but how much, exactly? He wasn't sure. And he wasn't ready for bad news. Still, he needed to see the numbers. The balance flashed on the screen: $189.45.

Jayden stared. Did the math quick.

Twenty a day on food. Fifty a week on weed. Random Uber rides.

He had about a week's worth of money left. And that wasn't even factoring in what he'd spend on Sonia.

A tightness curled in his chest, but then he heard Milton Money Maker's voice in his head: Your value doesn't come from your bank account. It comes from the vault of your ideas.

Jayden nodded to himself. He had million-dollar ideas, which meant, in essence, he was already a millionaire. And Inner-G always said, trust the process, let the universe provide.

With those two thoughts, Jayden shook off the anxiety. He was good.

When the clock hit 11:00 AM, he resisted the urge to call Sonia right away. Didn't want to look pressed. At 11:04, he dialed.

The phone rang. And rang. And rang.

No answer.

A sharp pang hit his stomach.

Why didn't she pick up?

His mind flashed back to Gina's rejection after the consulataion, and suddenly, Sonia not answering felt heavier than it should have. Ten minutes passed. Then twelve. Then, finally, his phone lit up.

It was Sonia.

"Sorry I missed your call," she said. "Had to talk to my professor about a project."

Relief washed over him. He let out a short breath, made his voice casual. "No problem. Wasn't sweating it."

Sonia didn't waste time. "So how'd your consultation go?"

Jayden had already rehearsed his answer. "She was looking for more Western-based methods. Not really into the holistic stuff I do."

Sonia made a sound of understanding. "Her loss. I know you're good at what you do."

Jayden felt something warm spread through his chest. At last, a woman who supported his vision.

He shifted gears. "You ever heard of the Science of Manifestation?"

"Nah, what's that?"

Jayden smiled. This was his moment. Fresh off his lessons, he was about to impress her, put her on game. "It's about attracting what you desire, bringing things into reality."

"Oh," Sonia said, "so kinda like when the Bible says, 'Ask and ye shall receive, knock and the door will be opened'?"

Jayden paused. He saw where she was coming from, but comparing the universe to a man-made book? It didn't sit right.

"It's like that," he said carefully, "but manifestation doesn't rely on a fake god. It depends on the divine within you."

Silence. Just for a beat.

Then Sonia's voice, quieter now. "You don't believe in God?"

Jayden could hear something in her tone, like he'd brushed against a nerve. He wasn't trying to debate. Not yet.

"It's not that I don't believe in God," he said smoothly. "I just believe we have more power than we give ourselves credit for. We've got divine power within us."

That seemed to satisfy her. Jayden could tell she wasn't looking for a battle either. They both wanted this to go smoothly. No rocking the boat. Not yet.

"Tomorrow at the bookstore," he said, "I'll go deeper into manifestation, all that."

"I'd like that," Sonia said.

They talked for another forty-five minutes, easy and flowing, until Sonia had to get ready for her next class.

"Call me after seven," she said.

"Will do. It was good talking to you."

"You too."

Jayden hung up, leaned back against his pillows, and smiled.

Tomorrow was about to be a good day.

After they hung up, Jayden flipped over onto his stomach, phone in hand, thumb tapping into social media. Consistency was key. That's what all the business gurus said, and he was taking it to heart. Build your brand. Keep showing up.

Five likes. Two new messages.

He used to brush off likes, didn't see the point of them. Likes didn't pay bills. Likes didn't book clients. But now, he was shifting his mindset—likes meant eyes. And eyes meant potential.

He checked his messages.

The first was from @Firesign2365. I'm interested in learning more about your services.

Jayden sat up, blood rushing, heart thumping in that hopeful way. A potential client.

He flexed his fingers, let them hover over the screen for a second before typing back: I am a master healer, studied in holistic wellness. Whatever your illness is, it can be healed through natural methods. What services are you looking for?

He sent it, then closed his eyes and pictured it—
@Firesign2365 booking a session, spreading the word, his business blowing up. He could manifest this. He knew it.

The second message was from @Treehugger4368. This is dope.

Jayden tilted his head, rereading the words. Was it just encouragement? Or another lead? He wasn't about to leave it to chance. He copied and pasted his response, hit send.

One failed consultation wasn't about to stop his healing empire. His mind flashed to the founders of Cobra Pose and how they built from the ground up, took hits, stayed resilient. If they could do it, so could he. He had that same grit, that same fire.

His stomach grumbled, snapping him back to the present. Lately, he'd been spending too much—gas station snacks, quick sub shop runs. Money was tight. Time to adjust.

Peanut butter and jelly. Tuna.

That's how he'd stretch his budget. He could get a can of tuna for just a dollar.

Jayden headed to the store, grabbed bread, peanut butter, jelly, and four cans of tuna. As he walked back, plastic bag swinging at his side, he nodded to himself. A little sacrifice while I build my kingdom.

At 7:06 PM, Jayden called Sonia. Not right at seven—didn't want to seem too eager.

They talked for fifteen minutes before Sonia cut it short. "I got a lot to do," she said. "But I'll see you tomorrow."

That was fine. That was cool. But as soon as the call ended, Jayden felt restless. It was early, and the night stretched ahead of him, wide and empty.

He thought about hitting up Pharaoh, but neither of them had a car.

He thought about going out, but money.

So, he settled on a night in—weed and videos.

His stash was too low for a full blunt, and he wasn't in the mood for the pipe. He needed a plug that delivered.

He scrolled through his contacts. Landed on Bird.

Bird didn't always have the best weed or the best prices, but he was reliable. And right now, reliability mattered.

Jayden hit call. "Yo, I need a twenty."

Twenty dollars wasn't much. Not for what he was used to. But now? Saying it out loud felt different. Like his budget was shrinking by the second.

Bird didn't hesitate. "I got you, bro. See you in ten."

Ten minutes later, the weed was in his hands. Jayden rolled up, cracked the window, and lit up, exhaling slow, careful, watching the smoke swirl out into the night.

His thoughts drifted to Sonia.

He picked a movie—Love Song in the Hood.

Laid back. Sank into it. Let the scenes play out in his mind like a preview of his own life. He was the leading man. Sonia, the love interest. The soundtrack swelling, the chemistry building, the kind of romance that felt real.

By the time the credits rolled, Jayden was halfway to sleep, slipping into his own dream world, where everything played out just the way he wanted.

Tomorrow was another day. Another chance to make it all real.

Jayden woke up with a buzz running through his body, that kind of excitement that made the day feel lighter. He grabbed his phone first thing, scrolled straight to Sonia's pictures.

One of her at work, looking all focused, eyebrows slightly raised, like she was about to call somebody out on something.

One at home, stretched out on her couch, casual, cozy, like she wasn't even trying but still looked good.

And then the third one. The one that made him stop.

Sonia at the beach last summer, sun hitting her skin just right, the curve of her body highlighted in a way that made Jayden exhale slow. Man, she looked fine.

They had plans to meet at 3:00 PM. Jayden had already given her a heads-up: Make sure you eat first. Black Pyramid Bookstore only sold vegan desserts and herbal teas—not real food.

He was relieved he wouldn't have to buy lunch but a little tight about the prices. Six dollars for a muffin? Add in a three-dollar tea, and that's a ten-dollar snack that won't even fill you up. When he came alone, he rarely bought anything, but he knew he couldn't be cheap on a first date.

Alright. A muffin for her. Two teas. Fifteen dollars. Not bad.

Jayden was more excited to show her the spot than anything else. Black Pyramid was more than a bookstore—it was a hub, a place for the conscious and enlightened, where people knew him. He wanted her to see that, to see how he moved in these spaces.

Before heading out, he checked his social media, still hoping for a quick-money miracle. Two new messages.

The first was from @Firesign2365. Jayden sat up. This is it. I know it is. He tapped the message open.

Thank you.

Jayden squinted at the screen. Thank you? That's it? No follow-up, no commitment? He inhaled, then typed back:

You're welcome. Would you like to schedule a consultation?

This was the part he hated—people tiptoeing, half-interested, wasting his time. He didn't want thanks. He wanted bookings.

Be like grease, he told himself. Keep sliding through.

The next message was from @Kryptcard7209, some spiel about crypto. Not today. He deleted it without a second thought.

As the day moved forward, so did Jayden.

1:00 PM – He made a tuna sandwich, something simple to hold him over. 2:00 PM – Ordered his Uber. 2:20 PM – The car pulled up, and Jayden slid in, tapping his knee. Let's get it.

When he got to Black Pyramid at 2:45 PM, he felt good. He wanted to be there before Sonia, pick a table, set the tone.

He glanced around. The only people he recognized were Zeda, one of the cashiers he'd chopped it up with before, and Prime. Prime was always around—at the bookstore, at events. They had built a cool vibe over time.

Jayden dapped him up. "Meeting a queen," he said, grinning.

Prime nodded, approval in his eyes. "Enjoy, bro." Then he went back to flipping through a book.

Jayden checked his phone. 2:55 PM. A text from Sonia popped up.

Running 15 minutes late.

No problem, Jayden texted back. I'm sitting at the table next to the snack bar. See you soon.

He leaned back, scrolling mindlessly. Another message from @Firesign2365.

I'll let you know.

Jayden rolled his eyes. What does that even mean? Either you want the service or you don't. He exhaled, shook it off. Whatever. I got a fine queen walking through that door any minute now.

And then—at 3:20 PM, she did.

Chapter 10

The Date

Jayden saw Sonia before she saw him.

She stepped in wearing a tight-fitted T-shirt with the Ethiopian Lion of Judah stretched across her chest, dark blue jeans hugging her curves, sandals on her feet, and a head wrap covering her locs like a crown.

Jayden felt his breath slow.

Man, she looked good.

He waved her over. She smiled—that smile—and walked toward him, smooth, unbothered, like she knew the effect she had.

When they hugged, a scent wrapped around him—sweet, warm, maybe sandalwood. It clung to the air between them, stirred something low in his gut.

He pulled back, held her eyes for a second longer than usual.

This was about to be a good date.

"I like your shirt," Jayden said, nodding toward the bold lion emblazoned across her chest. "Looks like you're representing for Lion Heart Healing."

Sonia laughed, her eyes lighting up. "You know it."

He knew the Lion of Judah was a big symbol in Rasta culture, especially around places like Black Pyramid Bookstore. Plenty of Rastas came through, talking liberation, chanting scriptures, burning incense. But he wasn't exactly sure what the lion meant to them. He knew Jesus was called the Lion of Judah from his church days, but that connection? Fuzzy. And he wasn't about to let on. He'd brought her here to impress her with his wisdom, not to get schooled.

"Do you know about the Lion of Judah?" Sonia asked, tilting her head, testing him.

Jayden nodded coolly. "Sure. It'll break every chain." He'd heard that line in a Bob Marley song. He just hoped she didn't press him for details.

"That's right." Sonia snapped her fingers. "Every chain."

Jayden exhaled. So far, so good.

"You want anything?" he asked, figuring food would shift the conversation to safer ground.

Sonia's face lit up. "That would be great. I love vegan junk food."

They both laughed as they stepped to the counter. She studied the menu like a scholar, eyes darting back and forth, reading each item with intent. "This all looks so good," she mused. "I wanna try everything."

Jayden chuckled, but inside, his stomach tightened. How much was 'everything' about to cost?

"I'll take the kale chips, the energy balls, and the vegan muffin," Sonia said, grinning like a kid in a candy store.

"Wow, three things?" Jayden thought, feeling his wallet get lighter by the second.

"I can buy my own," she offered, noticing his hesitation.

"Nah," he said quickly, shaking his head. "I got you, Queen."

Part of him wanted to let her pay. But the part of him that wanted to win her over? That part was stronger.

Then it hit him—he couldn't just sit there sipping tea while she feasted. That'd look weird. He added a vegan muffin for himself. When the cashier rang it up, the total flashed on the screen: $27.50.

Ouch.

Jayden kept his face neutral, sliding his card like it was nothing. But inside, he felt every dollar. He was still processing the damage when Sonia suddenly perked up.

"Oh! I forgot to get a drink."

Jayden exhaled, praying she meant tap water.

"I think I'll get the chai tea," she said, smiling.

Ouch again.

"I got you," he said, the words automatic now. He added her tea and got himself a water.

When they finally sat down, she took a bite of her muffin, let out a soft "Mmm," and grinned at him. That smile made him forget the sting of the bill.

Alright, Jayden thought. Thirty bucks for a fine woman and good vibes? Maybe that wasn't so bad after all.

Then she leaned in. "So tell me, King J," she said, her voice teasing. "What's your take on manifestation?"

Jayden grinned. Now we're talking.

Ever since Jayden brought up the *Science of Manifestation*, Sonia hadn't been able to shake one thing he said: *fake god*. The rest of it—manifesting, energy, the universe responding to our thoughts—sounded interesting enough. But *fake* and *God* in the same sentence? That stopped her cold.

Sonia had never even considered the idea that God wasn't real. Sure, she wasn't religious like her grandmother, but she had always believed there was *something*—a higher power, a divine presence guiding things. She'd never met anyone who flat-out denied that. And now, here was Jayden, talking like the idea of God was some kind of elaborate hoax.

She wasn't looking to argue, but she needed to understand where he was coming from. *Who does he think created the sun, the moon, the stars?* she wondered.

Jayden saw her question as a green light. She was *open*—ready to receive the knowledge he'd spent the last six years gathering. He leaned in, his voice smooth, assured. "See, we have the power to manipulate the universe in our favor," he said. "We can create whatever reality we choose. There are ten steps to mastering the *Science of Manifestation*."

Sonia could tell he was about to launch into a long explanation, so she cut straight to what was really on her mind. "So, this divine power we have... it doesn't include God?"

Jayden hesitated. He knew he had to ease her in. If he pushed too hard, too fast, she'd shut down. He wasn't about to make that mistake. Instead, he flashed a knowing smile and changed the subject—just enough to keep her intrigued.

"You ever heard of *Kundalini energy*?" he asked. "It's the divine force lying dormant within us. When we activate it, we unlock our true power. We become creators."

Sonia frowned. "Okay... but *what about God?*"

Jayden's jaw tightened. She wasn't following the script. He wanted to talk about manifestation, not keep circling back to *God*. But she was persistent.

Finally, he decided to be blunt. "God is a man-made construct," he said, locking eyes with her. "Designed to strip us of our own divine power."

Sonia sat back, arms crossed. She wasn't buying it. "So... who created the sun, the moon, the stars?"

Jayden exhaled sharply. He saw where this was going, and he didn't like it. But he had an answer ready. "Science tells us that everything came from the *Big Bang*—an explosion that brought the universe into existence."

Sonia nodded slowly. She'd heard all about the Big Bang in school. But to her, that explanation had always felt... incomplete. "Okay," she said, "but science also tells us everything has a cause. *Who* created the Big Bang?"

Jayden clenched his jaw. He wished she'd stop questioning and just *listen*. He wanted her to be *enlightened*, to see what he saw. But Sonia wasn't playing along.

"Thirteen-point-eight billion years ago," he started, his voice smooth but clipped, "the universe started as a singularity—an unimaginably hot, dense point. Then, in an instant, it expanded, forming physics, subatomic particles, and later, atoms."

He paused, waiting for that moment—the moment where she'd look at him, eyes wide with realization. But instead, Sonia just shook her head.

"That doesn't make sense," she said simply.

She wasn't interested in arguing. She'd heard enough. To her, Jayden's beliefs weren't all that different from the theories she learned in school. And if that's what he wanted to believe, fine. But she saw things differently.

Jayden, though, wasn't satisfied. Her response—*That doesn't make sense*—felt like a rejection. A dismissal. He wasn't about to let that slide. He wanted to be her teacher, her guide. But a student had to be *willing* to learn. *Willing* to submit to the lessons of their master.

If she wouldn't accept his teachings outright, then he'd have to dismantle her beliefs first. Expose the foolishness.

This was where things got tense.

"Do you believe in the Bible?" Jayden asked, leaning in slightly.

Sonia tensed. She didn't like the question. Not because she was unsure of her answer, but because she could already feel where this was going. She wanted to understand more about his views, but she wasn't in the mood for a debate about her own beliefs. "Yes, I believe in the Bible," she said, keeping her tone neutral, hoping to move on quickly.

Jayden smirked. "Why?"

Sonia sighed, shifting in her seat. "Does it matter why I believe in it?"

Jayden nodded, as if he was about to impart some great wisdom. "Most people believe things just because they were taught to. They don't do their own research, don't ask their own questions."

Sonia felt her face heat. She didn't like the implication. He was basically saying she was just blindly following what she'd been told, that she hadn't thought for herself. "So you're saying I don't think for myself?" she shot back.

Jayden's smirk faded for a second before he recovered. "I'm not saying that, but if you really look into it, you'll see the Bible is a man-made book."

Sonia felt her patience thinning. She had come to this date excited to learn more about Jayden, but now she was starting to think he just liked to argue. "Sounds like you have all the answers," she said, her voice laced with sarcasm.

Jayden's eyes flickered with something—irritation? He didn't like the way she said that. He wanted her to believe he had all the answers, but not like this. "I've studied a lot over the years," he continued, his voice steady, controlled. "And I realized a lot of what we were taught growing up? Fairy tales."

Sonia crossed her arms. "I'm happy for you," she said, her voice cool. "I've done research too."

Jayden's jaw tightened. He had been warned about women like her—women who thought they knew something, women who refused to listen. He wanted Sonia to be open, to be teachable. "You obviously didn't dig deep enough," he pressed. "I can put you on to some real wisdom."

Sonia exhaled sharply. "I'm sure you can," she said, forcing a smile. "But maybe we should just agree to disagree."

Jayden stiffened. Agree to disagree? That wasn't the plan. He wasn't here to agree to disagree—he was here to enlighten her. "We wouldn't disagree if you were willing to do the research."

Sonia was irritated. She glanced at the clock on her phone. If she wanted to enjoy the rest of this evening, she was going to have to steer this conversation somewhere else. "Maybe," she said lightly. "Anyway, tell me more about your business."

Normally, that question would have made Jayden light up. But right now, his mind was locked in. How could she understand his business if she was still clinging to fairy tales? "You probably won't fully get it until you realize we've been lied to," he muttered.

Sonia blinked. That was it. She was done. "This has been interesting, King J. I appreciate you taking me here, but I have some essays due on Monday. I should probably get back and finish them up."

Jayden checked his watch. Forty-five minutes. That's how long they'd been here. That was unacceptable. He needed more time. "Oh wow, you're a busy woman," he half-laughed. "Can you give me just a little more time? You told me you were gonna share your social psychology essay with me."

Sonia hesitated. Part of her wanted to leave, but another part of her wanted to see if the conversation could recover. She sighed. "Alright, I'll show it to you."

Jaden read it and they talked about what she wrote.

After that, things smoothed out. They were laughing now, vibing over music, trading stories about their childhoods, and for the first time since she sat down, Sonia actually seemed engaged. Jayden was feeling good about the shift—until he heard the front door chime.

Something in his gut twisted. He looked up, and there she was.

Phoenix.

And she wasn't alone.

She walked in, laughing, her arm brushing just a little too close to the man beside her. Jayden knew exactly who he was—the father of her daughter. He had only met the dude twice, but he knew enough about him to resent his entire existence. A so-called co-parent who never seemed to step up unless it was convenient. A man Phoenix swore she wasn't interested in anymore, yet here they were, walking into the bookstore together, looking comfortable.

Jayden froze for a second, eyes locked on them. A heat climbed up his neck, slow and simmering. He turned back to Sonia before she could notice his shift in energy, but he wasn't all there anymore. His body was at the table, but his mind was over at the entrance, trying to figure out if what he saw was just two people co-parenting—or something else.

He snuck another glance. Phoenix didn't see him yet, but he knew it was only a matter of time.

His stomach tightened.

How could she sit there, laughing with that dude after everything she put Jayden through? After all the times she called him, complaining about how exhausting she was dealing with her child's father? All that crying about how she was done with him—how he stressed her life and didn't pull his weight. And yet, here she was. Back in his presence like none of that mattered.

Phoenix had always been good at playing both sides. Keeping one foot in the past while pretending to step forward. It pissed him off, but what pissed him off more was the fact that he even cared.

Sonia must have noticed his energy shift. "You ok?" she asked.

Jayden exhaled sharply. "Yeah, I'm cool. Just saw someone I know."

But he wasn't cool. Not even close.

The more he watched Phoenix and her daughter's father settle into their table, the more that old bitterness bubbled up. It was like seeing a bad investment flash before his eyes—a woman he had poured so much into, only for her to turn around and entertain the same man she claimed was beneath her. And she wasn't even being low about it. She was laughing. Smiling. Looking like she didn't have a care in the world while Jayden sat here stewing.

He couldn't let this slide. He had to address it—had to at least acknowledge the situation to Sonia, even if it was just to process it out loud.

"My ex-girlfriend just walked in," he admitted, his voice edged with frustration.

Sonia raised an eyebrow. "That's a funny coincidence."

Funny wasn't the word Jayden would use. More like infuriating. More like proof that Phoenix had no respect.

Sonia was curious. She wasn't sure she wanted to meet this Phoenix woman, but she kind of did. Before she could stop herself, she blurted out, "I'd love to meet her."

Jayden narrowed his eyes, trying to figure out if she was serious. Why would she want to meet Phoenix? Did she not catch the aggravation in his voice? Maybe this was some kind of test. Maybe Sonia just wanted to size up the woman who had Jayden in his feelings. Either way, he decided to lean into it. "Okay," he said with a half-smile. "She needs to see what a real woman looks like anyway."

He didn't go over right away. Instead, he stole quick glances at Phoenix, waiting to see if she noticed him.

Ten minutes passed. Then, finally, she looked up. Their eyes met.

Jayden nodded. Phoenix nodded back. Then she turned to her daughter's father and whispered something. Jayden knew exactly what she was saying.

Another twenty minutes passed, and Sonia really did have to go this time. As they stood up, Jayden realized they had to walk past Phoenix's table to leave. He figured this was the time for his reluctant introduction.

When they reached the table, Jayden greeted Phoenix's daughter's father, then turned to Phoenix. "Hey," he said, keeping his tone casual. "This is my friend, Sonia."

Phoenix barely looked at Sonia before smirking. "Oh," she said, tilting her head. "Is she your new cab driver?"

Jayden's stomach tightened. This bitter woman.

Sonia frowned. She didn't get the joke, but she caught the edge in Phoenix's tone.

Jayden kept his expression neutral and the interaction brief. "As I said, she's my friend. Anyway, good seeing y'all."

With that, he started walking toward the door. Sonia followed.

Outside, Sonia turned to him. "Your cab driver?"

Jayden had already prepared for this. He shrugged. "Phoenix is always making bad jokes."

Sonia wasn't sure if she believed him, but she let it go.

Jayden walked her to her car. They hugged, exchanged polite goodbyes.

Sonia reflected on the date. It had started rocky, but once they got past the heavy topics, Jayden seemed like a decent guy. As long as the subject of God didn't come up, they could probably get along.

Jayden, on the other hand, had different thoughts. He wasn't planning to avoid the topic of God. No, he would take his time. Slowly, methodically, he would strip away Sonia's old beliefs.

This wasn't over.

Chapter 11

Winning a Client

After Sonia pulled off, Jayden ordered an Uber and headed back to his sister's house.

When Jayden got back to his sister's house, he didn't even take off his shoes before dialing Pharoah. He needed to debrief. The date had been a rollercoaster, and he wasn't about to process it alone.

Pharoah picked up on the third ring. "What's good, King?"

Jayden exhaled. "Man, let me tell you about this date." He laid it all out—the rough start, Sonia's resistance to his wisdom, the way she kept trying to dodge the truth. "She a work in progress," Jayden said, stretching out on his mattress. "But she's workable."

Pharoah chuckled. "I hope you right, bro. Otherwise, you in for some headaches."

Jayden nodded to himself. Sonia wasn't quite there yet, but he had faith in her potential. If she was smart enough to be in college, she was smart enough to wake up. He just had to lead her.

But then his tone shifted.

"Bruh, you won't believe who walked in while we was there."

Pharoah already knew from the way Jayden's voice dipped. "Nah… don't tell me."

"Phoenix. And guess who she with?"

Silence.

"Her baby daddy."

Pharoah groaned. "Man. That's some foul energy right there."

Jayden sat up, heat rising in his chest again just thinking about it. Phoenix didn't just walk in. She strolled in, looking real comfortable, laughing at whatever her baby daddy was saying like he was the funniest dude in the world. Like she ain't spend all that time with Jayden talking about how he wasn't good for her. Jayden had been done with Phoenix, but seeing her like that—so at ease, like their history didn't even matter—unsettled him.

And then she had the nerve to throw that jab.

"Asked if Sonia was my new cab driver." Jayden exclaimed, feeling heat in his rising.

Pharoah sucked his teeth. "These women be straight vengeful. She just mad 'cause she see you moving on."

Jayden wanted to believe that. But something about Phoenix's presence, about the way she looked right past him, like he wasn't even there, gnawed at him.

They talked for over an hour, circling around the same conclusions. Women didn't appreciate a good man until it was too late. Phoenix was just trying to get under his skin. Sonia had potential, but she needed guidance.

After the call, Jayden stared at the ceiling, his stomach growling. That muffin wasn't holding him. He thought about how much he had spent—Ubers, Sonia's snacks, that little muffin of his own. Sixty dollars gone. He hadn't even checked his account yet, but he already knew—his balance was creeping toward dangerous territory.

He slapped his hands together and sat up. Triple-decker peanut butter and jelly it was.

As he made his sandwich, he thought about Sonia. He liked her. She was different. And she was smart—smart enough to see the truth once he showed it to her. He'd form her into the conscious queen she was meant to be.

He shot her a text: *Had a great time tonight. Looking forward to seeing you again.*

She didn't reply right away.

Sonia, meanwhile, sat on her bed, rereading his message. She had enjoyed the second half of the date, but there were things she couldn't shake. The way Jayden talked about God, like he was trying to rewire her. The way Phoenix looked at him—like she knew something Sonia didn't.

She wasn't cutting him off. Not yet. But she needed to see more before she let herself get pulled in. Eventually, she texted back: *I had a nice time too. We should hang out again sometime.*

That *sometime* didn't necessarily mean soon.

Over the next two weeks, their conversations became shorter. Sonia stayed busy with school and work—or at least, that's what she told Jayden. When they did talk, it was never for long, and when he asked to hang out, she always had something else going on.

Jayden didn't think too much of it. He figured she really was busy. It didn't cross his mind that their conversation about God had rubbed her the wrong way. That she was starting to avoid certain topics altogether.

But Jayden was itching for another *real* talk. The kind that peeled back layers and forced people to think. He wanted to enlighten her, not just skim the surface.

Still, part of him didn't mind the space. Dates meant spending money, and money was something he needed to hold onto. Instead of meeting up, he threw himself into his business, Lion Heart Healing.

But the business wasn't exactly booming. In two weeks, despite posting twenty-seven times to his thousands of followers, he'd only gotten two serious inquiries.

One was from a guy named Howard, a security guard who suffered from chronic migraines. Howard didn't trust doctors and was looking for natural remedies. Jayden set up a free consultation—he figured even if he didn't make much, at least he'd get a testimonial.

The other was a woman named Hope. She wanted help for her mother, who had cancer and was struggling with chemo side effects. Hope said her mother was skeptical. Jayden knew that meant she'd be a harder sell.

His consultation with Howard was set for Thursday. Howard told him he'd tried both herbal and Western medicine, but nothing worked. Jayden assured him that he could help and they could work out a price.

As he prepared for the consultation, Jayden spent hours researching migraines and energy imbalances. He couldn't afford to be caught slipping.

The irony, though? His own energy was shot. He felt it—his peanut butter and jelly diet catching up to him. But his bank account had dipped below $100. Until Lion Heart Healing started bringing in real money, this was what it was.

For now, he'd focus on the business. And on Sonia. She just needed time. He'd get through to her eventually.

She just didn't know it yet.

The morning of Jayden's consultation with Howard he got to the library an hour early, walking in like a man with purpose. He needed a private meeting room, something professional, something that would make a client feel like they were in the hands of someone who knew exactly what they were doing. But when he asked the librarian, she barely glanced up before shaking her head.

"All booked."

Jayden exhaled through his nose. *How?* He had been counting on that room, had envisioned himself sitting behind a polished table, setting the tone of authority. Instead, he was going to have to hold the consultation out in the open like some amateur. It wasn't ideal, but the show had to go on.

He scanned the space and found a table tucked near a window in the back. It would do. Except there was a woman sitting at the next table, just close enough to eavesdrop. Jayden sent up a silent request to the universe: *Move her along.*

By 3:25, his phone buzzed.

Howard: *I'm parking.*

Jayden straightened his shoulders. Me: *Sounds good. I'll meet you up front.*

He walked to the entrance just as a tall, heavyset man in a flannel shirt and jeans approached. Jayden caught the way Howard's eyes flickered over him, assessing.

"You Howard?" Jayden asked.

"Yeah... King J?"

Howard's expression said it all. He had been expecting someone older, someone with more years behind their wisdom. But all he saw was a young man, maybe early twenties, looking more like a student than a master healer.

Jayden wasn't new to this reaction. People always measured his knowledge against his age, waiting for him to prove himself. But Howard was here, which meant he was searching for something. And if Jayden played this right, he'd be the one to provide it.

"C'mon," Jayden said, leading him to the back.

The woman at the next table looked up as they sat down. Jayden clocked her sideways glances. *Nosy.* But he forced himself to focus.

Howard wasted no time. "So how long you been doing this?"

Translation: *You sure you know what you're talking about?*

Jayden smiled, already prepared. "Six years." He counted all the time he had spent studying, experimenting, learning since his mother's death. "I've dedicated my life to the healing arts."

Howard nodded, but his eyes still held that doubt. Jayden wasn't about to give him the chance to poke holes. He leaned forward and launched into his prepared introduction.

"The most effective approach to mitigating cephalalgia—commonly referred to as a headache—lies in addressing both its etiology and symptomatic manifestations." He paused, letting the weight of his words settle. "We will address causes such as dehydration, which can precipitate vascular constriction, exacerbating cranial discomfort."

Jayden had practiced that line in the mirror for two days straight. And from the way Howard was sitting up now, the effort had been worth it. Jayden could see it—the shift. The respect.

Howard nodded. "Man… okay."

Jayden allowed himself a small smile. That's right. He wasn't some kid playing doctor. He knew what he was doing.

Howard exhaled and leaned back in his chair. He started talking—about the headaches that had followed him for years, the sluggishness, how it was interfering with his life. Jayden listened intently, nodding at the right moments, offering sympathy where it was needed.

"I can help you with that," Jayden assured him.

Howard sat with that for a moment before nodding. "I'm interested."

Jayden's heart jumped. *This is happening.* His first paying client.

Then Howard hesitated. "Thing is… I can't afford the full price."

Jayden kept his face neutral. He had been prepared for this too. "How much are you able to invest?" he asked. "Remember, your health is your wealth."

Howard sighed. "I can do twenty a session. And when I get back to working full time, I'll pay more."

Jayden hesitated for a second. *Twenty wasn't much.* But it was more than zero.

"Deal," he said.

They set the first session for three days later, at a location yet to be determined. Jayden was about to move into the Violet Light House, so the library wouldn't be within walking distance much longer. He'd have to figure out a new meeting spot.

But for now, none of that mattered.

Because he had done it. He had sealed his first paying client. And this? This was just the beginning.

Chapter 12

The Big Move

Jayden was supposed to move into the Violet Light House a week earlier, but when some brothers from out of town said they were crashing there, he decided to push it back. No big deal. He figured it gave him more time to get things in order. He had talked to Inner-G briefly about the house rules, but Inner-G had been busy. "I'll fill you in later, bro," he'd said. Jayden let it slide.

But now, fresh off his consultation with Howard—his *first paying client*—he needed to talk. He pulled out his phone and shot Inner-G a message. He wanted to tell him how he'd killed it, how he had this man hanging on his every word, ready to pay for his healing work. And, while he was at it, he needed more details about VLH.

Inner-G texted back: "Yea bro, hit me up in 5."

Exactly five minutes later, Jayden hit call.

"You're boy making his professional debut!" Jayden announced the second Inner-G picked up. "Got my first paying client."

"That's what's up, King J!" Inner-G laughed. "Knew it was just a matter of time. You got this!"

Jayden grinned. He launched into the play-by-play—how he'd wowed Howard with his knowledge, how the man was excited to start sessions. Inner-G hyped him up the whole way through.

For about twenty minutes, they talked *Lion Heart Healing*, Jayden riding the high of his first success. But then he switched gears.

"So, what's up with the VLH? Give me the deets!"

"Yeah, King, you gonna love it there." Inner-G's voice warmed with excitement. "The house is owned by a Black real estate investor named Joe. Big community guy. He don't live there, but he pops in from time to time."

Jayden nodded, taking it in.

"Two people pretty much run the place—Wize and Egypt. It's a three-bedroom spot, but everybody got their space. The third bedroom? That's Panther's. He been there for two years now. And then there's Royal and Diamond. Diamond has been staying in the back room for about five months and Royal has been in the den for two months.”

Jayden listened, trying to picture it all. Sounded like a full house already.

“And me?” Jayden asked.

“You got the patio, bro,” Inner-G said, matter-of-fact. “It’s converted into a room, but it gets a little chilly at night, so I’d grab a heater if I were you.”

Jayden let that sink in. He wasn’t mad at it. A space was a space, and this was the start of something bigger.

By the time they hung up, Jayden felt good. Ready.

It was Thursday evening. Move-in day was set for Saturday.

He figured it was time to let his sister know.

Jayden had told Trinity a while ago that he was moving, but after he pushed back his move-out date, she stopped taking him seriously. “Okay, as soon as you’re ready,” she had said, but he could tell what she was really thinking: *He’s not going anywhere.*

Now, though? Now it was real.

Jayden could hear her in the kitchen, putting dishes away. He walked in, leaned against the counter.

"Well, Saturday's the day, sis," he said. "Your brother's out of here."

Trinity turned, eyebrows raised. "Oh really? For real this time?"

Jayden caught the shift in her tone. This time, she believed him.

"For real," he said. "Think you can give me a ride with my stuff?"

She sighed, but not in a bad way. More like she was wrapping her head around it. Then she nodded. "Yeah, I got you."

She looked at him for a beat, then said, "Just keep praying, Jayden. And remember, God still loves you."

That part rubbed him the wrong way, just a little. He knew it was coming from a good place, though, so he let it slide.

"Appreciate it," he said.

And just like that, it was official. Saturday, he was gone.

The night before his move, Jayden was restless, itching to tell Sonia all about it. He figured this would be the spot where she'd come to see him, where they could really build. More than that, he was craving a deeper conversation—one that could open her mind, maybe even change the way she saw the world. Lately, their talks had been surface-level, cool but not *transformative*. He wanted more.

He dialed her number. No answer.

A second later, his phone buzzed with a text.

"Hey King J, a little busy. Can we talk tomorrow?"

Jayden frowned. *Busy?* What could she possibly be doing at 8:15 on a Friday night? He knew she wasn't working. Wasn't in school. So what was so important that she couldn't pick up?

He shot back: "Hey, I really wanted to talk to you. Can you call me back when you're free?"

On the other side of the city, Sonia sat on her bed, staring at the message. She wasn't doing much of anything—just avoiding a conversation she wasn't in the mood for. She liked Jayden, liked his energy, but she wasn't ready for another one of his deep dives into the *truths of the universe*. Still, she knew she couldn't dodge him forever.

"Ok, I'll call you in 30 minutes."

When the time was up, Sonia dialed. Jayden picked up on the first ring. She apologized for not being available earlier.

"No problem, beautiful. Good to hear your voice," he said smoothly.

"Yeah, likewise," she replied.

He wasted no time getting to the news. "I'm moving into the Violet Light House tomorrow." His voice brimmed with excitement. "It's a hub for conscious people, a real think tank. Being in that energy is gonna take my work to the next level."

Sonia smiled. "That's great, Jayden. I hope it works out for you."

She meant it. She had never lived on her own, so the thought of someone making that move without parents or family felt grown—it was something she hadn't experienced yet.

Jayden went on, talking about the enlightened minds he'd be around, the deep conversations he was looking forward to having. And then, he pivoted.

"Man, it's gonna be so good to be around people who think outside the box. Who don't just accept the programming. Did you know the story of Jesus actually came from the Egyptian god Horus?"

There it was. *The Jesus conversation.*

Sonia sighed, but only inwardly. She'd grown up hearing different takes on the Bible—her mother and grandmother teaching her from a traditional Christian perspective, her father coming from a Rastafarian angle, telling her about the Solomonic kings of Ethiopia, King Selassie, and the ancient texts that he informed her held timeless truth. She wasn't a Bible reader like them, but she respected it, turned to it when she had questions.

Still, she knew this moment was coming. Might as well get it over with.

"No, I wasn't aware of that," she said carefully. "I always thought it was an original story."

She wasn't about to drop everything she knew just because a guy she was still getting to know said so. But she'd humor him.

Jayden took her response as a green light. "Yeah, the whole Bible has been plagiarized from ancient Egyptian stories and other religions. The virgin birth? That came from Horus. Hinduism has a virgin birth story with Krishna as well."

Sonia frowned. The idea intrigued her, but something about it rubbed her the wrong way. This was the book her family held dear, the book her grandmother quoted every Sunday morning before breakfast.

"How do you know the Bible got its stories from them? Maybe they all just had similar stories," she countered.

Jayden chuckled. "Come on. How could the details be *so* similar if they weren't copied?"

Sonia narrowed her eyes. "You sound so sure of yourself. You really think *millions* of people could be fooled?"

Jayden didn't even hesitate. "Of course. The masses are asleep. Blind to reality!"

For the next hour, he went in. He talked about God being a man-made construct, how prayer didn't work, how religion was forced onto Black people through slavery. He went on about systems of control, the ways people were kept docile, obedient, unaware.

Sonia listened, mostly. She asked a few questions, pushed back here and there, but a lot of what he said was new to her. She wasn't going to argue something she hadn't fully looked into.

By the end, she sighed. "This all sounds far-fetched to me. But I'll look into it."

Jayden smiled to himself. She was *listening*. She wasn't shutting down. That was all he needed.

They agreed to talk again tomorrow.

After they hung up, Sonia sat with her thoughts. Jayden was passionate, confident, *knowledgeable*. But was he really dropping wisdom, or was he just another conspiracy theorist with a good vocabulary?

Jayden, on the other hand, felt solid. Sonia was workable. She wasn't resisting. And that meant she was already halfway there.

Jayden woke up early, his body humming with energy. Today's the day, he thought, stretching his arms wide, letting the anticipation settle in his chest. Moving into the Violet Light House felt like stepping into a new chapter—one where he'd be surrounded by like-minded souls, deep conversations, and a real sense of purpose. He had high hopes for this place, believing it could be the kind of life-changing experience he'd been craving.

And he wouldn't have to wait long to dive in. Inner-G had already told him about the plant medicine ceremony happening that night. Jayden didn't know much about plant medicine, but if it was about healing, he was ready to learn. Maybe this could be something to incorporate into his own work.

He got to packing, methodically folding clothes, stacking books, and tossing out loose papers that had gathered over time. He stripped his bed, wiped down the dresser, and ran his hands over the space, feeling a quiet gratitude for what his sister had done for him. But he was ready—more than ready—to go.

After an hour of tidying up, he sat down with his phone and pulled up a map, searching for a place near the VLH where he could meet with clients. He needed something close, professional, and—most importantly—free. The arts district had plenty of spots, but when he saw a community center less than two miles away, he paused. The pictures looked promising. They rented out meeting spaces, but they also had free quiet study areas. That sounded like exactly what he needed. He made a mental note to check it out.

At 10:30, Trinity's voice floated up the stairs. "Jayden! Breakfast!"

He smiled, pushing back from the desk. One last meal with the family before he left. That felt right. He washed his hands, took a deep breath, and headed to the kitchen.

Jayden slid into his seat at the kitchen table, feeling lighter than he had in weeks. Most mornings, breakfast felt like a silent negotiation—him trying to fit into a rhythm that wasn't his. John would say the blessing, Trinity would talk about the kids, and Jayden would sit there, half-listening, half-waiting for the moment he could retreat upstairs. He wasn't about to start talking about Kundalini energy or Egyptian pyramids over pancakes. But today felt different. Today, he wasn't just an extra seat at the table—he was a guest of honor. He had one foot out the door, moving toward a world where he belonged.

Trinity picked up on it right away. "So," she said, narrowing her eyes at him, "you seem ready for this move. Who will you be living with?"

"Some folks from my community," Jayden said. "Conscious folks."

Trinity didn't know exactly what that meant. She knew about Phoenix, she'd met Pharaoh, and a few of Jayden's other friends had passed through, but she never fully understood them. They were polite, respectful even, but something about them felt... off. She couldn't put her finger on it, but it was like they were searching for something and had convinced themselves they'd already found it. She kept that thought to herself. Instead, she smiled softly and said, "I just want the best for you, Jay. You've always had so much potential."

She didn't add the rest—he's wasting a lot of his potential with this lifestyle.

John, who had been buttering his toast, cleared his throat. "How's the business going?"

Jayden grinned. "Great. I meet with my first client tomorrow."

Trinity and John exchanged a glance. They'd already had conversations about Jayden's healing business, how he needed more training, more certification, more something before jumping in. But it was his last day in the house. No need to start a debate.

"Oh, okay," John said, nodding. "Good luck with that."

After breakfast, Trinity agreed to drive Jayden to his new place in an hour. She cleaned up while Jayden went upstairs to call Inner-G. The phone barely rang before he picked up.

"Peace, King. Your castle awaits."

Jayden smiled. That was exactly how he felt.

Inner-G promised to meet him at the house to introduce him to everyone. Jayden had seen Wize and Egypt at events but never had a full conversation with them. The others? He had no clue who they were. But that didn't matter. This was his tribe.

"Are you joining the plant medicine ceremony tonight?" Inner-G asked.

"You know it," Jayden said, sitting up straighter.

"Brother about to take that Shaman journey," Inner-G mused.

Jayden nodded like he knew exactly what that meant. Truth was, he didn't. He didn't know what plants they'd be using or what the ceremony was even for. But he trusted Inner-G, and there was no way he was about to sound clueless.

He glanced at his backpack on the floor, the weight of his dwindling funds creeping back in. Less than $75 to his name, and Inner-G had told him he needed to buy a heater, which would take another $25. That meant he had $50 to his name until he got more clients for Lion Heart Healing—whenever that happened.

Pharaoh had brought up selling weed before, but Jayden had shut it down. No car. Living at his sister's house. Too risky. But now? Now he had options. The Violet Light House was a hub for smokers, and that meant business. He decided he'd talk to Pharaoh again. It wasn't just about money—it was about control. Stability. Survival.

At 12:20, Jayden brought his bags downstairs and set them by the front door. Trinity met him there, and together they walked to the car. The drive was about 35 minutes, through streets Trinity knew well since John worked nearby.

Halfway there, she glanced at him. "Have you talked to Aunt Patrice lately?"

Jayden scoffed. "No. I don't have anything to say to her."

Trinity frowned. "You used to be close. What happened?"

"She's just another judgmental Christian," he shot back. Then, realizing how that might sound, he added, "You're cool. You let me be myself. But she's different."

Trinity sighed, keeping her eyes on the road but shaking her head slightly. "She loves you, Jay. You know that, right?"

Jayden let out a breath through his nose, arms crossed over his chest. "Love? If love means constantly criticizing my choices and telling me I need to 'come back to the Lord,' then sure. She loves me." His voice was edged with sarcasm.

Trinity tightened her grip on the steering wheel. "She just worries about you. She sees your potential, Jayden. She doesn't want you to get lost."

"Lost?" Jayden let out a dry laugh. "I'm not lost, Trin. I've never been more found. I'm building something for myself—Lion Heart Healing, the community, my own path. But she can't see that because it doesn't fit in her little church box."

Trinity hesitated before speaking again. "Maybe she doesn't understand your path, but does that mean you just cut her off? You know she asks about you all the time. She was just telling me last week how she prays for you every day."

Jayden exhaled sharply and rubbed a hand over his face. "Look, I appreciate the prayers, but I don't need saving. And I don't need someone constantly telling me I'm wrong for choosing something different than what we were raised on."

Trinity let a few moments of silence settle between them, the hum of the road filling the space. She stole a glance at her brother, taking in the set of his jaw, the way he stared out the window as if watching his thoughts pass by like the trees lining the freeway.

"I get it," she said finally. "I do. Aunt Patrice can be... intense. But family is family, Jay. And no matter how different your paths are, I just don't want you to let resentment close doors that don't need to be shut."

Jayden scoffed again but softer this time. "Doors swing both ways, Trin. If she wants a relationship with me, she has to respect me. Not try to 'fix' me."

Trinity nodded slowly. "That's fair." Another beat of silence, then she added, "You ever think about reaching out? Setting some boundaries, but still keeping that connection?"

Jayden shrugged. "Maybe. Not now. I just need space from all that."

Trinity sighed again, nodding. "Alright. Just... don't let space turn into silence forever."

Jayden didn't respond. He just stared out the window, watching the city blur by.

When they pulled up to the house, her eyes widened. Three people sat in the open garage, passing a blunt back and forth. Trinity stiffened. She wasn't used to being around smokers, and the sight of it unsettled her.

Jayden reached for the door handle, but she grabbed his arm. "Listen," she said, voice soft but firm, "you are one of the most intelligent, good-hearted men I know. Don't lose track of yourself. The Lord has a calling on your life. Sometimes pain and sorrow can make us forget who we really are. But the Lord loves you, and so do I."

Jayden nodded, her words warming something in his chest. But she didn't understand. Her world was her world. His was his.

"Thanks, sis," he said, flashing a grin. "I'll never lose track of my dreams."

She just nodded.

They got out of the car, Trinity grabbing one of his bags while Jayden stacked the others in his arms. Inner-G was one of the ones outside smoking, and Jayden introduced him.

"Greetings, Queen," Inner-G said, bowing slightly. "Pleased to make your acquaintance."

Trinity raised an eyebrow but remained polite. "Nice to meet you too, sir."

"Your brother is a powerful soul," Inner-G said. "He'll be in good hands here."

Trinity smiled, though she wasn't convinced. "I hope this is a safe and good environment for him."

Inner-G gestured toward the house. "Come on in. Let me give you the tour."

The moment they stepped inside, a thick cloud of smoke wrapped around them, and Trinity coughed into her elbow. Inner-G chuckled. "Oh, my bad, sis. Guess you're not a smoker."

She waved a hand in front of her face. "Not at all."

Two people lounged on the couch, blunt in hand, and Inner-G motioned for them to take it outside. They nodded and left without hesitation.

"Welcome to the VLH," Inner-G announced, arms wide. "Renaissance hub for mystical thought."

Trinity scanned the space—drums, guitars, hookahs, ashtrays, religious quotes from every tradition pinned to the walls, wooden statues, ankhs. The place reeked of weed and incense. It was cluttered, disorganized, nothing like her house, which smelled of lavender and was spotless.

Inner-G led them to the kitchen. "This is the infirmary," he said proudly. "Our food is our medicine. The healing starts here."

Vegetable scraps littered the counter, alongside a juicer, a blender, and an assortment of herbs and spices. The fridge was plastered with magnets promoting animal rights, free Africa, and vegetarianism.

Trinity took it all in, her expression unreadable.

Jayden, meanwhile, was grinning. I can definitely make this home.

The tour continued as Inner-G led them into the living room, which he grandly referred to as the "conference room." He spread his arms wide, as if unveiling a sacred space. "Many enlightening conversations have been had in this very room," he declared. The space was cluttered but lived-in—pillows and blankets scattered on a worn-out sectional couch, a low wooden table covered in books on metaphysics, healing, and African spirituality. Incense burned from a brass holder, its smoky tendrils curling into the air. Posters of Malcolm X, Bob Marley, and various African kings and queens hung on the walls alongside vibrant paintings of Egyptian gods and goddesses. A djembe drum rested in the corner, next to a tapestry featuring the Eye of Horus.

From there, Inner-G led them down the hallway, stopping at the bathroom. He grinned and said, "I don't think I need to explain this one," with a small chuckle. Trinity and Jayden peeked inside. The bathroom was small and well-used, with an overflowing laundry hamper in the corner and a stack of mismatched towels hanging from hooks. A bottle of sage spray sat on the sink, and a handwritten affirmation was taped to the mirror: *You are divine. You are powerful. You are whole.*

Finally, they reached Jayden's new room. Inner-G swung open the door with a flourish, revealing a narrow, enclosed patio that had been converted into a bedroom. The wooden-paneled walls gave the space a rustic feel, and sunlight streamed through a row of windows, casting long shadows across the dusty floor. A cracked pane in one of the windows let in a slight draft, and a few cobwebs clung to the corners of the ceiling. There was no furniture yet, just a pile of blankets in one corner and a small wooden crate doubling as a makeshift nightstand. A single bulb dangled from the ceiling, flickering slightly as it buzzed to life.

"You got your own exit door, King," Inner-G pointed out, motioning toward a door that led directly to the backyard.

Jayden stepped inside, taking it all in. It wasn't much, but it was his. The independence of having his own entrance sparked something in him—an opportunity, a new beginning. "Yeah," he said with a slow nod, "this will definitely do."

Trinity, on the other hand, took a more critical view. She noticed the dust, the dead insects in the corners, the thin walls that would offer little protection from the elements. Her protective instincts kicked in, but she held her tongue. Instead, she simply said, "As long as you're happy." She had her doubts. But she knew Jayden. And Jayden had already made up his mind.

Chapter 13

The Housemates

After ten minutes at the Violet Light House, Trinity was more than ready to go. The walls vibrated with incense smoke and soft drum beats from a speaker in the corner, but she was done soaking in the scene. She turned to Inner-G with a polite smile. "Thanks for the tour. This place is... definitely something."

Inner-G grinned knowingly. "It's home."

She nodded, then pulled her brother into a quick hug. "Take care of yourself, Jay."

Defensive, Jayden replied, "You know I always do."

She shot him a look, one that said she wasn't so sure, but she let it slide. With a final nod at Inner-G, she headed for the door.

Jayden lingered in the living room as Inner-G flopped onto the couch, stretching his long arms across the back. "So," Inner-G said, watching as Jayden reached into his pocket and started rolling a blunt, "what you think? You vibin' with the spot?"

Jayden licked the edge of the paper, sealing it with precision. "Yeah, man. It's solid. I feel like I can really build something here."

Inner-G nodded. "For sure. And you ain't even met everybody yet." He stood, motioning toward the door. "Come on, let's fix that."

Jayden tucked the blunt behind his ear and followed. Outside, two men sat perched on stools like kings on thrones. One was bald with a thick beard, the other had long dreadlocks and a nose ring. They both looked up as Inner-G approached.

"Family, meet King J," Inner-G announced, slapping a hand on Jayden's shoulder. "New king in the VLH palace."

The bald man, introduced as Finesse, nodded in approval. "Welcome, young king."

Inner-G grinned and gestured toward the man with dreads. "And this here is Royal. He was the rookie till you showed up."

Royal chuckled, shaking his head. "Guess I'm a vet now."

Jayden dapped both of them up. "Looking forward to building with y'all."

Inner-G nodded in satisfaction. "You will. We all got a role to play." Then he turned toward the door. "Come on, still got some folks for you to meet."

Inside, they moved down the hallway, stopping at a door next to the bathroom. Inner-G knocked, and when it swung open, an older man—maybe in his late forties—stood there. He wore a dreadlock hat, a red, black, and green scarf draped over his shoulders, and his partially graying beard gave him the air of an elder.

"This right here is the man with the plan—Panther," Inner-G said with a grin. "If you got questions about how this revolution gon' pop off, he's the one to ask."

Jayden gave him a respectful fist bump. "Pleased to meet you, brother."

Panther studied him for a beat, then nodded, his deep voice rumbling like distant thunder. "I already see it in you—a warrior spirit. We need more brothers like you."

The words landed heavy, but in a way that made Jayden stand a little taller. He felt seen. Not as someone running from something, but as a man stepping into something. "Yes sir," he said, meaning it.

Inner-G let the moment settle, then clapped his hands. "Still got one more stop. Let's keep it moving."

Upstairs, three doors lined the hallway. One, slightly ajar, revealed a bathroom. The other two were closed.

Inner-G knocked on the door to the left, and when it opened, a tall woman with locks adorned with beads stepped out. She moved with a presence—regal, confident, unshaken. Her long skirt swept the floor as she regarded Jayden with a knowing smile.

"This is King J," Inner-G introduced. "He's the one I told you about."

The woman's smile deepened as she leaned in for a warm hug. "Pleased to meet you, King J. I'm Egypt. If you need anything, just ask. We're happy to have you here."

Jayden nodded, feeling something shift in his chest. There was warmth in her, something grounding yet electric at the same time. "Appreciate that," he said.

Egypt took a moment to fill him in on the house rules—cleaning schedules, trash pickup days, shared bathroom etiquette. He listened, taking mental notes, but mostly, he was taking in *her*. The way she carried herself. The way her voice held both authority and ease.

As she finished, Inner-G said, "Gotta introduce him to Wize."

Egypt nodded at Jayden. "Will I see you later at the plant medicine ceremony? I'll be leading it." She tilted her head slightly, studying him.

Jayden opened his mouth, but before he could respond, Egypt continued. "It's a sacred journey, a chance to open yourself up, cleanse old energy, and receive divine insight. The plants are our ancestors' teachers. They show us what we need to see—sometimes what we're ready for, sometimes what we've been avoiding." She paused, her dark eyes locking onto his. "It's not just about getting visions. It's about transformation."

Jayden held her gaze, feeling the weight of her words settle over him. He didn't hesitate this time. He squared his shoulders and nodded. "I'm in. I'm ready for whatever the ancestors have to show me."

Egypt's lips curled into a satisfied smile. "Good. Then tonight, we begin."

His interest piqued. "Looking forward to it."

They exchanged parting words, and Inner-G knocked on the adjacent door—the one marked with the Eye of Horus. Thirty seconds passed before it opened, revealing a man of medium build, short afro, vest, and cargo pants. His gaze was sharp but calm, like he saw more than what was in front of him.

"Brother, this is King J," Inner-G said, exchanging daps with the man. "And King J, this is Wize. When it comes to herbs and metaphysical sciences, he's the truth. This brother and I go way back—been building, learning, growing together. From street knowledge to ancient wisdom, we've been through it all. If there's one person I trust when it comes to the science of the soul, it's Wize."

Wize nodded, "Fifteen years deep. This my brother" his eyes steady as he studied Jayden. He extended his fist. "Good to have you, King J. We family here. This ain't just a house—it's a temple, a training ground, a space for elevation. You ready for that?"

Jayden met Wize's fist with his own, nodding with quiet confidence. "Been ready."

Wize gave a small approving smile. "Good. Then let's build."

As Inner-G and Wize caught up on an event they had both attended recently, Jayden listened with half an ear. The other half of his mind wandered—turning over the faces, the names, the energy of it all. This place was different. *These* people were different. Mystical.

When the conversation wrapped up, Inner-G clapped Jayden on the back. "Alright, let's finish this tour."

Jayden followed him back downstairs, knowing one thing for sure—he wasn't just moving into a house. He was stepping into something bigger.

The last stop on the tour was Diamond. Inner-G led Jayden toward the back of the house, glancing over his shoulder. "Diamond's a trip, but she's cool. Y'all should get along. She's into healing like you."

As they rounded the corner, Jayden noticed a space sectioned off with a folding screen. The scent of burning incense curled through the air, mingling with the sound of neo-soul music drifting from the room. Inner-G didn't hesitate, calling out, "Yo, Diamond!"

A moment later, a slim woman with medium-length twists and a flowing African dress appeared from behind the screen. Jayden recognized her immediately—he'd seen her before, but never knew her name. A memory flickered—talking to her at a booth, something about sea moss.

Inner-G grinned. "Peace, queen. This is King J. He's gonna be stayin' in the patio."

Diamond studied Jayden for a second, then a spark of recognition lit her face. "I know you," she said, tilting her head. "Didn't you stop by my booth?"

Jayden nodded, smiling. "Yeah, we talked about the benefits of sea moss."

"Oh yes," she said, her voice warm. "I remember now. Good to have another healer in the house." She pulled him in for a hug, and he embraced her, feeling the same welcoming energy she carried before.

They talked for a few minutes, picking up where they had left off at the booth, but Inner-G cut in, shaking his head. "Glad y'all vibin' already, but me and the king got some business to handle."

Jayden and Diamond exchanged smiles. "We'll finish this later," he told her, and she nodded, a knowing look in her eyes.

Back in the living room, Jayden sank onto the couch. Inner-G sat next to him, stretching out his legs. "So, what you think, King?"

Jayden grinned. "I love it."

Inner-G nodded, satisfied. "Good. 'Cause I need your help vending at an event tomorrow."

Jayden thought for a second. "I got my healing session with Howard in the morning, but I can do both."

Inner-G lifted a brow. "Bet."

That reminded Jayden—he still needed a spot for his session. "Hey, I need a spot for my healing session. What about that community center nearby? You think that'll work?"

Inner-G nodded. "Yeah, that could work. I know the assistant director. Might even be workin' today. C'mon, let's check it out."

He pulled a small pipe from his pocket, packed it, and passed it to Jayden. They took a few hits in silence, the air between them thick with smoke and contemplation. Finally, Inner-G stood. "Let's roll."

Minutes later, they pulled into the nearly empty lot of the Arts District Community Center. A large sign marked the entrance. Inside, a receptionist at the front desk looked up. "Hello, are you members?"

Inner-G leaned in with his usual charm. "Nah, but we're looking for Mr. Brown."

She shook her head. "He's off today."

Inner-G didn't miss a beat. "Well, my boy here is new to the neighborhood. Thought we'd stop by, maybe see about a membership."

The receptionist softened, nodding. "Hold on, I'll get Sylvia, our manager."

Five minutes later, a Latina woman in khaki pants and a blue polo with the center's logo walked up, her presence commanding but friendly. "Welcome! I'm Sylvia. Let me show you around."

She led them through the center, pointing out the computer lab, the weight room, and a conference space in the back. When Jayden asked about membership, she smiled. ""It's free. Only rentals cost money," Sylvia explained, her voice warm with encouragement.

Jayden's eyes swept across the open space, landing on a quiet corner where a cluster of small tables and chairs sat neatly arranged. The natural light streaming in from the tall windows made the area feel peaceful, almost sacred. It was perfect—private enough for one-on-one healing sessions, yet open enough to feel connected to the community. He wouldn't need to pay for a rental, he could utilize that area.

Without hesitation, he filled out the membership form, the process surprisingly quick. As soon as they stepped outside, Jayden pulled out his phone, typing a message to Howard: "Got a spot for the session. Arts District Community Center. Meet me there at 10 AM."

He hit send, a surge of excitement running through him. This wasn't just a meeting place—it was his new office.

Back at VLH, Inner-G parked in front of the house and stretched. "I gotta dip for a bit, get ready for the plant medicine ceremony. Starts at seven. You good?"

Jayden nodded. "Yeah, I just need a mattress."

"I got an air mattress. I'll bring it when I come back."

Jayden exhaled in relief. "Bet. Thanks, man." They dapped up, and Inner-G pulled off.

Stepping inside, Jayden found Royal and Essence lounging in the living room, passing a blunt. Royal caught his eye and held it out. "C'mon, King, join us."

Jayden didn't hesitate, sinking into the couch. They were deep in a conversation about a community in Ghana where some of their people had relocated. Jayden listened, nodding along, intrigued.

Then Royal turned to him. "You got a girl, King?"

Jayden hesitated, then shrugged. "I just started talking to someone. We still feeling each other out."

Royal smirked, shaking his head. "King, leave these Western women alone."

Jayden chuckled as Royal leaned forward, his eyes gleaming with amusement. "My boy moved to Mali—three wives. They cook, clean, don't give him no lip." He took a slow pull from the blunt, exhaling a cloud of smoke before continuing. "Man, he livin' like a king. No stress, no back talk, just peace. He tells me all the time, 'Brother, you need to get out here and live this life. I'm planning on going this year.'" Royal shook his head, laughing to himself. "He swears it's the best move he ever made."

Jayden thought about Sonia. Thought about how hard it had been to break through her walls. He wouldn't lie—Royal's words made sense in a way that unsettled him. Maybe it could be easier. But even as the thought crossed his mind, he pushed it away. He wasn't done trying to work it out with Sonia.

Still, he laughed along with them, keeping it light. "I hear you, bro. I done had my own experiences with these controlling Western women."

Phoenix flashed in his mind. Her sharp tongue, her unyielding opinions, the way she always had to have the last word. At first, he'd been drawn to her fire—it was intoxicating, the way she carried herself like she was untouchable. She spoke with conviction, never hesitated to challenge him, to push back on anything she disagreed with. It was exciting... until it wasn't.

Their arguments had been exhausting, like a battle where neither of them could ever surrender. One time, she had gone off on him for an entire hour because he didn't text her back fast enough. Another time, she accused him of not "leading" enough, not "stepping up" as a man. But the craziest moment—the one that stuck with him most—was the night she called him weak for showing emotion. He had opened up about something personal, something deep, and instead of support, she had scoffed, telling him to "man up."

Jayden took another hit, shaking the thought away. He wasn't trying to go down that road tonight.

Royal, still lounging back with the blunt in his hand, smirked. "See? You know what I'm talkin' about. They got too much mouth, too many expectations."

Jayden exhaled slowly, nodding. "Yeah, I hear you." He wasn't about to spill his whole history with Phoenix, but he couldn't deny that part of what Royal was saying hit home.

They passed the blunt around for another thirty minutes before Jayden excused himself. He needed space.

In his room, he shut the door and let out a breath. The quiet felt good. Real good. The day had been a whirlwind—new faces, new connections, new possibilities. He grabbed a chair from the hallway and sat in the center of the room, letting it all sink in.

Wize, Egypt, Essence, Panther, Diamond, Royal—each of them had left an impression, their energy lingering in his mind like the scent of incense after a ceremony.

Wize carried wisdom like an heirloom, his every word laced with knowledge that made Jayden want to sit at his feet and just listen. He had a presence that demanded attention without needing to raise his voice, a quiet confidence that came from knowing things most people overlooked.

Egypt... she was something else entirely. Regal, magnetic. The kind of woman who made you rethink everything you thought you knew about yourself with just a glance. He had never been the type to get easily flustered, but one conversation with her and he could already feel himself tripping over his words.

Essence and Royal were laid-back, their energy easy and familiar, like a perfectly rolled blunt passed between friends. He could already tell they'd be the kind of people he could unwind with—no pressure, no expectations, just good vibes and deep conversations.

Diamond had a different energy. She was a healer, a builder. Someone who spoke the same language he did when it came to wellness and spirituality. He could already see the potential for long talks and shared knowledge, for exchanging remedies and philosophies.

And then there was Panther. Intense, sharp, the kind of man who looked right through you and saw what you were made of. Jayden respected that. Panther didn't sugarcoat things—he spoke in raw, unfiltered truth. Being around him felt like standing next to a fire; you either got warmed by it or burned, depending on how strong you were.

Each person at VLH was different, but together, they formed something powerful. And now, he was a part of it.

Then there was the community center. A free, quiet space. His home office. Things were lining up.

After a while, he pulled out his phone and dialed Pharoah. He had too much to share. He needed to talk about VLH, about the vibe, about what was next. And, more than that, he needed to pick Pharoah's brain about his next move—weed distribution.

Chapter 14

Plant Medicine

When Pharoah picked up, Jayden didn't waste a second. "Man, this place is dope!" His words tumbled out fast, his excitement too big to hold back. He ran down the list of housemates, painting quick sketches of each—Wize, deep and deliberate; Egypt, so smooth she had him fumbling his words; Essence and Royal, laid-back, smoke-in-hand kind of people; Panther, sharp-edged and intense. But when he got to Diamond, he lingered. Maybe a little too long. Mentioned their easy flow, the way she remembered him from before. Talked about how she was into healing, just like him.

Pharoah caught it. "Oh, word? Sound like you already settin' up shop," he teased.

Jayden laughed, brushing it off. "Man, chill." He shifted gears, telling Pharoah about the Arts District Community Center, how he'd already locked down a space for his healing work. The possibilities felt endless.

"That's what's up, King. I'm glad things lining up for you," Pharoah said, his voice warm with approval.

They vibed for a while, talking about plans, visions. Then Jayden dropped his tone, got serious. "So…" He let the word hang before laying it out. "You think you can put me on to flippin' that green?"

Pharoah had been waiting for this. He knew Jayden had big dreams, but dreams didn't always pay the bills. He had wondered how long it would take before Jayden saw the easy way to stack money. "I got you, bro. When we link, I'll put you on." That was all he needed to say. No deep explanations. Some things didn't belong in a phone conversation.

Jayden grinned, nodding even though Pharoah couldn't see him. "Bet." His money problems were about to be a thing of the past.

They talked for another thirty minutes, the conversation stretching and winding, before Jayden finally hung up. The weight of the day—the moving, the meeting, the smoking—had settled deep into his body. The blankets piled in the corner looked like a promise. He needed a quick recharge before the plant medicine ceremony started. Within minutes, sleep took him.

It wasn't until the deep, rolling boom of a djembe drum shook him awake that Jayden stirred. His eyes fluttered open to darkness—night had crept in while he slept. He reached for his phone. 7:20 PM. He'd been out for more than two hours. The drums told him everything he needed to know: the ceremony was starting. He figured they'd be on that "divine timing"—things in this community never ran on schedule—but still, he didn't want to be too late.

Stretching, he pulled himself up, changed into fresh clothes, and made his way toward the central part of the house.

The living room was different now. Two unfamiliar men sat on the couch, and a third was in the corner, hands moving over the djembe, pouring rhythm into the space. Jayden scanned the room, looking for a familiar face, a signal on where he was supposed to be. Nothing. He nodded at the men and kept moving, slipping into the kitchen.

Two women sat at the table, locked in deep conversation, their voices a low hum over the steady beat of the drum. They barely noticed him as he passed, heading for the fridge. He didn't recognize them either. Something about the moment made him feel out of place, like a guest in his own house.

He poured himself a glass of water and retreated to his room. Better to wait it out than hover like he didn't belong.

For twenty-five minutes, he sat in the quiet, sipping his water, listening as the house came alive. More voices. More instruments. The energy shifting. That was his cue.

When he returned to the living room, the space had transformed. About fifteen people had gathered, the air thick with drums, shakers, tambourines—sounds layering, blending, creating something bigger than all of them. And this time, his people were there. Egypt. Wize. Diamond. Inner-G, posted up on a small couch in the corner.

Jayden moved toward him. They dapped up, exchanged nods, but words were pointless now. The music had taken over.

The instruments carried on for another fifteen minutes, the drumming and rattles winding through the air like a spell being cast, until Egypt rose to her feet.

And just like that, silence.

The room stilled, every voice quieted, every movement stilled, as if Egypt had pressed a mute button on the space. She didn't have to demand attention—she commanded it just by being. Jayden sat up a little straighter, drawn in by her presence, the quiet authority in her stance, the way her voice seemed to wrap itself around the room.

She began with a libation to the ancestors, her voice rhythmic, deliberate, each chant cascading over the next as she poured water into a ceramic vase. Three candles burned around it, their flickering light casting shadows against the walls, mingling with the thin trails of incense curling toward the ceiling.

Jayden watched, transfixed.

Egypt spoke then of the history of plant medicine, of rituals passed down through generations, of the sacredness of communing with the spirit world. She lifted an Ankh, holding it high, invoking the order of Ma'at—balance, harmony, divine alignment.

Jayden soaked it in, drawn deeper. Some of this was familiar—he'd experienced similar rituals before—but there was something different here, something unspoken but powerful, humming beneath it all.

Then Egypt pulled out a small container.

"This," she said, "is our sacrament tonight."

Jayden squinted. He could feel the anticipation rippling through the room. He leaned toward Inner-G and whispered, "What is the plant?"

Inner-G grinned, his voice low, amused. "Mushrooms."

Jayden's stomach tightened.

Mushrooms?!

This wasn't what he expected. He thought plant medicine meant something for the body—liver cleansing, kidney flushing, something like that. Not this. Not a full-on mind-altering substance. He had homeboys who did shrooms, heard them talk about how it twisted time, warped reality, made the world pulse and breathe like a living thing. But he'd never considered doing it himself. Weed was his lane. Weed was safe.

Now, here he was. His first day in the Violent Light House, about to take a leap he never planned for.

His pulse picked up, but he couldn't back out. Not in front of Inner-G. Not in front of Diamond. Not in front of Wize. And especially not in front of Egypt.

He swallowed hard as she passed around the small containers. He took his and peered inside.

The shrooms looked nothing like he expected—small, shriveled, white with little gray patches, almost alien. He glanced around the room, scanning faces, wondering if anyone else was new to this. But they all seemed calm, at ease, like this was just another Saturday night.

When Egypt gave the word, everyone lifted their mushrooms and ate. No hesitation. No ceremony. Just business as usual.

Jayden followed suit, picking up the smallest piece. The texture hit him first—rubbery, tough, nothing like the mushrooms he threw on salads. The taste was worse, earthy and bitter, like dirt mixed with something spoiled. He forced it down, barely chewing, then looked into the container.

Two pieces left.

He glanced at Inner-G, who had already finished his and slipped into meditation. Jayden exhaled. Just get this over with. He took the next piece, chewed it just enough to make it swallowable, and downed it. Then the last.

And then... nothing.

Not like weed, where a hit to the chest lets you know it's working. No slow climb, no creeping haze. Just stillness.

Jayden sat back, watching the room. Some people talked like nothing had happened, deep in conversation. Egypt and Wize stood in the corner, looking serious. Inner-G was breathing deep, eyes closed, already sinking into whatever trip was coming.

Then he spotted Diamond.

She sat cross-legged on the floor, her head moving to the rhythm of the djembe drum that had started up again. Alone, in her own world.

Jayden needed answers.

He made his way over, sat beside her. She turned to him, smiling like she already knew what was coming.

"You ready for this voyage?" she asked.

He tried to play it cool. "We're doing what shamans do," he said. But the words felt fake coming out of his mouth. He dropped the act. "How long does it take to start working?"

She studied him, amused, like she'd seen this a hundred times before. "Usually about thirty minutes." Then, as if realizing something, she asked, "You ever done shrooms before?"

Jayden hesitated, then admitted the truth.

She smiled, slow and knowing. "You're gonna love it."

Jayden and Diamond's conversation flowed easy, like they had just hit unpause from before. She talked about herbs—how certain roots could calm the nervous system, how different leaves could cleanse the blood—and he matched her, throwing out facts about the body, the way organs worked together, the importance of fasting. He wanted to impress her, wanted to keep up, but the more she spoke, the more he just wanted to listen. Her voice was smooth, her energy light, like a gentle current pulling him in.

Every few minutes, Jayden checked his phone. Checking for that magic thirty-minute marker when the mushrooms were supposed to kick in.

Ten minutes in. Nothing.

Fifteen. Still nothing.

At twenty-five minutes, he wasn't sure. But the djembe drum—it sounded closer, like it was right beside him, the sound waves not just hitting his ears but wrapping around him, vibrating through his skin.

Thirty-five minutes. Nothing major, but something was shifting. Diamond's presence had a glow now, an almost golden aura around her. The peace she radiated wasn't just something he noticed—it was something he could *feel*.

By forty-five minutes, their words had started to taper off. The conversation became less about talking, more about being. Just sitting in her presence felt good, like basking in the warmth of the sun. Jayden's thoughts drifted—thinking about masculine and feminine energy, the way they danced, the way they pulled at each other without trying. Diamond, with her soft presence, was like water, flowing, inviting, effortless. He wanted to reach out, to feel her in a way beyond words. A hug, a touch, something. But he hesitated, afraid of seeming too strange, he was aware that the mushrooms had kicked in.

Then, the room shifted.

It was subtle at first, like the space had expanded, stretched wider than it had been before. The voices around him weren't separate anymore—every conversation was layered, like different frequencies all playing in perfect harmony.

Diamond turned to him then, eyes knowing. "How do you feel?"

Jayden exhaled, the words coming easy. "I feel great. I can feel the energy of the entire room."

She nodded, smiling. "These are some good shrooms."

Jayden let his eyes linger on her. He had always thought she was pretty, but right now, in this moment, she was more than that. She was magnetic. Ethereal. He could smell the oil on her skin, something soft and sweet, and it pulled at him, made him want to lean in closer, to close the space between them.

He fought the urge, tried not to overthink, but his body moved on its own. Just a little. Just enough so their shoulders brushed.

A spark. A warm, tingling current rushed through him, starting at the point where their skin met, spreading through his chest, his arms, down to his fingertips.

She didn't move away. Didn't react at all, lost in her own world.

But Jayden *felt* it.

He stayed there, soaking in the warmth of her, until his body told him to rest. He grabbed a cushion, lay his head down, and let his eyes wander.

Everything looked different now. The ceiling wasn't just a ceiling—it was holding the light fixture like it had arms, cradling it. The cracks in the wall's paint weren't flaws; they were stories, intricate, intentional. The colors in the artwork weren't just paint; they were alive, shifting, pulsing with a quiet rhythm only he could see.

The whole room had slipped into another dimension.

Jayden let it take him, let the rhythm of the space lull him, until, finally, he drifted off, sinking into sleep like the universe itself was cradling him.

Jayden woke up to silence so deep it felt sacred. The house was still, wrapped in the last whispers of night. From his spot on the floor, he could see the window, a faint purplish hue creeping in. No sun yet. He reached for his phone—5:15 a.m. The air held that cool, in-between feeling, the kind that blurred the line between late night and early morning.

The only light came from the hall, casting soft, golden shadows across the room. Jayden let his eyes adjust, scanning the space. A man on the couch, another curled up in the corner, and across the room, a couple lay tangled together—her body draped across his chest like a blanket. Everybody was still deep in it, the last echoes of the ceremony settling over them like dust.

Jayden searched for Diamond, hoping she was still nearby. But she was gone.

His mind drifted back to the night before. The way the room had come alive, colors pulsing, sound vibrating like a heartbeat he could feel under his skin. And then there was Diamond—how her energy had wrapped around his, how the pull between them had felt like something ancient, something cosmic. Masculine and feminine, yin and yang, interwoven like strands of DNA.

He exhaled. *That was real.*

Jayden sat up, rolling his shoulders, then pushed himself to his feet. His body still felt light, like he was floating just above the ground. As he stepped into the hallway and made his way to his room, the temperature shifted. The air inside was crisp, almost cold. He frowned, rubbing his arms. He'd definitely need a heater before the next night. He was grateful he'd crashed in the living room. Something about that space—about being with everyone, about being with *her*—had made the experience feel fuller, like he wasn't just witnessing something sacred but *inside* of it.

His mind wandered back to Diamond. The way her presence had grounded him, how she made him feel safe even in the middle of something unfamiliar. A small thrill ran through him—he was living in the same house as her now. There'd be more moments like last night. More energy to share, more quiet exchanges that didn't need words.

On impulse, Jayden grabbed his phone, fingers moving instinctively to search for Diamond's social media page. But before he could pull it up, a message notification caught his eye.

Sonia.

Sent at 9:30 p.m. the night before.

Hey King J, I didn't know if you were still calling. I'm going to bed soon, have a good night.

Jayden exhaled sharply. *Damn.* He'd completely forgotten. Between moving into the house, the ceremony, the trip—Sonia had slipped from his mind entirely.

Normally, seeing a message from her would have made him sit up a little straighter, would have put a small smile on his face. But now? It just felt like something he had to deal with. Like an obligation. *Like accountability.*

His interest flickered, wavered. Not because Sonia wasn't beautiful, not because she wasn't intriguing in her own way, but because *she wasn't Diamond*.

Still, he couldn't just leave her hanging. He told himself he was still invested, still had a role to play. Sonia was listening to him more, becoming more open to his knowledge, his guidance. And that meant something.

Jayden typed back quickly:

Sorry, queen, I was in a plant medicine ceremony. I'll give you a call this evening.

Then, before he could think too much about it, he went back to what he *really* wanted to do.

Diamond's page.

Her pictures, her posts—it was all a reflection of what he had felt in her presence. Soft, powerful, magnetic. He scrolled, studying her, resisting the urge to like any of her pictures. Not yet. Too soon. He didn't want to look pressed.

Ten minutes passed before he finally put his phone down.

He pulled the blankets tighter around him, willing himself back into rest. In just a few hours, he had a healing session with Howard. He needed to be sharp. But as he drifted toward sleep, the last thing on his mind wasn't the session, wasn't even Sonia.

It was *her*.

Chapter 15

Healing Connections

Two hours later, Jayden woke up to a world already in motion. Sunlight streamed through the window, stretching golden fingers across the floor. Birds outside were deep in morning conversation, their chirping layered over the distant hum of city life. He checked his phone—8:15 a.m. Just over an hour to pull himself together and make it to the community center. It was a fifteen, maybe twenty-minute walk, and he wanted to arrive early to set up.

He remembered the tray of vegan muffins he'd spotted on the kitchen counter the night before. He didn't know who they belonged to, but figured one wouldn't be missed. Moving quickly, he hopped in the shower, got dressed, grabbed a muffin, and was out the door by 9:20 a.m.

At the community center, the same woman from yesterday sat at the reception desk. He greeted her with a nod before heading straight to the table he had scoped out the day before. The place was nearly empty—a couple of people hunched over computers in the computer lab, two men lifting weights in the gym, and a few employees moving about. Otherwise, the quiet stretched. Jayden settled in, spreading out his notes, going over the treatment plan he had crafted for Howard.

Right at 10:00 a.m., his phone buzzed. A message from Howard: I just arrived. Jayden texted back: I'll meet you at the desk.

A minute later, Howard stepped inside, and Jayden led him to the table.

"How you holding up, man?" Jayden asked, scanning his face.

Howard let out a deep sigh. "Man, these migraines been kicking my butt. Had to call out of work yesterday. I hope you got something for me."

Jayden nodded, his confidence steady. "I got you. But you know I deal with health holistically. That means real lifestyle changes. Migraines can be serious, but there are natural ways to ease them—even prevent them. Hydration is key. Dehydration triggers migraines like crazy. You gotta drink plenty of water, maybe add in some coconut water for electrolytes. And magnesium?

A lot of people don't realize they're deficient. Leafy greens, nuts, seeds, bananas—those will help."

He had practiced this opening line over and over, making sure it flowed naturally. Howard leaned in, listening. Jayden kept going, asking about his diet, his stress levels, how much sugar and salt he was consuming. Howard admitted he needed to clean things up.

They talked for forty minutes, mapping out a plan. Before they wrapped up, Jayden handed Howard a sheet summarizing everything, his CashApp and Zelle details printed at the bottom. Howard nodded in appreciation, pulled out his phone, and sent the payment right then and there.

They scheduled another session for the following week, but Jayden told him to check in before then, let him know how he was feeling. As Howard walked out, Jayden sat back, exhaling deeply.

This—this right here—was what he was meant to do.

Inner-G told Jayden he'd pick him up at 1:00 p.m. for the vending event. Jayden agreed to help, and instead of getting paid, his cut would go to Wize for his portion of the rent. It felt like the right thing to do. After wrapping up his session with Howard, Jayden walked home, his steps steady, his mind still turning over the conversation from earlier. When he checked the time, it was 11:20 a.m.

As soon as he stepped inside, voices carried from the kitchen—sharp, rising, the kind of tension that made a space feel smaller. A man and a woman. Arguing. Curious, Jayden edged around the corner and found himself staring at Diamond and Royal, locked in the middle of a heated exchange.

His heart kicked up when he saw Diamond. But this wasn't the soft-spoken, glowing energy from the night before. No, this was a different side of her—sharp, unyielding, fire where there had been water. She stood squared off against Royal, her tone edged with challenge, her body language pointed. When Jayden stepped into the room, both of them turned to him at once, looking like they wanted backup.

Diamond spoke first. "Jayden, do you think a man should have more than one wife?"

Jayden blinked. Wow. That was not the conversation he expected to walk into. He could feel the weight of their stares, both waiting for him to tip the scale. Royal, who he was trying to build a bond with. Diamond, who he was quickly—too quickly—developing a thing for.

He measured his words carefully. "Well," he started slowly, "I think it's up to the individual. If a man and a woman agree to that, then that's their decision."

It was the safest answer he could think of, but it didn't satisfy Diamond.

She scoffed, turning back to Royal. "Be careful what you pick up from Mr. Royal here," she said, folding her arms. "Brother got hurt in one relationship and now he can't handle the emotional depth of a real one."

Royal's laugh was short, dismissive. "See, Jayden, these Western women are all the same. In Africa, the women get it. Sister wives are productive for the life of the village."

Diamond rolled her eyes. "You can't even take care of one woman," she shot back. "Why don't you learn how to protect the feelings and emotions of one woman first? Then maybe—maybe—you can have this conversation. You're barely making it yourself financially. You really think you're gonna take care of three wives? You're living in a fantasy, my brother."

Royal turned to Jayden, shaking his head. "You see, king? These women be tripping."

The words hit Jayden sideways, stirring up something Inner-G had said before—She's a trip, but she's cool. Maybe there was more to Diamond than what he had seen so far. Maybe there was more to all these "Western" women—Sonia included.

At the same time, Diamond had a point. Maybe Royal really had been hurt before, maybe he was trying to rewrite his story in a way that made sense to him. Jayden wasn't sure. When it came to relationships, he was still figuring things out himself.

One thing he did know? He wasn't about to get stuck in the middle of this debate.

"Aight, y'all, I gotta get ready for this event. Inner-G's coming in a little bit." He didn't mention that "a little bit" was actually an hour and a half later.

Diamond exhaled, then looked at him with something softer in her expression. "King J," she said slowly, "you seem like a good man. Don't let these hurt men rub off on you."

Jayden smiled, gave a nod, and walked off, but inside, something buzzed.

She thinks I'm a good man.

He let that sit with him as he made his way back to his room.

Inner-G pulled up to the Violet Light House right at 1:00 p.m., his car packed to the brim. A canopy, folding table, chairs—everything necessary for the day's work. In the backseat, nestled between boxes of dried herbs, books on Qi Gong and Reiki, and an array of polished crystals, Jayden sat wedged against the door, knees pressed uncomfortably against the dashboard. The passenger seat had been pushed up to make space, leaving him barely any room to breathe.

As soon as Inner-G caught his eye, he grinned. "You ready to make this money?"

"Let's do it," Jayden shot back.

On the way there, Inner-G kept the energy high, talking about the event like it was the biggest opportunity of the year. "Plenty of people, bro. Good traffic. Good energy. You just hold it down at the table, and I'll be moving through the crowd, making connections."

"Cool, sounds good to me," Jayden agreed. Easy enough.

But as they pulled up to the park, something felt… off. Jayden expected the usual scene—drum circles, incense smoke curling through the air, people wrapped in bright African prints, Ankhs gleaming in the sun. That wasn't what he saw. Instead, the park was full of what he could only describe as regular folks. Families pushing strollers, older couples in walking shoes, teenagers in jeans and sneakers. No headwraps. No pan-African colors. No familiar signs of the conscious community.

Jayden frowned. "What kind of event is this?"

Inner-G chuckled, pulling into a parking spot. "Community-wide health and wellness fair. This is where you make the real money, brother."

Jayden didn't respond, just stepped out of the car and grabbed the canopy. The two of them carried their supplies about fifty feet to the reserved spot in the grass. This was Jayden's first time vending, so he followed Inner-G's lead—unfolding the table, spreading out the merchandise. Inner-G draped a cloth over the table, its deep blue fabric stamped with a massive Eye of Horus at the center. Then, piece by piece, he laid out the books, herbs, crystals, and gold-tone Egyptian statues, adjusting them like sacred offerings. Around them, other vendors were doing the same, setting up their spaces, preparing for the day's flow.

As Jayden worked, a memory flickered to life—this park, years ago. He had been here before. Back then, it wasn't about vending, it was about wandering. His mother and sisters beside him, weaving through the different tables, sampling food, listening to live music. The sun had been warm on his skin, and he remembered the feeling of his mother's hand tightening around his whenever he strayed too far. It felt like another lifetime. Now, he was here as an adult, sitting on the other side of the table, seeing the world through an entirely different lens.

Once everything was in place, Jayden settled into his seat. He let his eyes drift over the setup around him—a life insurance booth to his left, a chiropractor's table across from him. A few tables down, handmade soaps and lotions were being arranged with careful precision. He was taking it all in, getting a feel for the space, when something unexpected happened.

Three tables down, a banner caught his eye.

New Life Church.

For a moment, Jayden just stared, his mind slow to register what he was seeing. Then, like a puzzle snapping into place, the faces came into focus. Regina. His mother's old friend from church. Next to her, Charles, her husband. And then, standing beside them, two teenagers—except they weren't kids anymore. Jayson and Amiyah.

Jayden exhaled sharply. Last time he had seen them, they were maybe twelve or thirteen, gangly and full of youthful energy. Now, they were practically grown, eighteen or nineteen at least. Which meant it had been six years. Six years since he last set foot in New Life. Six years since he walked away.

His body tensed.

This was the last thing he expected.

Jayden immediately looked away, heart thudding against his ribs. He had come here for business, not for a reunion. The last thing he wanted was to dredge up old conversations about why he left, what he believed now, or the inevitable "We've been praying for you" that would come with those knowing smiles.

He lowered his head, eyes on the table, hoping—praying, even though he didn't do that much anymore—that if he just kept his energy low, if he didn't send any mental waves in their direction, maybe they wouldn't notice him. Maybe the universe would let him disappear.

But the irony of it all wasn't lost on him.

Here he was, sitting under the all-seeing Eye of Horus, trying to be invisible.

And the past was three tables down, staring right at him.

By the time they finished setting up, the sun had shifted, settling higher in the sky, casting a warm glow over the park. It was 2:30 p.m., and the event was scheduled to kick off at 3:00. Inner-G ran through the rundown, rattling off the prices, reminding Jayden to talk up the healing properties of the crystals, the benefits of Qi Gong, and the alternative paths to wellness. Jayden listened, nodding along. A year under

Inner-G's teaching had given him confidence in the lingo, the philosophy, the pitch. This was his world now—or at least, he was trying to make it his.

Before the crowds rolled in, Inner-G pressed a $10 bill into Jayden's palm. "Get yourself something to eat before things get busy."

Jayden took the money and, without hesitation, veered in the opposite direction of his old church's table. He had no desire to run into familiar faces before he absolutely had to. He found a food truck, grabbed a turkey burger and fries, and made his way back, arriving at his table just as the event officially began.

At first, the scene was slow-moving. People wandered in, easing into the rhythm of the event, pausing at tables, checking out the displays. Jayden sat, eating, watching. At 3:20 p.m., his first customers arrived—a young couple, early twenties, eyes flickering with curiosity.

"We just felt drawn to these," the woman said, fingers hovering over the crystals like they were humming with energy.

Jayden leaned in, slipping into the flow. He explained each stone's purpose—one for abundance, another for protection, another for health. The woman picked up the abundance crystal; the man chose the one for health. A solid start.

After they left, the lull returned. Jayden kept his head down, but his eyes betrayed him, darting every so often toward the New Life Church table. He didn't want to be seen, didn't want to be recognized. Yet, he couldn't stop himself from checking.

By 3:45 p.m., the foot traffic picked up. More people stopped by, some buying crystals, some flipping through books, others just wanting to talk. Jayden got caught up in the momentum, explaining how "Qi Gong is a meditative practice incorporating breathing, movement, and sound," and how "crystals can increase confidence, strengthen the immune system, and regulate the body's rhythm." He was deep in his element, wrapped in the moment.

Until he wasn't.

He was mid-sentence, explaining the properties of a stone to an interested woman, when his gaze lifted—and locked onto a familiar face. Regina.

She stood just behind the woman, watching him.

Jayden's breath hitched, but he recovered quickly, offering a stiff nod in her direction before finishing his spiel. The woman thanked him, pocketed her wallet without buying anything, and walked away.

Regina stepped forward.

"My gosh," she said, eyes scanning him, taking in the transformation. "Jayden, it's so good to see you. You look so different."

Different was one way to put it.

Gone was the clean-cut kid from New Life's youth group. Now, Jayden had a full beard, thick dreadlocks, a presence that no longer fit the mold of the boy she once knew.

Jayden forced a half-smile. "Hey, Ms. Regina. Good to see you too."

She wasted no time. "What have you been up to? We haven't seen you in so long. Why haven't you come back to church?"

Jayden exhaled slowly, keeping his voice even. "I'm on a different path now."

Regina nodded, but there was something behind her eyes. Something that said she already knew. Jayden's aunt and sisters had probably kept her informed, kept him in those prayer circles, kept his name lifted in hopes he'd "come back into the fold."

She pressed her lips together, then said carefully, "Jayden, Jesus is the way, the truth, and the life. I heard you telling that woman that crystals can heal her."

Jayden exhaled, keeping his face neutral, but inside, something twisted. Before he could come up with a response, she leaned in slightly, her voice softer now, but no less firm.

"Do you know my son got off drugs the minute he accepted Jesus?" She shook her head, a mix of disbelief and gratitude in her eyes. "You don't know what it was like. He was lost, baby. Stealing from me. Lying. Staying out all night, high out of his mind. I tried everything—therapy, rehab, locking up my purse, begging him to just stop." She pressed a hand to her chest, steadying herself. "But nothing worked. Not until he surrendered, for real. And when he did?" Her eyes glistened. "He ain't touched that stuff since. That was two years ago."

She let the weight of her words settle between them before shaking her head again, this time with a small, knowing smile. "No crystal could have done that."

Jayden swallowed. He wanted to dismiss it, wanted to tell himself she was just emotional, caught up in her beliefs. But the conviction in her voice... it reminded him of something. Something he used to have.

Jayden forced a tight-lipped smile and nodded, pretending her words didn't stir something deep inside him. He told himself it was just her perspective, just another person clinging to faith because they needed something to believe in. Pushing the feeling down, he shifted his weight. Still, something inside him stirred. A flicker of anger. A memory.

He swallowed hard and said, barely above a whisper, "Jesus didn't save my mother."

Regina's expression barely faltered. If anything, her voice only grew stronger. "Jayden, ultimately, God decides who lives and dies. Death isn't a punishment—it comes for us all, the righteous and the wicked. Your mother was a woman of faith. She's with the Lord now."

Jayden felt the weight of her words pressing against him. He had spent years wrestling with questions, coming to his own conclusions. He heard what she was saying, but he wasn't sold on it. And this wasn't the time or place to get into it.

He took a breath. "I hear you, Ms. Regina. But I've learned a lot about healing, and that's what I'm focused on now."

Regina's gaze dropped to his table, scanning the books, the crystals, the Egyptian statues. Then, she looked back at him—really looked at him. Past the beard, past the locs. Deep into the parts of him that still carried hurt.

"Jayden," she said softly, but with conviction, "rocks, stones, and statues can't save souls. Let the Holy Spirit guide you to a personal relationship with Jesus Christ. There is only one way to Yahweh's kingdom."

Jayden's throat tightened. He shifted, glancing at the growing line of customers. "I appreciate you stopping by, Ms. Regina, but I got a lot of people to tend to."

She held his gaze a beat longer, then nodded, a trace of sadness in her eyes.

"It really was good seeing you," she said, reaching into her bag. She handed him a church pamphlet, her and her husband's phone numbers written neatly on the back. "Call us. Stop by."

Jayden took it, slipping it into his pocket. "Thanks. You take care."

She lingered a second longer, then turned and walked away.

Jayden exhaled, his fingers twitching against the pamphlet in his pocket. He thought about throwing it away right then and there, but something stopped him.

Instead, he shoved his hands into his lap, straightened his back, and greeted his next customer.

Regina went back to her table while Jayden turned his attention back to vending, but something had shifted. The rhythm was off. His words felt rehearsed, his movements mechanical. He handed out information, explained the properties of the stones, but his mind wasn't in it. His thoughts tangled around his mother, the church, the conversation with Regina. The crystals—once vibrant, humming with energy in his hands—suddenly looked like nothing more than polished rocks, cold and lifeless.

A little while later, Inner-G returned, moving with his usual easy confidence, eyes scanning the table. "Jayden, my man! I made some solid connections," he said, nodding toward the items that had sold. "And look at you, doing your thing. Proud of you, brother."

Jayden forced a smile. "Yeah, appreciate it."

Inner-G clapped a hand on Jayden's shoulder. "Go take a break, walk around, see what else is going on."

Jayden hesitated. Before, he would've wandered, maybe checked out some holistic booths, talked to like-minded folks. But now, his cover was blown. Regina had seen him. It was only a matter of time before others did, too. He exhaled sharply. Might as well get it over with.

He walked over to New Life's table, already bracing himself.

Charles spotted him first. His face lit up, his handshake firm. "How's it going, son? Been a while."

Jayden nodded. "Yeah, it has." He told Charles about moving into his new place, about the business.

Charles listened, nodding, a proud smile settling onto his face. "That's good, real good. We miss you at church, though. You know you're an anointed young man, right? Your understanding of scripture was always impressive."

Jayden shifted his weight. "I appreciate that, but... I'm on a different path now."

Charles studied him for a moment, then rested a hand on his shoulder. His voice was steady, knowing. "Trust in the Lord with all your heart and do not lean on your own understanding. In all your ways acknowledge Him, and He will make straight your paths."

Jayden felt the words settle into him. He knew that verse inside and out. Back in youth group, he used to say it to others—kids with questions, kids curious about other religions, kids searching. He had been the one guiding them, grounding them. Some of those same kids had thanked him later, saying his words had given them clarity.

And now here he was, on the other side of it.

A quiet unease crept in, something he couldn't name. His mind flickered between the Qi Gong and crystals he'd spent the afternoon talking about and the teachings he used to believe in so fiercely. The conviction he once had, the clarity—where had it gone?

No, he told himself. I've moved past that Christian stuff. I've elevated.

Before he could sit with the feeling too long, movement caught his eye.

Jayson and Amiyah.

At first, they didn't recognize him. But then, as realization dawned, their faces lit up.

"Jayden? No way!" Amiyah squealed.

Jayson grinned. "Man, it's been forever! You used to run our whole youth group."

They rushed over, their excitement undeniable. Jayden met them with the same energy, commenting on how much they'd grown, asking about life.

"So, who are you here with?" Jayson asked.

"I've got a table a few rows down," Jayden said.

"What are you vending?" Amiyah asked.

Jayden hesitated. "Crystals. Healing books."

The shift was almost imperceptible, but he caught it. The way their smiles faltered just a bit, the slight exchange of glances.

Amiyah spoke first. "Why'd you stop coming to New Life?"

Jayden exhaled, already knowing where this was headed. "I'm just on a different path now. I've been studying other spiritual traditions, learning a lot."

Jayson's face tightened, his brows knitting together. "So you don't follow the Way of Christ anymore?"

Jayden shook his head. "That's just not for me anymore."

Jayson's voice softened. "I remember you teaching me that He was the Way, the Truth, and the Life. That there was no way to the Father except through Him." He swallowed hard. "I was about to run away from home when you pulled me aside that night after Bible study. I don't know where I'd be if you hadn't talked to me."

Jayden felt something shift in his chest. A weight. A strange, unexpected heaviness.

Amiyah's voice came next, quieter, almost hesitant. "I used to hate how I looked. I used to cut myself. You probably never knew, but I did. And your Bible classes… they changed my whole outlook on myself. My grades got better. I made better choices. I stopped hanging with the wrong people. And now…" She glanced at Jayson, then back at Jayden. "We lead the youth ministry."

Jayden nodded slowly, taking it all in. He did remember them coming in rough around the edges. He didn't know their full stories, but he had seen the transformation in them. He just never thought about the fact that he had been part of that transformation.

Amiyah continued, telling him about the work they'd been doing—feeding the homeless, helping kids struggling with addiction, raising money for school supplies.

Jayden listened, nodding, but his mind was somewhere else. As Amiyah spoke, one thought hit him like a jolt: he needed to make sure they didn't see him smoking weed.

They had once looked up to him.

And here they were, still standing in that same faith. While he...

Jayden shook off the feeling, forcing a smile. "I'm proud of you both. Really. That's good work you're doing." He cleared his throat. "I should get back to my table, though."

They nodded, saying their goodbyes, telling him to stop by again.

Jayden turned, heading back toward his booth, but something sat heavy on him. He should've felt good—these were kids he had helped, kids who were doing well. But instead, something about the conversation gnawed at him.

Something didn't sit right.

When Jayden returned to the table, Inner-G was mid-conversation with a couple of potential customers, hands moving fluidly as he spoke, weaving words about crystals, chakras, and the power of energy healing. Jayden stood back, watching, listening. Normally, he'd be right there with him, nodding along, adding his own insights. But tonight, his mind was somewhere else.

As soon as the customers walked away, Inner-G turned to him with a grin. "Welcome back, my guy. I saw you over there politicking for a minute—what kind of connections you making three tables down?"

Jayden exhaled, rubbing the back of his neck. "That was my old church."

Inner-G's eyes widened before a smirk played on his lips. "Oh wow, so that's the brainwash camp you came from?"

That was the kind of joke Jayden usually laughed at. A quick chuckle, maybe a shake of the head, but this time, the words hit different. He thought about Jayson and Amiyah, the way their eyes lit up when they saw him, the way their voices carried that kind of conviction he used to have. He thought about how they had held on to the very thing he had let go of.

He just shook his head, his response quiet. "Yeah... that's them."

Inner-G wasn't paying attention to his shift in tone. "They need to drop that Jesus talk and come get some of this energy healing," he said, tapping the table where the crystals sat gleaming under the sunlight.

Jayden heard him, but it was like the words floated somewhere outside of him, unable to land. He nodded, forced a weak chuckle. "Haha, yeah."

But he didn't feel it.

They vended for another four hours, but Jayden was just going through the motions—smiling, selling, answering questions, but his mind kept circling back to the young adults at the New Life table. The things they said. The way they looked at him. The gratitude in their voices.

He kept trying to shake it, telling himself the same things he always did—*We're enlightened. We're on a higher frequency. We're doing the real healing work.* But tonight, those words felt flimsy, like paper-thin affirmations that even he didn't believe.

By the time the event wrapped up, Jayden felt drained in a way he couldn't explain. They broke down the setup—collapsed the canopy, folded the table, packed everything into the car.

Inner-G clapped his hands together, grinning. "We did good, king. These people were looking for what we offer."

Jayden nodded, forcing a smile.

Inner-G reached into his pocket and pulled out a crisp twenty, handing it to him. "I appreciate you rolling with me today. You're definitely earning your spot at the VLH."

"Appreciate it," Jayden said, tucking the bill into his pocket.

As they packed up the last of their things, Jayden glanced at the time. "Yo, can we stop at the store real quick? I need to grab a heater."

"Yeah, no problem."

They made the stop and got back to the Violet Light House at 9:10. Jayden let out a deep breath as they pulled into the driveway. He was ready to just go inside, maybe play some music to drown out his thoughts, but Inner-G wasn't done vibing yet.

They sat in the car, rolling up a blunt, passing it back and forth, talking about the event, the people they met, the money they made. Jayden nodded along, responding when he needed to, but his mind wasn't fully in the conversation.

They hung out for another hour before Inner-G stretched, exhaled, and patted Jayden's shoulder. "A'ight, I'm out. Catch you tomorrow."

Jayden nodded. "Yeah, later."

As he walked up to the front door, the cool night air hit him, and suddenly, his mind shifted—Sonia. He was supposed to call her.

He pulled out his phone. 10:30.

Was it too late?

Maybe. But he still wanted to hear her voice.

As soon as he got inside, he decided he'd send her a quick text. Just to see if she was up. Just to see if she had time.

Maybe a conversation with her would settle him. Maybe.

Chapter 16

Open for Business

Jayden stared at his phone for a moment before sending the text. "You up?"

Sonia's reply came quick. "Yes, but getting ready for bed."

"Can I call you?" he typed back, already knowing the answer.

"Can we talk tomorrow?"

Jayden exhaled, rubbing his hand over his face. He knew she probably thought he'd been brushing her off all weekend. Maybe he had. But exhaustion weighed on him, thick and heavy from everything that had gone down. "That's fine, talk to you tomorrow," he replied. No point in pushing it.

He unpacked the heater, plugged it in, and watched as the small red light flickered on, casting a weak glow in the dim room. Heat seeped into the cold air, slow and steady. Jayden let out a deep breath. He needed movement, distraction. He grabbed his phone and called Pharoah.

"Peace, king," Pharoah answered on the first ring.

"Peace, I'm at the VLH. What you doing?"

"Up the street at Jewelz's spot. I can slide through in a few."

"Bet. Come around back," Jayden said, a little too eagerly.

Thirty minutes later, a knock came at the door. Jayden let Pharoah in, rolled up a blunt, and settled into the comfort of familiar habits. As the smoke curled in the air, Jayden leaned back, exhaling slow.

"Man, the room came alive," he said, eyes gleaming as he recounted his shroom trip. "I could feel everybody's energy, their vibrations, like waves moving through me."

Pharoah's eyebrows raised. "That sounds dope. Let me know next time y'all doing some of that plant medicine."

Jayden chuckled but didn't linger on it. He had other things on his mind.

"So about this distribution thing..." he said, shifting the conversation.

Pharoah grinned. "King tryna come up," he teased.

They talked shop. Pharoah broke down his connections, the flow of the product, the numbers. "How much you tryna start with?"

Jayden thought about his bank account, the reality of his finances pressing in. "Fifty."

Pharoah scoffed, shaking his head. "Bruh, that's a personal stash. I thought you was trying to flip something." He laughed, then leaned forward, voice dropping. "Look, Imma hit you with an ounce and a scale. Just pay me back when you flip it."

Jayden nodded, his mind made up. This was the move. No second-guessing, no hesitation. They locked in the plan for the next day, and then Pharoah bounced.

The next morning, Jayden woke up with the weight of yesterday pressing in on him. He thought about the Health and Wellness Fair—his vending, the crystals, the conversations that still lingered in his mind. Regina. Charles. Amiyah. Jayson. He hadn't expected to be confronted with his past like that, hadn't realized how much of a mark he'd left.

He sat up, running a hand over his head. His best days couldn't be behind him.

Inner-G had that relentless hustle, that drive. Jayden needed to match that. He still wanted to change lives—

just in a bigger, more enlightened way. Maybe he hadn't been pushing hard enough. He had let the lack of response to his social media posts get in his head, let the slow growth of Lion Heart Healing drain his motivation. Howard was a client, sure, but one client at $20 a week wasn't enough.

The weed hustle was about money, but Lion Heart Healing—that was purpose.

He decided to spend the morning posting, reaching out to contacts, making moves. He barely got ten minutes in before his phone rang.

"King J, meet me at the 7-11 on Main Street," Pharoah's voice was all business. "You about to get your first pickup."

Jayden grinned. "Bet."

He got himself together and headed out. The 20-minute walk to the store was quiet, giving him too much time to think. By the time he arrived, Pharoah was already there, leaned against the wall, talking on his phone.

Five minutes later, a black Chevy truck pulled up, the bass from the speakers rattling the curb. Pharoah threw up a hand in greeting, then nodded at Jayden. "Let's roll."

Jayden slid into the back seat, sizing up the driver as Pharoah made introductions. "Peace, fam. This is King J. King J, meet Buffalo."

Buffalo had thick, unkempt locs and a mouth full of gold teeth. A heavy chain hung around his neck, a picture of a little girl inside the pendant. His daughter, Jayden guessed.

"Peace, King J," Buffalo said, his Southern drawl thick.

Jayden nodded. "Peace."

Buffalo tapped his fingers on the steering wheel, eyeing Jayden through the rearview. "Pharoah tells me you getting in the game. Just keep it cool and you'll be alright."

Jayden nodded again, but this time, something tightened in his chest.

Buffalo and Pharoah talked shop—quality, pricing, how the game had shifted since dispensaries started taking over. Jayden listened, absorbing it all, but his mind flickered back to yesterday. To Charles's words, to the look in Amiyah and Jayson's eyes. To a past life that felt too close, yet too far away.

Buffalo dapped them up before pulling off, leaving Jayden and Pharoah standing under the buzzing fluorescent lights of the 7-11. Jayden clenched his jaw, pushing the thoughts down.

He had made his choice.

Hadn't he?

Pharoah stretched, exhaling the last of the blunt's smoke before clapping Jayden on the shoulder. "Aight, I'm out. Gonna go back to my spot."

Jayden nodded, dapping him up before heading out. The walk back home was quiet, the cold air clearing some of the haze from his mind. He didn't regret linking with Pharoah, but he had to stay focused. Too many things were pulling him in too many directions.

When he stepped inside, the scent of fresh fruit and herbs hit him. Panther was in the kitchen, blending up a smoothie, his arms flexing as he worked the blender.

"Salute, warrior. How you feelin'?" Panther greeted, eyes steady as he poured the thick, purple liquid into a tall glass.

"I'm good, man. Just maintaining," Jayden said, leaning against the counter.

Panther nodded knowingly. "I hear you. Gotta stay fueled, though. The body is our first defense."

Jayden watched as Panther took a sip, eyes closing like he could taste every nutrient, every vitamin soaking into his system. "People don't understand, man. The food industry, the healthcare industry—it's all a setup. They get you addicted to sugar, salt, chemicals, all that poison. Then when your body breaks down—diabetes, cancer, high blood pressure—they got you spending money at their hospitals, taking their pills."

Jayden's stomach twisted as he glanced at his own breakfast—a frozen cheese burrito and a bottle of sugary juice. Panther caught his eye and grinned. "See? That's what I'm talking about." He pushed a second glass across the counter. "Here, try this king."

Jayden hesitated, then took the smoothie, sipping cautiously. The flavors—banana, berries, something green—exploded on his tongue. He had to admit, it was good.

"The body is a temple," Panther said, leaning against the counter. "Even the Bible says that. But I see so many so-called believers trashing their bodies while their own book tells them to honor it. That's sacrilege."

Jayden nodded, feeling a pang of guilt. "I hear you, bro. I wish my family ate better. Maybe they'd live longer."

Panther gave a slow, approving nod. They finished their smoothies in silence, the faint buzz of the city outside seeping into the room. As Jayden rinsed his glass, his mind wandered to Sonia. He needed to call her.

Jayden sat on his bed, phone in hand, heart thudding lightly. He called. No answer.

His stomach tightened. Maybe she was still upset. Maybe he'd messed things up. He tossed the phone onto his pillow, jaw tightening.

Five minutes later, it vibrated. Sonia.

"Hey," she said, voice unreadable. "I was starting to think you forgot about me."

Jayden exhaled, forcing a smile into his voice. "Never that. Just been busy. It's good to hear your voice."

The conversation eased from there—he told her about his shroom trip, about the way the room had come alive, how he could feel people's energy in waves. Sonia listened, but he could hear the hesitation in her voice. She wasn't sold on it. Then she switched gears, talking about her weekend—flea markets with her mom, a get-together with friends. It was easy, flowing, until she said,

"I asked my dad about what you said about the Bible."

Jayden sat up straighter. "Oh yeah?" His pulse quickened. He wanted to know every word. "Did he know the Bible was forced on us in slavery?" He let the words drip with disdain, expecting her to agree.

But Sonia's voice sharpened. "No. He said the Bible was in Africa way before it ever reached Europe. That the people who wrote it were Black."

Jayden blinked. That was not the answer he expected.

"He said people think Armenia was the first country to become Christian, but it was actually Ethiopia."

Jayden felt something rise in his chest—frustration, impatience. The shift in her tone told him everything. She believed her dad more than him.

"So your dad knows about Africa," he said, his voice edged with sarcasm. "But does he know the Jesus story comes straight from the ancient Egyptian god Horus?"

Sonia didn't even pause. "No. He said the Bible is an original story. That your research is weak and just something you probably Googled."

Jayden's fingers gripped the phone tighter.

"He said that just because something has similarities doesn't mean one thing comes from another. It's false correlation. And he said—" she hesitated, then continued, "he said you don't have the Holy Spirit, which is why you don't know Jesus walked in the flesh."

A slow heat crawled up Jayden's spine. He could feel her slipping away, back into their grip. Before she talked to her father, she had been open. She had been listening. Now?

Now, she was back in their world.

He leaned forward, voice low, urgent. "Well, that's what your dad thinks. But what do you think?"

Sonia hesitated. "Well…" she said slowly. "I don't think millions of people could all be wrong."

Jayden sat up straight. "They're wrong about a lot of things!" he shot back, louder than he meant to.

Sonia sighed. "Jayden, you're free to believe what you want. Just don't force your views on me."

That stung. That wasn't how this was supposed to go. He could feel her closing the door on the conversation.

He exhaled, forcing himself to pull back. "Okay, queen. Just… stay open-minded."

They moved on, talked for another twenty minutes—safe topics, lighter things. But Jayden felt it in his gut.

This wasn't over.

Jayden hung up and stretched, the weight of the conversation with Sonia still sitting somewhere in his chest, but he shook it off. He wasn't about to let it ruin his night. Voices floated in from the living room, low and relaxed, the kind that came with smoke in the air and time to kill. He decided to bag his weed and check it out.

When he stepped in, Essence and Royal were sprawled on the couch, the thick scent of weed wrapping around them. Blunt smoke curled toward the ceiling, moving slow, lazy.

"Peace, fellas. What's good?" Jayden said, easing into the room. He kept his tone light, casual, but he had a purpose. It was time to let people know he was open for business. "I got that fire if y'all need."

Royal raised an eyebrow with a half-smile as he passed the blunt to Essence. "Okay, young king. I didn't know you was holdin'. Imma definitely check what you got."

Jayden pulled out his stash, and just like that, the transaction was made—smooth, effortless. Essence and Royal each copped a little, rolling another blunt before Jayden could even put his money away.

Essence took a long pull, exhaled, then nodded approvingly. "This that sour diesel. Good stuff. Imma put my people on to you."

Jayden watched as Essence pulled out his phone, thumbs moving fast. "My man at the VLH got that good green if you need."

The replies came quick—two people, ready to buy.

Over the next few hours, people came and went from the VLH like clockwork—some just passing through, others staying to lounge and soak in the vibe. But plenty had a purpose. Word spread fast that Jayden had the goods, and one by one, they found their way to him. A handshake here, a nod there. Cash discreetly folded into palms, small bags slipped into pockets. Some lingered, rolling up on the spot, letting the smoke curl into the air like incense at an altar. Others made their transactions quick, dipping out as fast as they came, eyes always shifting, always aware.

Jayden felt the rush of it, the control. Supply met demand, and he was the middleman making it happen. Every exchange reinforced what he already knew—this was easy money. The kind of hustle that didn't require a punch clock or a manager breathing down his neck. By the time his last bag was gone, Jayden leaned back on the couch, exhaling deep. This was just the beginning.

Within three hours, Jayden was sold out. Doubled his money. Just like that.

He leaned back, blunt in hand, the slow burn of the high settling into his limbs. Man, he thought, watching the smoke dance in the air. That was almost too easy.

They sat for another thirty minutes, vibing, letting the weed pull them deeper into the couch. Jayden listened to Royal and Essence go back and forth about music, about women, about everything and nothing. But his mind was somewhere else—on the cash in his pocket, on the ease of it all. Already, he was that dude. The one with the good stuff. And people were taking notice.

Back in his room, Jayden hit up Pharoah, his excitement bubbling over.

"Bro, this stuff flew. I'ma need more."

Pharoah chuckled on the other end, like he already knew. "I'm tellin' you, king. You in the perfect location. You sittin' in a hub for that green."

Jayden grinned, running his fingers over the bills in his lap.

"I'll tell Buffalo to double up on your next batch," Pharoah continued. "And don't even worry about paying me back till your next flip."

Jayden nodded, feeling the weight of trust in those words. "Bet."

"I'ma hit Buffalo now. I'll call you back."

Ten minutes later, his phone buzzed again.

"Buffalo said he good to meet in an hour. Same spot— 7-Eleven."

"Say less."

Jayden leaned back, staring at the cash in his hands. Over $400. And all he did was be in the right place with the right product.

Before he even got up to leave, his phone pinged—two more texts. More people looking for him.

This is it, he thought.

By the end of the day, half his new supply was gone.

The next morning, his phone wouldn't stop buzzing.

Every time he checked, another text, another knock at the door. By late afternoon, seven people had come through, cash in hand. Jayden sat on his bed, counting. Six hundred dollars. And he still had some left to sell.

He leaned back, letting the reality sink in. His mind drifted—back to the warehouse, the endless hours on his feet, sweating for a paycheck that barely made it feel worth it. It shifted to Lion Heart Healing, the hours spent posting on social media, trying to make something out of nothing. Twenty dollars a week. That's what all that effort got him.

His phone buzzed again. Another customer. Another stack in his pocket.

He was supposed to meet with Howard tomorrow, but now, the idea felt distant. Like something from another life. His excitement for those sessions was slipping.

Why grind so hard for slow money when fast money came this easy?

Jayden had watched people struggle his whole life—his mom working doubles just to keep the lights on, his aunt Patrice constantly reminding him about "hard work and responsibility," as if breaking his back for a paycheck that barely covered rent was something to be proud of. He thought about the people who clocked in every morning, dragging themselves through the same routine, waiting two weeks for a check that barely lasted one. And for what? Stability? Security? Even that wasn't guaranteed. He'd seen plenty of hardworking folks still end up broke, still evicted, still begging for extensions on their bills.

But this? This was different. The cash was in his hands before the sun set. No waiting. No taxes. No boss telling him what to do. He had product, people wanted it, and they paid. Simple. No resumes, no interviews, no proving himself to anybody but the game itself.

And the rush—it was addictive. The way people came looking for him, needing him, treating him like he was somebody. This wasn't just about money. It was power. It was status. It was walking into a room and knowing he had something everybody wanted.

Slow money might be safe, but it wasn't built for someone like him. Fast money moved, and Jayden was ready to move with it.

Jayden exhaled, thinking back to the manifestation lessons with Inner-G.

"Emotional alignment," he murmured to himself.

That was the key, right? The energy behind manifestation. And right now, he could feel it— success, abundance.

Maybe the universe had been waiting for him to get here all along.

That evening, Jayden's phone buzzed, the screen lighting up with a name he didn't expect but definitely welcomed—Diamond.

Blessings, King J. I heard you got the good stuff. Why didn't you let your girl know about this?

Jayden stared at the message for a second, lips pulling into a slow smile. They had exchanged numbers, but she had never used his before. Until now.

You know where I'm at, he texted back.

See you in a few, she replied.

Chapter 17

The Chariot Card

Five minutes after Diamond texted Jayden, a knock echoed through his door. When he opened it, Diamond stood there, hip cocked, eyes low-lidded but sharp. "People been talking about your sour diesel," she said, stepping inside like she belonged there. "Had to see for myself. Gimme twenty dollars' worth. I get paid tomorrow—I'll get more then."

Jayden nodded, handed her the bag, and before long, they were sitting cross-legged on the floor, smoke curling between them as Diamond packed her pipe. The conversation drifted, light at first, circling their last trip, the way the universe worked, how divine energy flowed through everything. Then her gaze sharpened, lips curving like she knew something he didn't.

"You want me to do a reading for you?"

Jayden hesitated. A flicker of the past brushed against his mind—his church days, warning the youth group against divination, against tarot cards and anything that even smelled like witchcraft. He had the verses memorized. There shall not be found among you… a consulter with familiar spirits, or a wizard, or a necromancer. For all that do these things are an abomination unto the LORD.

And yet, here he was. The weight of those old teachings pressing against the man he was becoming. He had spent years listening to voices outside of himself, letting them dictate his path. Maybe it was time to listen to something else.

Jayden exhaled, pushing past the hesitation. "Yeah," he said, voice steady. "Go ahead."

Diamond shuffled the deck with a slow rhythm, the scent of sage thick in the air. The candlelight flickered, casting long shadows on the wooden table. Jayden sat still, watching, curiosity tightening his chest. He wasn't sure if he believed in any of this, but there was something about the moment—about her—that made him lean in.

She placed three cards on the table, tapping the first.

The Past – Eight of Swords

Diamond studied the card, her voice soft but certain. "This is where you've been. The Eight of Swords? It's about feeling trapped. Like your own thoughts, your own circumstances, been keeping you locked up.

Maybe you've been second-guessing yourself, stuck between choices. But look—those swords ain't holding you. The only thing keeping you in place is you."

Jayden felt that. Felt it deep. The way he'd been moving lately, caught between decisions, between women, between paths he wasn't even sure he was meant to walk.

The Present – The Lovers

Diamond flipped the second card, a knowing smile ghosting across her lips. "Well, well. The Lovers." She glanced at him. "Before you jump to conclusions, this ain't just about romance. This is about choice. Alignment. It's about deciding what's real, what's true. You can't be in two places at once, Jayden. Can't keep straddling two different energies. It's time to choose."

His body tensed. He didn't need a deck of cards to tell him that. He'd known it—he just hadn't wanted to face it.

The Future – The Chariot

Diamond turned over the last card and hummed, like she had already known what was coming. "The Chariot. Now this is what you need. This card is about movement. About focus. About willpower. Once you decide? You gotta own it. No looking back. No hesitation. The Chariot is telling you—step into your power and move forward. And if you do that? Can't nothing stop you."

Jayden let the words settle in his chest. The message was clear. Trapped. A choice. Forward motion.

Diamond sat back, eyes on him. "So," she asked, "what do you think?"

Jayden exhaled, staring at the cards, then at her.

"I think…" He paused, feeling the weight of his own voice. "I think it's time to stop overthinking and start moving."

Diamond smiled, slow and approving. "Now that," she said, "is the right answer."

Jayden sat there, the energy of the moment still thick in the air. And as he thought about what the cards were telling him, two things became clear—two things he needed to move forward with. His weed distribution business. And Diamond.

Diamond stretched, her fingers idly stacking the cards. "Well, it's getting late," she said, standing. "I better head back to my room."

Jayden watched her, then sat up a little straighter, pushing through the nervous edge in his voice. "I appreciate the reading. It was great spending time with you." He hesitated, then went for it. "I got a healing session tomorrow, but after that—maybe we could grab lunch?"

A flicker of something crossed Diamond's face, but then she smiled, warm and slow. "That sounds great. I'd like that."

Jayden nodded, keeping it cool, but inside? He felt good. Real good.

He had money. He had a date with Diamond. What could be better than that?

The next morning, Jayden woke up feeling good—ready for the day, but not for his meeting with Howard. He used to care about these sessions, used to spend hours researching ways to help. Before their first meeting, he had gone deep, reading about natural migraine remedies, learning about magnesium, aromatherapy, meditation. He had been eager then, wanting to see results, to make a difference.

But now? Now his mind was somewhere else.

Fifteen minutes before he had to leave, he grabbed his phone and did a quick Google search. He skimmed an article, found a couple of new things to suggest. It'd be enough. Probably.

At 9:55, he glanced at the time. Five minutes to get to the center. Damn. He jumped up, threw on a hoodie, and hit the streets, speed-walking, knowing he wouldn't make it by ten but hoping to shave some minutes off the usual twenty it took.

By the time he walked through the doors of the community center, it was 10:16. He had sent Howard a text on the way, but still—Howard was sitting at the front, waiting, his expression blank, unreadable.

"Hey, Howard, sorry I'm late. Ready to get started?"

"Hey, Mr. King J, yeah, I'm ready."

They took their usual spot in the back. Jayden leaned in, tried to bring some focus to the moment.

"So, how's it been going? Any improvements?"

Howard shook his head. "Not much. Still getting migraines."

The words irritated Jayden. He wanted to hear Yeah, man, I'm doing better already, thanks so much. But no. Instead, Howard sat there, waiting for Jayden to fix something he probably hadn't even followed through on himself.

"You been doing everything I told you?" Jayden pressed.

Howard hesitated. "Well...I haven't been fully consistent with the meditating. But I upped my magnesium and did the aromatherapy a few times."

Jayden exhaled. "That's the reason, then. You gotta do everything. It only works if you commit." He leaned back, trying to muster some patience. "Alright, this time, add Tiger Balm to your temples. And take ginger."

"Okay," Howard said. "I'll try that."

Fifteen minutes in, and Jayden was already done. He repeated the same thing he had told Howard last time—consistency was key. Howard nodded, but there was a look in his eyes, like he was expecting more.

Jayden caught it but brushed it off. Man's paying me twenty dollars and expecting miracles. I make that in two minutes.

Howard pulled out his phone, sent the payment, and just like that, they were done.

On the walk back, Jayden's mind stayed on the session. Howard was starting to feel like a waste of time. Traveling all this way, putting in research—for what? For somebody who wasn't even serious? It didn't sit right with him. Maybe it was time to cut him loose.

His thoughts shifted, quick and easy, to something better. His lunch date with Diamond. Now, that—that was something worth investing in.

He thought about the Tarot reading. The Chariot card. Moving forward.

His mind flickered to Sonia, to how she resisted everything he tried to teach her. He exhaled sharply. Probably gotta move forward from her, too.

Weed distribution and Diamond. That's the focus.

As soon as he got back to the Violet Light House, he shot Diamond a text.

"Hey queen. 12:30 good for lunch?"

"Perfect. See you then," she replied.

At 12:30 on the dot, Jayden was outside her room, calling for her. She stepped out in an African dress, a matching headwrap, gold hoops catching the light.

Man, she looks good.

"I like that dress," he said, keeping it cool.

They had picked a Mediterranean spot a few miles away.

"Mind driving?" Jayden asked. "My car's done for. Gotta get a new one."

"Oh, sure."

Her ride was an old red Hyundai, the passenger seat piled with papers and bags. She had to clear it out before he could even sit down.

At the restaurant, they chose an outdoor table, the air warm, the breeze just right. Jayden didn't waste time. He wanted to see if she was really about this life.

"You know the Bible was plagiarized from older Egyptian texts, right?"

Diamond laughed. "Oh yeah. And King James? A whole homosexual."

They both cracked up.

Yeah. Jayden nodded to himself. She's legit.

She told him she never really went to church. Her dad was in the streets, her mom was always working. She was raised by TV. Jayden told her about his church days, how he was deep in it until his mother passed, how that loss made him see it all as a fraud.

Diamond was his age, been doing Tarot and astrology readings for five years. Jayden admitted he had been skeptical, but her last reading? It had made too much sense to ignore.

Then she hit him with something new.

"I believe humans came here as an alien species," she said. "And I think the mothership is coming back."

Jayden leaned in, intrigued. He had done some research on UFOs, had read things that made him wonder.

Her theory was different, but at the very least he was just glad she didn't believe in Jesus.

Even though the date was vibing, Jayden kept checking his phone. Notifications kept coming in—customers looking for him.

Money waiting to be made.

"I got a few people to meet back at the VLH," he told her.

Diamond nodded. "I get it."

They drove back. He told her she could chill in his room while he handled business, and she agreed.

Within twenty minutes, two customers knocked, cash in hand.

The rest of the day, Jayden and Diamond stayed in his room, smoking, talking. Aliens. Meditation. Government conspiracies. The way the body worked.

By nightfall, they were kissing.

"I like how you think different," Jayden murmured against her lips. "Not like everybody else, caught up in the system."

At 11:30, Diamond pulled away. "I need to get back to my room."

"Stay a little longer," Jayden urged.

She shook her head, smiling. "Nah. But today was nice. Thank you."

Then she was gone.

After that evening, Jayden and Sonia had a few more conversations, each one starting with good intentions but ending in the same place—frustration. No matter how hard they tried to find common ground, religion kept pulling them apart. Jayden felt like Sonia was unteachable, too stubborn to even consider a perspective outside her own. Sonia, on the other hand, saw Jayden as controlling, always trying to force her beliefs instead of just accepting them. It became clear that neither of them was willing to bend, and after one particularly heated debate, they both sat in silence, the weight of their differences settling between them. Finally, Sonia let out a tired sigh and said, "Maybe this just isn't working." Jayden nodded, not angry, just resigned. They cared about each other, but some gaps were just too wide to bridge.

The next few months followed the same rhythm for Jayden.

People knocking—at all hours, day and night. Some loud, some discreet, some fiending so hard they barely made eye contact. Jayden barely had to step outside anymore. The VLH was a revolving door, money exchanging hands as quick as a handshake. Cash piled up—stacks in shoeboxes, rolled bills shoved in drawers. The more he sold, the more they came, word spreading like wildfire through the community.

Transactions made—quick, clean, routine. No unnecessary talk, no hesitation. Some came through for a quick sale, others lingered, trying to make conversation, trying to get friendly. The product moved, and as long as the money was right, he didn't ask questions.

Diamond continued coming through as well—her presence a break from the business, a moment of something softer. She'd breeze in smelling like vanilla and weed, dropping onto the floor like she belonged there. They'd smoke, talking about nothing and everything, laughing in between lazy exhales. She'd run her fingers through his locks, her voice low and sweet, telling him she had his back no matter what. And when words weren't enough, their bodies did the talking—intense, unspoken promises exchanged in the dim light of his room.

Jayden wasn't thinking about anything else. Right now, everything was smooth—money flowing, supply steady, Diamond by his side. The days had a rhythm, and he was content riding the wave. This was his world, and for now, that was enough.

Jayden stopped seeing Howard. Lately, every session had started feeling like an interrogation. Howard kept circling back to the headaches, pressing him about the migraines—when they started, how often they came, what triggered them. Jayden didn't have answers, and didn't feel like Howard was serious enough for him to put in the work to research it. He was tired of talking in circles, tired of Howard's concerned expression like he was some kind of case study. So when Howard finally said, "Maybe this isn't working," Jayden just nodded.

No sweat off my back.

With the money rolling in, Jayden upgraded his life. Bought a real bed. New clothes. Two months in, he dropped $7,000 on a used car.

Started paying $700 a month for rent at VLH.

He barely talked to his family. A few texts, some random calls with Trinity. But that was it.

As far as he was concerned, they were his past.

The Tarot reading stayed in his mind. Moving forward.

When Diamond wasn't around, Jayden kept himself occupied—mainly with some of his female customers. A few were just friendly, but others wanted more, and

Jayden wasn't one to turn down the attention. He enjoyed the company, the way they laughed at his jokes, the way they leaned in a little closer when they talked. Sometimes, that connection came with perks—free weed hookups, favors exchanged without much being said. He didn't overthink it. As far as he was concerned, he was enjoying himself, making money, and living life on his terms.

The 420 festival was just days away, and business was booming. Jayden's phone stayed buzzing, customers stocking up for the weekend's festivities. Diamond had gone out of town to visit family but planned to be back in time for the event. Jayden didn't mind her absence. It gave him space to move how he wanted.

It was 8:30 p.m. when the text came through: "Hey, I hear you're the guy. I need 4oz. Can you help me?"

Jayden was sprawled across his bed, tangled up with one of his regulars—a woman who only seemed to come around when Diamond was gone, always expecting free smoke. He barely glanced at her as he sat up, his mind locking onto the opportunity. This was the kind of customer he loved. Not the ones nickel-and-diming him for twenty dollars' worth, wasting his time. Four ounces? That was five hundred dollars in one move.

He was halfway listening to the woman ramble about her day when he cut her off telling her to put her clothes on. "I gotta make a run."

She groaned, stretching lazily, but he was already typing out his reply. "I got you. Where you at?"

While he waited, he lit another blunt, passing it to the woman. She took a slow drag, watching him as he exhaled. His phone vibrated. "Meet me at the gas station on MLK Blvd at 9:30."

"See you there," Jayden texted back.

The gas station was a twenty-minute drive from the Violet Light House. He figured he'd head out early, grab some snacks—smoking always gave him the munchies. He pulled up at 9:10, stepping into the bright lights of the convenience store. He lingered in the aisle, debating between chips and a muffin, when he heard his name.

"Jayden!"

The voice stopped him cold. Nobody from this life called him Jayden. Everyone knew him as King J.

He turned toward the front of the store and saw Jayson from New Life Church, standing behind the register, grinning wide. "Wow! It's good to see you again, man!"

Jayden's stomach tightened. Damn. He wasn't in the mood for this. He was high, his eyes low and red, and the last thing he wanted was a trip down memory lane. But he forced a smile and walked up, muffin in hand.

"Oh hey, Jayson. You work here?"

Obvious question—the name tag on Jayson's shirt made that clear.

"Yeah, been here about six months. It's cool, helping me pay for college."

College. That tripped Jayden out. His mind flashed to the scrawny 12-year-old kid who used to come to youth group, eager and wide-eyed, hanging on to his every word. It felt like not so long ago and yet, a different lifetime.

Jayson peered at him, his expression shifting. "Man, I told everybody at New Life I saw you at the Health and Wellness Festival. You're like a legend in that church. You know we're still doing the purity challenge you started?"

Jayden's smile faltered. "For real?"

"Yeah! No sex before marriage, no porn. We got thirty-three people in it right now. We even had eleven graduates who kept their purity and are married now. We still talk about you, how you changed our lives."

Jayden's stomach twisted. His mind flashed to the woman sprawled out in his bed earlier, trading her body for a high. He forced another smile. "That's cool", he mumbled "Glad it's working for y'all."

Something about Jayson's admiration stirred him, made him want to teach him again, to drop some knowledge. "Jayson," Jayden leaned in, voice low squinting through his high. "You believe in UFOs?"

Jayson frowned. "Umm, I guess they could be real."

Jayden nodded like he was revealing sacred knowledge. "We're an alien species, and the mother ship is coming back. But there are reptilians—shape-shifters—trying to stop it. We're gonna have to use telepathy to communicate when the ship returns."

Silence. Jayden figured Jayson was just processing. Eventually, he'd be grateful for the enlightenment. "Yeah, bro," Jayden nodded, "the world ain't ready for this stuff."

Jayson's confusion turned to something else. A quiet, deep disappointment. This wasn't the Jayden he remembered. The pure-hearted, righteous leader who had once helped so many youth. Now, he just seemed... lost.

Jayson cut the conversation short. "Alright, man. Thanks for the info. You buying that muffin?"

Jayden shook his head, grabbed a bottle of juice too. "And this."

They exchanged awkward goodbyes. Jayden stepped out into the night, checking the time. 9:25. Perfect. He tore into the muffin, enjoying the soft sweetness, then his phone buzzed.

"I'm here. Black Ford, parked up front."

Jayden spotted the car immediately. He nodded at the driver, who nodded back and stepped out.

"Let's go around the side," the man said. "Don't want people watching."

Jayden followed him to a dark, empty corner of the building. He grinned. "You know I got that good stuff."

He pulled out the bag—four ounces of high-grade Sour Diesel. The man inspected it, then reached for his wallet. But instead of cash, he flipped it open, revealing a badge.

Jayden's heart stopped.

"Detective Lawson," the man said, smirking. "Your name's been coming up a lot."

Two other men got out of a second black Ford and walked over. "Yeah, this is him," Lawson said to them with a chuckle. "The infamous King J."

Jayden tried to keep his face blank, his hands steady.

"Turn around," Lawson ordered. "Hands behind your back."

Jayden obeyed, feeling the cold snap of cuffs around his wrists. As they led him toward the car, he saw people watching, eyes wide, whispering. He glanced through the gas station window and locked eyes with Jayson, who stood frozen behind the counter, his face stricken.

Jayson ran out. "Wait! He paid for that muffin and juice. He just didn't take the receipt."

The officers laughed. "That's not what we're here for, son. He's being arrested for possession with intent to distribute."

Jayson's face went pale. He looked at Jayden, searching for something—an explanation, maybe.

Jayden gave a half-hearted shrug. "I don't know what they're talking about."

The officer pushed his head down and guided him into the backseat of the black Ford. As the door slammed shut, Jayden stared blankly ahead. The mother ship wasn't coming.

The chariot wasn't moving forward.

Only thing moving now was the car, pulling away, taking him with it.

Chapter 18

Unexpected Visitation

The ride to the precinct was the longest, most uncomfortable ride Jayden had ever taken. The cuffs dug into his wrists like they had been cinched extra tight on purpose, and every sharp turn sent him sliding, bumping his head against the window. Detective Lawson was driving like he was late for something, but Jayden knew better—this was intentional. A little extra humiliation, just because he could.

"So, your highness, King J," Lawson drawled, his voice thick with amusement. "Hope you don't mind if I just call you Jayden." He barely paused before continuing, "You do know carrying anything over two ounces with intent to distribute is a felony, right?"

Jayden said nothing. He didn't know the difference between a misdemeanor and a felony, not really. He'd never had to. But he knew "felony" meant serious. It meant time.

Lawson glanced at him in the rearview mirror, smirking at the silence. "We got people ready to testify that you're their dealer. You might want to start being more careful about who you do business with."

Jayden's stomach twisted. Somebody snitched. But who? He mostly sold to people connected to the VLH. They were supposed to be solid—cool people, down for the cause.

His mind raced, trying to piece together who might've turned on him. His mouth was dry, his heart pounding, but he forced himself to play it cool. He'd seen enough cop shows to know the only thing to say in moments like this.

"I want to talk to my lawyer."

Lawson let out a laugh, deep and mocking. "I don't care if you talk to Jesus Christ himself," he said, shaking his head. "It doesn't change the fact that you had four ounces of marijuana with intent to distribute. That's a felony charge in this county."

Jayden stared out the window, jaw clenched. His mind flipped through the names of people he could call. Pharoah was the first to come to mind. That was his boy—he'd come through for him. Then there was Diamond, but she was out of town. His older sister, Trinity, crossed his mind for a split second before he shut that thought down. No way. He didn't need her knowing about this.

Then his mind landed on Jayson.

His stomach dropped. Jayson had seen the whole thing. If he told anyone at the church, the news would spread like wildfire. His aunt would hear about it, and that thought shook Jayden more than anything. She had already been disappointed enough. If she found out about this? He didn't even want to think about what she'd say. And his sisters—he couldn't have them knowing either.

For a second, just a split second, he almost prayed. Almost. But when he caught himself, he stopped. He wasn't that guy anymore.

At the precinct, they sat Jayden on a cold wooden bench and left him there. Nobody said a word to him for an hour. He watched as officers brought in more people, one after another, cuffed and escorted. One guy came in with a mesh hood over his head and face, screaming at the top of his lungs. Jayden didn't get it until someone muttered, "He's a Spitter."

Finally, an officer walked over and motioned for him to follow. At the desk, they laid out everything from his pockets. His keys. Wallet, with $450 in cash. His pipe. His phone. "You'll get everything back," the officer said, bored, "except the marijuana and the pipe."

Jayden barely nodded.

Then came the moment.

"You can make a call."

Jayden reached for the phone, and it hit him—his phone had all his contacts. He didn't know anybody's number by heart except Pharoah and Trinity.

Pharoah. He was the only real option.

He dialed. The phone rang. And rang. And rang.

No answer.

Jayden stared at the officer. "I gotta call him back. He didn't pick up."

The officer nodded like he'd seen this play out a thousand times before. Jayden dialed again, hoping, willing Pharoah to pick up.

Ring. Ring. Ring.

Nothing.

His heart sank. How? Pharoah always picked up. Then it hit him—Pharoah probably didn't recognize the number. Jayden left a message the second time, just to make sure Pharoah knew where he was.

There was no way he was calling his sister.

The officer took him back to the bench. Another officer, this one older with a beer belly pressing against his uniform, grinned as he passed.

"Well, King J," the man chuckled, "I hope the state penitentiary is a suitable castle for you."

More laughter.

Jayden's jaw tightened. The way they said it—"King J"—like it was a joke, like he was nothing.

Then came the holding cell.

Two men were already inside, stretched out on bunks. Jayden was left with a thin mat near the toilet. He sat down, pressing his back against the wall, his mind spinning.

This wasn't what the Tarot cards said.

Jayden barely slept. His mind was a whirlwind, looping the same scene over and over—Lawson flashing the badge, wide-eyed onlookers whispering, Jayson's stunned face, his desperate attempt to smooth things over. The whole thing felt like a bad dream he couldn't wake up from. This wasn't supposed to be his reality. *Weed ain't even bad,* he told himself. *I shouldn't be in here for this.*

He was so deep in his thoughts that he almost didn't hear the voice above him.

"Yo, bruh. I gotta go."

Jayden blinked and looked up. The guy on the top bunk gestured toward the toilet—just sitting there, out in the open, like something you'd find in a stall at a rundown bus station, not in a cramped room of men. Jayden scooted to the side, turning his back. The sound of urine hitting metal felt like it was happening right in his ear. His stomach twisted. *This is disgusting.*

Morning light slashed through the narrow window, weak and gray. Jayden's stomach growled. He hadn't eaten since the gas station muffin, and he had missed dinner the night before. Soon, they made the breakfast call, leading him into the common area with about 80 other men. A line formed, slow-moving, shuffling feet and blank faces. Then came the trays—bologna sandwiches and cartons of milk. Jayden peeled open the sandwich and stared at the pale slice of meat. *Pork?* He glanced around. The guards didn't look like the accommodating type. No special dietary requests here. He yanked the bologna off and ate the bread, swallowing dry, flavorless bites. The milk tasted off, watered down and stale. But he forced it down. Hunger was a beast that didn't care about taste.

Back in his cell, he lay on the mat, staring at the ceiling. He imagined Pharoah walking in like a king, laughing, slapping paperwork down on the counter. *King, we outta here. They can't hold us.* The thought was the only thing keeping the hopelessness from swallowing him whole.

Jayden lay on the stiff mat, staring at the cracks in the ceiling, counting the hours. Three had passed before a guard finally appeared at his cell door.

"You got a visitor," the guard said, unlocking the bars with a slow, deliberate clang.

Relief surged through Jayden's chest. Finally. Pharoah must've come through. He could already see it— Pharaoh grinning on the other side of the glass, saying something slick like, *"King, they can't hold us. We outta here."*

As they walked down the hallway, stopping at locked doors that needed clearance, Jayden ran through possible ways to explain himself. He needed a solid story, something airtight. Maybe he could spin it as a mistake—wrong place, wrong time. Or maybe Pharaoh already had a plan. They'd put their heads together, figure it out like they always did.

But when the officer led him into the visitor's room and he looked through the glass, it wasn't Pharaoh on the other side. It was Trinity.

Jayden's stomach dropped. His worst fear had just come true.

It turned out, Jayson had gone straight to calling his Aunt Patrice after the arrest, and from there, the news traveled fast. His aunt wasted no time calling Trinity. Jayden could only imagine the conversation—how quickly his fate had been sealed in their minds.

Trinity didn't yell, didn't scold. Her voice was low, heavy with disappointment. "What is going on, Jayden?"

He swallowed, forcing himself to keep his expression cool. "This is all just a misunderstanding," he said, though he didn't even believe it himself. "I'll clear it up. But listen, can you message Pharaoh for me?"

Trinity shook her head, her eyes sharp. "Jayden, you're being charged with possession of over two ounces of marijuana—with intent to distribute. That's a felony. Do you even understand what that means? You could go to prison."

She was acting like it was already decided. Like he was guilty. Like he wasn't getting out.

"I told you, it's a misunderstanding!" he said, his voice rising. "I'm gonna fix this."

She exhaled, slow and deliberate. "Jayden, you used to be the one helping troubled kids. Now you're the one who needs help."

Her words hit him hard, knocking the wind out of whatever front he had left. His mind flashed to Jayson, the look on his face when the cops put him in cuffs. The shock. The disappointment. He wasn't supposed to be this guy.

He straightened up, trying to shake off the weight pressing on his chest. "Look, Trinity, just do me a favor. Take down Pharaoh's number. Text him. Tell him I'm at the Downtown Correctional Facility—he'll know what to do."

She sighed but pulled out her phone. "I'll text him. But I'm also calling a lawyer."

"Can you do me one more favor."

"Sure, what is it?"

"My car—it's still at the gas station. The night I got arrested, I left it there. Can you pick it up for me?"

Trinity nodded without hesitation. "I got you."

Relief washed over him. He hadn't even realized how much that had been nagging at him. The last thing he needed was for his car to get towed or stolen. "Thank you, Trin. For real."

Jayden rubbed a hand down his face. "What did Aunt Patrice say?"

Trinity hesitated. "She was shocked. She never agreed with your lifestyle, but she never thought you'd end up in a situation like this."

Jayden could picture it. Could hear her voice, the disappointment laced in every syllable.

They talked for another fifteen minutes, mostly Trinity lecturing him about his choices, about how he needed to get it together. He sat there, nodding, but his mind was already somewhere else—on Pharaoh, on his next move, on clearing his name.

When the visit ended, he thanked her and let the guard escort him back to his cell. But the weight of her words followed him, settling deep in his chest.

Time dragged. The hours bled together, stretching long and lifeless. Jayden spent most of the day watching the clock, waiting for Pharaoh to show up and fix this mess. Any minute now, he told himself. But the minutes turned into meals—rubbery eggs at breakfast, a stale sandwich at lunch, something gray and unidentifiable for dinner. The whole routine was already wearing thin. He kept to himself, only exchanging a few words with the other inmates, men locked up for everything from dealing and robbery to battery and assault. The second night was worse than the first. Sleep was a joke. The mat on the floor barely cushioned his body, and every sound in the cell—snoring, coughing, the rustling of someone shifting in their bunk—pressed down on him like a weight.

By the second day, his body forced his pride into submission. He had to use the toilet. Right there, out in the open, just feet away from the other men. Humiliation clawed up his throat, burning hot. He tried to be quick, to pretend it wasn't happening, but the shame settled over him like a second skin. The showers weren't any better—ice-cold water, no privacy, the stench of too many bodies packed into a tight space. This was no place for a king. Jayden longed for the VLH, for the life he knew.

On the third day, the guard appeared at his cell. "You got a visitor."

Jayden sprang up. Finally. Pharaoh had come with the plan. He walked with purpose, his mind racing ahead to how they'd get out of this. But when he looked through the glass, it wasn't Pharaoh's grinning face waiting for him. It was Trinity again.

He swallowed the lump of disappointment in his throat. "Did you reach Pharaoh?" he asked, his voice tight.

Trinity nodded. "Yeah. He said 'that sucks' and to hit him up when you get out."

Jayden felt the words land like a punch to the gut. That was it? No plan, no ride-or-die loyalty, no 'I got you, bro'? Just *hit me up when you get out*? His jaw tightened, anger rising fast. Did Pharaoh even realize what he was facing? Did he *care*?

"This is crazy," Jayden muttered, shaking his head.

But Trinity wasn't done. She leaned in, her voice steady and serious. "Jayden, a lawyer's coming to see you. We're working on your bond, but they might make you take a drug test first."

A drug test. Jayden felt his stomach drop. His urine was probably *green* from all the weed he'd smoked. This wasn't going how he thought it would. Not even close.

His chest tightened. He needed to get out of here. "Thank you for your help, Sis," he said, his voice barely above a whisper. Then, louder, more desperate, "Please. Help me get out of here. I need to go home."

He felt himself breaking, the weight of it all pressing down, squeezing the fight out of him. His eyes burned, the threat of tears creeping too close. But he clenched his jaw, swallowed it down. Kings didn't cry. Not here. Not now.

The next day, Jayden got another visitor. This time, it was Diamond.

Pharaoh told her what happened. As soon as she got back into town, she went straight to see him.

"Hey, queen. It's good to see you," Jayden said, and for the first time in days, he meant it.

Diamond's eyes filled with worry. "Oh my gosh, baby, how did this happen?"

Jayden exhaled sharply, shaking his head. "Somebody snitched. Had to be someone at VLH," he said, resentment thick in his voice. "But don't worry, I'll get out of this. I'll be home soon."

Diamond smiled, then pulled something from her bag. "I brought the cards." She held up the Tarot deck, like she was offering him a lifeline.

Jayden barely stopped himself from rolling his eyes. *The cards?* He wasn't trying to hear that right now. If they were so powerful, why hadn't they warned him about this? Why hadn't they told him how to stay free? He swallowed his irritation and forced himself to be polite. "Thanks, but not right now."

Diamond gave him a bewildered look, like she didn't understand the shift in his energy. She glanced down, adjusting the deck in her hands. "Well...I can wash some of your clothes when I get back," she said after a beat, trying to be helpful.

Jayden nodded. "I appreciate that," he said, even managing a half-smile.

A silence settled between them, heavy and unfamiliar. At home, they could have filled the void with blunt smoke and kisses. Here, there was nothing but cold glass and awkward pauses.

Finally, Diamond sighed. "I hope you get out soon. I miss you."

The words landed flat. Hope wouldn't get him out of here. It wouldn't fix this mess. He was grateful she came, but what he really needed was solutions, not sentiment. And deep down, he knew she didn't have those.

They said their goodbyes, and Jayden walked back to his cell, feeling just as stuck as before.

By day five, Jayden felt like he was serving a life sentence.

The days bled together, one gray hour rolling into the next. He didn't know what was happening in the outside world—who was looking for him, what was going on at his house. He barely knew what day of the week it was. But worst of all? He couldn't escape it. No matter how much he tried to resist, the routine of the correctional facility was creeping into his bones. And he hated it. Hated the sound of metal doors clanking shut, the way the guards barely looked at him like he was just another number, the tasteless food that sat like a rock in his stomach. The toilet situation? Still disgusting. The showers? A daily fight to keep his dignity intact. And the cold cement pressing into his back at night? That wasn't something a person could ever get used to.

But time was moving, dragging him along with it. And that terrified him more than anything.

That afternoon, a guard called his name. Another visitor.

Jayden made his way to the visitation section, his heart knocking against his ribs. He wasn't sure who to expect, but when he got there, looking through the thick glass, he figured it out quickly.

The man sitting across from him looked sharp. Dark suit, crisp white shirt, a red-and-black tie knotted just right. His afro was neatly trimmed, beard lined up like he had just come from the barbershop. This had to be the lawyer Trinity called.

The man nodded, his face unreadable. "Hello, Jayden. I'm Stewart Cookman. I'm an attorney—and a friend of your Aunt Patrice. I've been talking to your sister, Trinity, about your situation."

Jayden barely heard the rest. A friend of Aunt Patrice. That meant she'd know everything. That meant she was already shaking her head, telling the family what a disappointment he had turned out to be.

Still, he needed help. And right now, Stewart Cookman was the only option sitting in front of him.

"Hello, Mr. Cookman," Jayden said, his voice tight with a mix of relief and desperation. He swallowed hard, gripping the phone a little tighter. "Man, I appreciate you coming."

The lawyer gave him a slow nod, then got right to it. "We're working on getting you out on bond, but the court may require a conditional drug test first. As for your case—you're facing two to eight years for a first-time felony charge."

Jayden's breath caught in his chest.

Two to eight years. He was barely surviving five days.

Cookman kept going, his voice steady, almost too calm. "I'll be pushing for probation or the minimum two-year deal, but—"

"Two to eight years?" Jayden barely stopped himself from shouting. This wasn't real. It couldn't be real. His mind scrambled for something—anything—to get him out of this.

"Sir, this is all a misunderstanding," he said quickly, words tumbling out. "I was dropping something off for a friend. I didn't even know what it was."

The best lie he could come up with after five days sitting in a cell.

Cookman exhaled, folding his hands in front of him. "Jayden, you were arrested attempting to sell four ounces of marijuana to an undercover officer. This isn't the kind of case you just 'get off' on. A reduced sentence is the best we can push for."

Reduced sentence. Conviction.

The words hit him like a punch to the gut. That's not what he was supposed to say. The lawyer was supposed to tell him he'd beat the case. That he'd be home soon. That this whole thing was a mix-up.

"What kind of lawyer are you?" Jayden shot back. "Ain't I innocent until proven guilty?"

Cookman's face didn't change. "Jayden, you have to understand—the state has evidence. And they have people set to testify against you."

Jayden's body went cold. He dropped his head, staring at the table, his fingers clenching into fists. People were going to testify against him? It was like he was already guilty, already being sentenced, and he hadn't even had a trial.

But he wasn't about to just take this.

Jayden lifted his head, forcing his voice to be stronger than he felt. "I'm pleading not guilty."

Cookman studied him, eyes sharp, unreadable. For a long moment, he said nothing. Then, slowly, he nodded.

"We'll weigh out all our options," he said. "The courts go by evidence. I'll meet with you again, and we'll see what kind of case we can build."

Jayden sat back, exhaling hard.

That's right. We gotta build this case.

Chapter 19

Class in Session

The meeting with the lawyer deflated Jayden in a way nothing else had. Now, it all felt real. No more waiting for someone to walk in and tell him it was a mistake, that he was free to go. Instead, he got hit with *two to eight years. Years.* Not days, not weeks—years in this place. His chest felt heavy, like the air had been sucked out of the room. Five days in here had already stretched him to his limit, and now they were talking about *prison.*

The thought of prayer crossed his mind again, quick as a flicker of light. And just as quick, he shot it down. *I don't need prayer*, he told himself. *I need a good story.*

That evening at dinner, Jayden barely tasted the food as he picked at it. His mind was too loud, his body too tense. He didn't want to talk, didn't want to think, just wanted to disappear into the background. But then, right in the middle of taking a bite, someone dropped onto the seat next to him.

Jayden stiffened. He didn't even have to look to know someone was about to disrupt the little bit of peace he had left.

"What's up, young brother?" The man's voice was deep, steady.

Jayden clenched his jaw. *Oh great, now he's talking to me.* He wasn't in the mood for small talk, wasn't trying to trade his pork, wasn't interested in another inmate's take on his case. He just wanted to be left alone. Still, he muttered, "Hey," just to be polite.

The man didn't take the hint. "You look like you're going through it. I know that look."

Jayden finally glanced over. The man was older than himself, late thirties, maybe early forties. Beard thick with strands of gray. Hair cropped low. A tattoo on his neck—praying hands.

"I'm just done with this place," Jayden muttered, hoping that would end the conversation.

The man nodded, like he understood. "Yeah, this ain't no country club," he said. "And it definitely ain't a place for a brother like you."

Jayden perked up at that. *Finally.* Someone who saw it. Someone who realized he wasn't supposed to be in here. He wished the lawyer had that much sense.

"I can tell you're a good brother," the man went on, "but you been through some stuff. You gotta get yourself back on point. Jesus will set you free."

Jayden's whole body tensed. *Did this man just say Jesus?*

His first instinct was to shut it down, hit him with the facts—tell him Jesus was just a story, another version of Horus from ancient Egypt. But that would take too long, and Jayden wasn't trying to draw out this conversation. Instead, he said, "You sittin' right next to me. I guess He didn't set you free."

The man laughed. A deep, knowing laugh. "Nah, brother. I'm paying my debt for some things I did *before* I met Jesus. I gave my life to the Lord a year ago. Before that?" He shook his head. "Man, I was doing the devil's work. Selling dope. Sleeping around. Partying. Barely did a thing for my own kids."

Jayden glanced at him again. *Why is he telling me all this?*

"My life's different now," the man continued. "I ain't angry all the time. I got a peace I never knew before. I reconnected with my kids. I got a vision for my life now—real direction. I already started an electrical certification program. They gave me library privileges I ain't had before. Even the length of the prison time I'm facing when I go to trial got reduced." He leaned in. "Jesus is the way, the truth, and the life, brother. He freed me, and He can free you too."

Jayden let out a slow breath. He'd heard all this before. Preachers in the streets. Family members who swore they had *found the light*. He used to believe in it, too. Used to think prayer changed things.

"Yeah, I used to believe in that," Jayden said. "It's just not for me anymore."

"Come with me to Bible study tomorrow," the man said. "Just come, see for yourself."

Jayden studied him. The man's eyes weren't hollow like the rest of the faces in this place. He had something—some kind of light in him.

Every day in jail had been bad. Dark. But this guy? This conversation? It felt like a small sliver of something good. And right now, Jayden needed all the good he could get.

"Okay," he said finally. "I'll check it out."

The man grinned. "That's what's up, lil' homie. I used to be just like you. Just give it a chance. Come with a ready spirit. Brother Joshua—the chaplain—he's a powerful man of God. I'll meet you after breakfast tomorrow." He held out a fist. "I'm Dre. What's your name?"

"Jayden."

Dre gave him a fist bump, nodded, then got up and walked away.

Jayden sat there for a long moment, staring at his food. *Bible study?* That was the last thing he expected to be doing. But for the first time in days, he didn't feel completely hopeless. The thought of it—of something different—lifted his mood, even if just a little.

The next morning, Dre slid into the seat across from Jayden at breakfast, eyes bright with excitement. "Come with questions, bro. Brother Joshua welcomes them all."

Jayden nodded, mulling it over. He thought about challenging the chaplain—asking if he really believed in the Jesus story, even though Jayden was convinced it was just a repackaged myth from Egypt.

Maybe the chaplain was just another brainwashed Christian, clinging to a story that gave him comfort while preaching to men looking for something to hold on to. But he decided against it. No need to start trouble before he even knew what this was about. He'd listen first.

After breakfast, they made their way to a small meeting room tucked away from the noise of the jailhouse cafeteria. Jayden took one step inside and froze. A banner stretched across the back wall, bold and unwavering:

The Spirit of the Lord God is upon me; Because the Lord has anointed me to bring good news to the afflicted; He has sent me to bind up the brokenhearted, to proclaim liberty to captives, and freedom to prisoners. Isaiah 61:1.

Jayden swallowed hard. *Good news and freedom?* His chest tightened. That's exactly what he needed right now.

The energy in the room was different—warmer, lighter. Men greeted him with fist bumps and open smiles, nothing like the cold stares and tense shoulders that filled the rest of the jail. Here, he wasn't a number. Wasn't just another body waiting out time. Here, he felt... human.

He scanned the room. Fifteen men, pens in hand, ready to soak in whatever was about to be said. Dre introduced him around, and each welcome felt genuine, like they were actually glad he was here.

"The chaplain's not in yet, but he'll be here soon," Dre told him before turning to chat with two men about last week's lesson. Jayden just listened. They were talking about the fruits of the Spirit, about patience, self-control, and how they had to *cultivate* those things, like tending a garden in the middle of concrete.

Then, a tall man in a polo shirt and medium-length locks walked in.

"That's Brother Joshua," Dre whispered.

The men straightened, pens poised, notebooks flipped open. Jayden felt something shift in the air, like an unseen presence settling over them.

"Brothers," Joshua greeted, his voice deep, steady. "Another glorious and blessed day to be in your presence."

The men murmured their agreement, voices blending into something that sounded like unity.

Joshua didn't waste time. "I want to start today by talking about pain." He let the word sit there for a moment, let it press against their chests. "Every man in this room has felt it. And for most of us, the way we handled that pain is what landed us here. Pain has a way of twisting our perception, making wrong feel right, pushing us off the path the Most High laid for us."

Jayden stared at his hands, jaw tight. *Pain*. He knew that word too well. Losing his mother. Losing his direction. Losing himself. His life was supposed to be different—college, a future, something *more*. But pain had rerouted him, detoured him straight into the trap he was in now.

Joshua's voice carried on, steady, unwavering. "The Bible says, *The Lord is close to the brokenhearted and saves those who are crushed in spirit*. But too often, we turn our backs on Him when we need Him the most. We see tragedy, we see suffering, and we start to believe the lie that God abandoned us. That He abandoned the whole world."

Jayden's spine went stiff. He wasn't sure if he was breathing. It felt like Joshua was speaking straight to him, cutting through every doubt, every unanswered question.

The chaplain leaned against the podium, his voice softening. "I know what that's like. College did it to me. I was nineteen, fresh out of my mama's house, still holding on to the religion she raised me in. But notice— I said *religion*, not *relationship*. When my professors came at me with their logic, their theories, their so-called wisdom, I started questioning everything. God, faith, the Bible. I turned away for ten years."

Jayden lifted his head, listening harder.

Joshua exhaled, his eyes dark with memory. "Then tragedy struck. My eight-year-old son died of cancer."

Silence fell over the room. A heavy, thick silence that pressed against the walls.

Joshua nodded, like he could still feel that pain sitting on his chest. "My intellect couldn't save me. My degrees, my book knowledge—none of it could fill the hole in my soul. So I turned to alcohol. Drank day and night. Lost myself. Lost my job. Ended up sitting in a cell just like this, just like you." He let that sink in before continuing. "I was a prisoner to my pain. But through that darkness, the Lord called me back. He lifted me up, put breath back in my body, gave me *peace.*"

Jayden swallowed.

Joshua swept his gaze over the room. "God moves in different ways. For some, the Holy Spirit speaks directly to them. For others, He uses the people around them—people sitting in this very room—to bring them home."

Jayden felt something shift inside him, something he couldn't quite name. A heat in his chest, an awareness pressing at the edges of his mind.

For the next hour, he listened. Really listened.

When the class ended, Dre led him up to the chaplain. "Brother Joshua, this is Jayden."

Jayden extended his hand. "I really appreciated your message."

Joshua took his hand, holding his gaze. "I see the light in you, brother. I also see the pain." His grip tightened just a little. "You'll be a powerful man of God when you turn that pain into purpose."

Jayden's breath caught in his throat. The words hit something deep, something raw.

All the way back to his cell, his mind buzzed. For the first time in a long time, he wasn't just thinking about getting out. He was thinking about *why* he was here. About pain. About purpose.

And for the first time, he wasn't so sure they were separate things.

Jayden hadn't expected Bible study to sit with him the way it did. The words lingered, unsettled something in him. He'd always thought he had outgrown all that— moved beyond the simplistic beliefs he was raised on. Losing his mother had caused him to see the world differently, made him dig deeper, search for truth beyond what he saw as the limits of Christianity. He prided himself on being enlightened, on understanding spirituality in a way that wasn't boxed in by church doctrine. But still, Brother Joshua's words pressed on him. The way pain could push people away from God. The way grief, anger, and survival could bend a person's path without them even realizing it.

At lunch, Jayden kept to himself, barely touching his food, lost in his own head. He thought about the slow unraveling of his faith, the choices that led him here, the eerie parallels between his story and Brother Joshua's. He wanted to brush it off, to tell himself that the chaplain was just another preacher feeding men false hope. But something about the way he spoke, the way he owned his past, made Jayden listen. Really listen.

As lunch wrapped up, Dre slid into the seat across from him. "So, what'd you think?"

Jayden hesitated, then nodded. "It was real. I liked it."

Dre grinned, his eyes lighting up. "That's what's up. Keep coming, bro. Some real solid brothers in there. You'll see."

Jayden nodded again, still processing.

Dre leaned back, a thoughtful look crossing his face. "Got visitation with my kids coming up. Relationship's stronger than it's ever been." He exhaled, almost like he still couldn't believe it himself. "Crazy, right? Locked up, but free in a way I never was out there. I'm a prisoner of the Lord now."

Jayden took that in, watching Dre's face—peaceful, sure. It was something he hadn't experienced himself in a long time.

The next morning, after choking down a tasteless breakfast, Jayden got another visit from his lawyer, Mr. Cookman. The man's pinstripe suit and crisp blue tie made him look like he belonged in a boardroom, not in a place like this. Seeing him, standing tall and put-together, gave Jayden a flicker of hope. Maybe this nightmare was finally ending. Maybe today was the day he'd get to go home.

Mr. Cookman wasted no time. "You'll be able to get bonded out," he said, flipping open his leather briefcase, "but they're enforcing drug testing."

Jayden's stomach dropped.

The lawyer adjusted his tie, his face unreadable. "I don't know what the results will be, but if they hold you longer, we'll appeal."

Jayden barely heard the rest. His ears were ringing. He was still stuck on those words—drug test. He knew the results wouldn't be clean. He knew what that meant.

"And your trial's set for six months from now."

Six months?

The words hit like a gut punch. Six months in here? Six months without fresh air, without Diamond curled up next to him, without the freedom to go wherever he wanted, do whatever he wanted? He thought about the VLH, about the endless flow of people coming in and out, the money moving through his hands like water. He thought about rolling up, passing the blunt, laughing about nothing with Royal. He even missed scrolling his phone, that mindless distraction that used to fill up the empty spaces in his day. Now, there was nothing but silence, nothing but his own thoughts pressing in on him.

"We have to appeal this," Jayden said, his voice sharp with desperation.

"We will," Mr. Cookman assured him. "But you'll have to take the test tomorrow."

The lawyer kept talking, laying out details about the case, the process, the next steps, but Jayden wasn't listening anymore. He was stuck, locked inside the thought of being here another six months.

When the meeting ended, he shuffled back to his cell in a daze. This was a nightmare.

This place wasn't for him.

He wasn't a criminal.

At lunch, Dre plopped down across from him, his tray clattering onto the table. "What's up, lil' homie? You looking like you seen a ghost."

Jayden let out a slow breath, then told him about the lawyer, about the drug test, about the six months hanging over his head like a death sentence.

Dre nodded, chewing thoughtfully. "Man, I hear you. Don't none of us like being in here. But listen—if you do gotta stay, you can't lose yourself. Don't spend six months drowning in misery. Pick your head up. Put it in God's hands. Use this time to build your relationship with the Most High." He took another bite, swallowed. "Matter fact, the brothers and I are having Bible study tonight during rec. Come through."

Jayden barely registered Dre's words—his mind was still spiraling—but one thing stuck. Bible study. That was the only thing in this place that had made him feel... something.

"Aight," he said, nodding slowly. "I'll check it out."

Dre grinned. "That's what's up, brother. I'll see you after dinner."

That evening, Dre led him to the library, where three other men were already gathered around a table, Bibles open in front of them. "Fellas," Dre said, clapping Jayden on the back, "this young brother wanted to join us again."

He introduced them—Joe, Brooklyn, and Junior. They welcomed Jayden like he belonged, sliding a Bible across the table to him. Jayden hesitated before picking it up. He hadn't held one in six years. The weight of it in his hands felt strange, like something foreign and familiar all at once.

Joe, the one who seemed to be leading the group, told them to open to the book of John. He looked like a clean-cut football player, mid-thirties maybe, with a steady, calm energy about him. Jayden wondered why he was locked up but figured it wasn't the time to ask.

Joe started reading. "'Jesus said unto him, I am the way, the truth, and the life: no man comes to the Father, but by me.'"

The words rubbed Jayden the wrong way. He shifted in his seat.

He'd studied different religions, opened his mind to different perspectives. The idea that there was only one path, one truth, felt small-minded. He told himself to let it slide, but it gnawed at him. Finally, he spoke up.

"Well, I think there's more than one way," he said, testing the waters. "People find spirituality in different ways."

The men didn't flinch. They didn't dismiss him. They just looked at him, nodding like they understood.

Brooklyn leaned forward, his voice steady. "Brother, some things in life only have one right answer. If I tell you five plus five equals ten, that's a fact—it doesn't change just because someone believes otherwise.

Truth works the same way. Different religions make claims that completely contradict each other. They can't all be right at the same time."

He held up one finger. "Take Buddhism. It teaches that there is no personal God, just a path to enlightenment through meditation and self-discipline. But the Bible says that God is real, personal, and actively involved in our lives."

He raised a second finger. "Hinduism, on the other hand, teaches that there are millions of gods—gods of nature, gods of fortune, even gods in the form of animals like the cow. It encourages people to make statues and images to worship them. But the Bible says there is one God, and He forbids making idols or worshiping anything but Him."

A third finger. "Then there's Islam. They say Jesus was a prophet, a good teacher, but that he didn't actually die on the cross. They believe God wouldn't allow that to happen. But the Bible says Jesus did die on the cross, willingly, as the Lamb of God, to take away the sins of the world. That's not a small difference—either Jesus was crucified and resurrected, or he wasn't."

Brooklyn spread his hands. "So you see, these can't all be true at once. Either God exists, or He doesn't. Either He's one, or He's many. Either Jesus died for us, or he didn't. Truth doesn't bend just because people have different opinions. At the end of the day, you gotta decide—will you follow the Most High, or will you follow alternative beliefs?"

It made sense. Jayden couldn't deny that. But he still wasn't convinced.

"So what makes you sure that Jesus is the right way?"

Brooklyn smiled. "Because Jesus said, 'By their fruits, you will know them.' Look around, brother. Jesus is healing the addicted, giving peace to the broken, pulling men out of darkness. No other way matches those fruits."

Jayden didn't know what to say. He'd seen people changed by Jesus, that was true. But he also knew good people who weren't disciples of Christ.

"I hear you, man," he said slowly. "I'm just not so sure."

Joe nodded. "That's okay, brother. Just keep studying. But don't just read with your mind—ask for the Holy Spirit's guidance. A lot of us had the same questions as you. This world is full of noise, full of ideas pulling people in every direction. It's good to seek truth, but you gotta be careful. Some paths lead straight into confusion."

Jayden sat with that.

"We'll finish this lesson," Joe continued, "but I'm free to talk more tomorrow if you want."

Jayden nodded. "Yeah that's cool."

The group continued their study for another thirty minutes, and for the first time that day, Jayden's mind felt a little quieter.

Jayden woke with a jolt, his body stiff from sleep, his mind slow to catch up. The clock on the wall read 3:30 a.m. The dim overhead light buzzed, casting shadows against the cold concrete walls. He squinted, trying to make sense of the figures standing over him. Two guards. Their uniforms, their smirks. Then came the voice, thick with mockery.

"Let's go, Weed King. Time for your test."

Jayden blinked hard, still groggy. What test? His mind dragged through layers of exhaustion, piecing things together. Then it clicked—the drug test. At this hour? He wanted to argue, but what good would it do? The system didn't care about fairness, only control.

They cuffed him and led him down the dim corridor, their boots echoing against the hard floor. The place was colder at night, the kind of chill that seeped into your bones. They shoved him into a small room, bare except for a toilet and sink. A plastic cup landed in his hand.

"Fill it up. Cap it. Put it in the bag," one of them said, barely looking at him.

Jayden gritted his teeth but did as he was told, cursing them in his head. This whole place was a joke. When they were done, they walked him back to his cell like he was nothing more than a task checked off their list. By then, it was too late to go back to sleep. Breakfast would start in a couple of hours at 6:00am. He lay awake, staring at the ceiling, resentment burning in his chest.

At breakfast, Joe slid onto the bench beside him, his presence calm but intentional.

"Brother, I know we didn't get to fully answer your questions last night," he said.

Jayden exhaled sharply. He wasn't in the mood for this. He was still irritated, still sleep-deprived. He told Joe what happened with the drug test, shaking his head as he spoke.

Joe nodded, understanding. "Get some rest. We'll talk later."

Jayden didn't argue. Right after breakfast, he went back to his cell and knocked out, his body too exhausted to fight.

By dinner, he was feeling more like himself. When Joe sat down across from him, he was ready to talk.

Chapter 20

Understanding Prayer

Joe began the conversation.

"So..." he said, stretching out the word, "You strike me as somebody who reads, who knows a little something. Before I came in here, man, I was a straight knucklehead. Only thing I studied was money and women. But you? You got a mind for this. What's your belief when it comes to God?"

Jayden paused, figuring out how to put it into words.

"Well," he started, "I believe all religions, all civilizations, started in Africa."

Joe nodded. "I can agree with that."

Jayden continued. "I think the Jesus story came from Egypt, from the story of Horus. And we—Black people—we were kings and queens. Egypt wasn't even called Egypt back then, it was Kemet, and the people looked like us."

He debated mentioning his other thoughts—the alien bloodlines, the mothership—but decided to keep those to himself.

Joe leaned back, thoughtful. "I hear you. And yeah, Africa is where civilization began. Even the Bible backs that up. The Garden of Eden? That river ran right through Ethiopia. The first man? Formed from the dust of the earth—our earth. But I gotta push back on what you said about Jesus and Horus."

Jayden folded his arms, waiting.

Joe leaned in. "Tell me this—Horus getting people off crack? Horus turning prostitutes into wives, saving marriages, changing people's lives? I don't know anybody out here calling on Horus and being redeemed. But Jesus? I've seen Him do it. I've seen men in chains walk free inside, I've seen addicts healed, broken people restored. That's power, brother. And I've heard testimonies—real people, flatlining, leaving their bodies, seeing Jesus. Not Horus. Not Osiris. Jesus.

And let's be real—Jesus ain't new. He didn't just show up 2,000 years ago. He's been here since the beginning. When God said, *'Let there be light,'* Jesus was that light. Before the pyramids, before Egypt, before any of this— He was. The Bible says, *'In the beginning was the Word, and the Word was with God, and the Word was God.'*

That Word? That's Jesus. He's not some new idea or borrowed myth—He's the foundation of everything."

Jayden frowned. Some of what Joe said sounded different than what he'd grown up hearing. He thought Jesus—the Jesus story—started just 2,000 years ago, with the New Testament. The Egyptian gods were older.

"Wasn't Jesus born 2,000 years ago, though? How can you say He was here since the beginning?"

Joe smiled like he'd been waiting for that one. "Brother, that's when He revealed Himself as the Christ, when the Word became flesh. But He's been here since the start. The Bible talks about Him from Genesis to Revelation. You ever read John 17? Jesus said, 'Father, glorify Me with the glory I had with You before the world was.' Before anything was created, He was there. And in Revelation, He says, 'I am the Alpha and the Omega, the first and the last, the beginning and the end.'" Joe leaned forward. "Jesus was around way before the pyramids, before Kemet, before any of that."

Jayden wasn't convinced. "Then why are the stories so similar? And the Egyptians wrote theirs first."

Joe didn't miss a beat. "Jayden, the virgin birth of the Messiah was foretold from ancient times. And from what I've read, the Horus story? That was mythology— a lesson, not a literal man. Jesus was real, flesh and blood, born to a virgin, walked this earth, died, and rose again."

Jayden exhaled. He'd heard that Horus was more of a myth, not a historical figure. He didn't have a counter for that.

Joe studied him, then said, "Look, young brother, you don't gotta take my word for it. Ask the Holy Spirit to teach you. Open your heart. Listen to testimonies. See what God reveals."

By the time dinner was over, Jayden still wasn't sure. But he had to admit—Joe gave him some things to think about.

Before Jayden left, he hesitated for a moment, then said with a grin, "Since you're a praying man, pray I pass that drug test."

Joe didn't blink. His voice was steady, firm. "If you did the drugs, I won't ask God to lie on the test. But I will pray that you have the strength to take responsibility for your actions."

That wasn't the reply Jayden expected. It cut deep, sharper than he wanted to admit. But it gave him something to chew on.

Jayden lay on his back, staring at the cracks in the ceiling, sleep nowhere in sight. His mind kept circling the same thought—prayer. What did Joe mean when he said he wouldn't ask God to lie for him? If God was real, couldn't He do anything? And if He was real, why would He want Jayden miserable in this place? Didn't the Bible say, *Ask and you shall receive*? But Jayden had asked before—begged, even. And what did he get? His mama still died. The world kept turning, and he kept losing.

But Joe had spoken about prayer differently, like it was more than just asking for things. Like it was about something deeper.

At breakfast, Jayden didn't waste time. The moment the guards let him, he put in a request for the library. He wanted a Bible. Not because he was suddenly a believer, but because he needed to see for himself. He was tired of taking people's word for it. If God was real, He'd have to show up in His own words.

When Jayden finally got his hands on the book, he opened it with a sense of urgency, flipping straight to Matthew 7. He knew that's where *Ask and you shall receive* came from. His finger skimmed over the thin pages until he found it:

"Ask, and it shall be given you; seek, and you shall find; knock, and it shall be opened unto you: For everyone that asks receives; and he that seeks finds; and to him that knocks it shall be opened."

Jayden scoffed. *That's a lie.* He'd been knocking all week, and all he got was a locked cell and a drug test at 3:30 in the morning. He almost slammed the book shut, but something made him keep going.

A few verses down, something caught his eye:

"Every tree that doesn't bring forth good fruit is cut down and thrown into the fire. Wherefore by their fruits you will know them."

That line. He'd been hearing it a lot lately. It clung to him like a song stuck in his head. Then came the next verses—verses that stopped him cold.

"Not everyone that says unto me, 'Lord, Lord,' shall enter into the kingdom of heaven; but he that does the will of my Father which is in heaven. Many will say to me in that day, 'Lord, Lord, have we not prophesied in your name? And in your name cast out devils? And in your name done many wonderful works?' And then will I profess to them, 'I never knew you: depart from me, you workers of iniquity.'"

Jayden swallowed hard.

So if someone asks for God's help but isn't doing God's will... the Father can actually turn them away?

Joe's words about the drug test came rushing back. *If you did the drugs, I won't ask God to lie on the test.*

Maybe prayer wasn't just about asking for stuff. Maybe it had something to do with who was doing the asking.

Jayden flipped back to Matthew 6, his eyes darting over the text. Then he found it.

"When you pray, don't use vain repetitions, as the heathen do: for they think they shall be heard for all their talking. Don't be like them: for your Father knows what you need before you ask Him."

That struck a nerve. If God was real, wouldn't He already know what Jayden needed? What was the point of asking, of pleading for things that were already known? His eyes scanned the page, searching for answers.

"When you pray, pray like this: Our Father which is in heaven, Holy is Your name. Your kingdom come, Your will be done, on earth as it is in heaven. Give us this day our daily bread. And forgive us our trespasses, as we forgive those that trespass against us. And lead us not into temptation, but deliver us from evil."

Jayden sat still, gripping the Bible tight.

Jesus wasn't teaching people to pray for whatever they wanted. He was telling them to pray for God's will to be done. To pray for strength to overcome temptation, so that when they called on the Lord, He wouldn't say, *I never knew you, you workers of iniquity.*

One last verse caught his eye, and it shifted something inside him.

"Therefore don't think about or say, 'What shall we eat?' or, 'What shall we drink?' or, 'How shall we be clothed?' (For after all these things do the Gentiles seek.) For your heavenly Father knows that you need all these things. But seek first the kingdom of God, and His righteousness; and all these things will be added to you."

Jayden exhaled slow.

Jesus wants us to pray for good character and righteousness.

That's why Joe wouldn't pray for him to pass the drug test. He'd pray for Jayden to have the strength to take responsibility.

Jayden leaned back, staring at the ceiling again, but this time, something had shifted. Maybe it wasn't that his prayers had gone unheard all these years—maybe he'd just been asking for the wrong things. He'd been praying like God was some kind of genie, like the whole point was to get what he wanted. But what if prayer wasn't about bending God's will to fit his own? What if it was about surrendering, about lining himself up with something bigger, something higher? Maybe that's why it never worked the way he thought it should. Maybe that's why he always felt let down.

He hadn't just prayed wrong; he had prayed selfishly, asking for escape instead of endurance, for shortcuts instead of strength. Maybe real prayer wasn't about changing his situation—maybe it was about changing *him*.

Three days after the drug test, Jayden sat across from Mr. Cookman, his lawyer, in the sterile visitation room. The walls, the chairs, even the air itself felt lifeless, but Jayden sat still, waiting. He had a feeling about what was coming.

Mr. Cookman adjusted his glasses and let out a small sigh before speaking. "Well, Jayden, the drug test didn't go in our favor. You didn't pass, and the state wants to deny you bond." He paused, watching Jayden's face for a reaction. "We're appealing it, though."

Jayden exhaled, slow and steady. A few days ago, this news would've rattled him, had him punching walls or cursing the system. But after everything, after the prayers he wasn't even sure counted as prayers, after the quiet moments in his cell where he let his mind open just a little—this? This didn't break him. He had already figured he wouldn't pass. A small part of him had still held onto hope for a miracle, but now, hearing the truth, he felt nothing but acceptance.

"Thanks for letting me know, Mr. Cookman," Jayden said, his voice even. "Go ahead with the appeal, and whatever happens, happens." He almost said, *we'll leave it in God's hands*—the words rose up in his chest, but he caught them before they slipped out. He wasn't there yet.

Mr. Cookman studied him, his brows knitting together slightly, as if this calm, measured Jayden was an entirely different client than the one he first met. But he moved on. "Now, about the case—you're still pleading not guilty, correct? The state's got a lot of evidence, but I'm working to get some of it thrown out, weaken their witnesses. It's an uphill battle, but—"

Jayden shook his head. "No need for all that," he said, a quiet certainty in his voice. "I did what they said I did."

Mr. Cookman blinked, thrown off. "So, you're looking to change your plea?"

"Yes, sir."

The lawyer leaned back slightly, studying Jayden like he was some kind of puzzle. "Well... considering this is your first offense, I can push for probation and community service. If the state fights for prison time, I'll argue for the minimum—two years."

Jayden nodded. "That's fair."

Mr. Cookman lingered a second longer, then gave a slow nod of his own. "Alright, then."

When the visit ended and Jayden walked back to his cell, something inside him felt... lighter. He should've been weighed down, should've been restless, but instead, a strange sense of peace settled over him. He didn't know what would happen next, but somehow, he knew he'd be okay. Maybe for the first time in his life, he wasn't running from the truth—he was standing in it.

Maybe that's what Dre meant when he said he felt freer in here than he ever had on the outside. Jayden had brushed it off before, but now? Now he was starting to feel it too. Nothing—not a failed drug test, not a prison sentence, not even fear—could bring him down.

Jayden spent the rest of the day lost in thought, turning his life over and over in his mind like a puzzle with missing pieces. He thought about the choices he'd made, the prayers he used to send up like demands, the relationships he had built—and the ones he had broken. He had spent so much time expecting the world to bend to him, expecting God—if He was even real—to work on his terms. But now, sitting in a jail cell, stripped of distractions, he saw the truth. His way had led him here.

He had been a prisoner long before he ever set foot behind bars. A prisoner to his own mindset, his own selfish habits, his own reckless desires. Jail was just the consequence. The real chains had been wrapped around him for years.

That evening, for the first time in six years, Jayden did something he had sworn he'd never do again. He prayed.

"Father... I don't even know if I have the right to call You that. I don't know if You hear me, if You care, if You're real the way people say You are. But if You are... I need You to show me."

"I've done wrong. More than I can count. I've hurt people, lied, wasted time, wasted chances. I've tried to do things my way, and look where it got me. Locked up. But I don't want to keep running in circles. I don't want to keep messing up. If You can forgive me... if You can change me... I need that. I need You."

"God, I don't even know what I'm supposed to be asking for. I used to pray for what I wanted. To get good grades. To get stuff. But now... I think I need something different. I need to understand what You want. What You see for me. If You have a plan, I want to know it. If You have a will for my life, I want to follow it. But I need help. I need You to teach me, to guide me, to open my eyes."

"Show me who You really are, not who people told me You were. Not the God I made up in my head, but the real You. The one who's been around since the beginning. The one who sees past the mess I've made and still calls me to something greater."

"I don't know how to do this. I don't even know if I'm saying this right. But I'm here. And I'm asking."

"Lead me. Change me. Save me."

"Amen."

When Jayden opened his eyes, nothing in the room had changed. The bars were still there, the cold air still wrapped around him, the hum of the fluorescent light still filled the silence. But something inside him felt different—like a door had cracked open. Like, maybe, just maybe, someone was listening.

Over the next week, Jayden poured himself into the Bible like a man starving for truth. Any chance he got, he read. Morning, afternoon, night—flipping through pages, underlining verses, making connections. He joined Joshua's Bible study class, sat in on small group sessions with Dre, Joe, Brooklyn, and Junior. This time around, the words hit different. He wasn't just reading to memorize or to prove something to somebody. He was reading to *understand*.

And what surprised him most? He didn't have to throw away everything he'd learned from the conscious community. He started seeing the connections, the overlaps, the confirmations. Like how Inner-G, Diamond, and Panther always talked about the body being a temple—he found that same truth in scripture. The Bible didn't just say it in passing; it laid out laws to keep God's people clean and healthy. Growing up in church, he'd seen too many people abusing their bodies—overeating, living irresponsibly—and for the first time, he realized that wasn't biblical. That was people, eating and living according to their lusts. He read Philippians 3:19 which said 'whose end *is* destruction, whose god *is their* belly'

He also saw the benefits of the cultural dignity and pride that he'd gained. The school system and pop-culture had subtly—and sometimes outright—taught non-Europeans to feel less than, measuring themselves against Eurocentric standards of beauty, intelligence, and success. But the conscious community had brought light to ancient civilizations—kingdoms in Africa, indigenous sciences, and the brilliance of Black philosophers and builders—that had been intentionally omitted from his textbooks.

That knowledge had affirmed him. It gave him a reason to walk tall, to stop apologizing for where he came from. And now, he realized he didn't have to choose between that and his faith. He could hold both—the truth of his ancestors and the truth of scripture—in the same hand. In fact, one made the other clearer.

And the idea that he was a king? He had heard it for years in the conscious community, but now, reading Revelation, he saw it in black and white:

"Jesus Christ, the faithful witness, the first begotten of the dead, and the prince of the kings of the earth. Unto him that loved us, and washed us from our sins in his own blood. And hath made us kings and priests unto God and his Father."

Jayden sat with that verse for a long time. It made him think about what his friend Caleb had said, about the Israelite kingdoms being part of Africa's history. He had spent years studying African empires, learning about Mansa Musa, the Ashanti, the Zulu. But now, his mind stretched further—King David, King Solomon—were they his ancestors too? Was this history *his* story?

Piece by piece, the puzzle was coming together. The more he read, the more things started making sense. And it didn't go unnoticed. In the Bible study group, the other men watched as Jayden connected dots with ease, flipping between verses, breaking things down in ways that even surprised himself. He had thought he was starting over. But maybe, just maybe, he was picking up right where he left off.

Chapter 21

Unwelcome Home

When Trinity stepped into the visitation room and saw Jayden, she knew something was different. It wasn't just the way he carried himself—sitting up straight, eyes clear, no trace of that heavy, world-on-his-shoulders look he always had. It was something deeper, something in his *spirit*.

"You look... good," she said, settling into the chair across from him. She tilted her head, studying him. "Jail food ain't treating you too bad, huh?"

Jayden chuckled. "It ain't the food, Trin. It's me. I've been reading. Studying. Thinking about my life, my choices. Trying to get right."

Trinity raised an eyebrow. "*Trying to get right*?" She crossed her arms. "And what does that mean exactly?"

Jayden leaned forward, eyes shining with an intensity she hadn't seen in years. "It means no more smoking, no more dealing. No more running in circles, making the same mistakes." He sat back, shaking his head. "The scriptures say, *Be sober, be vigilant; because your adversary the devil, as a roaring lion, walks about, seeking whom he may devour.*"

Trinity's mouth dropped open. "*You* quoting scripture?" She let out a laugh, shaking her head. "Man, if I didn't see it with my own eyes, I wouldn't believe it."

Jayden smiled. "I'm serious, Trin. I see things different now. I'm done playing games with my life. When I get out, I'm going back to school. I'm gonna get involved with New Life again. Really *be* about something, not just talking."

Trinity stared at him, the weight of his words settling in. She had spent years watching her brother slip further away, fading into the haze of smoke and bad decisions. But now? Now, he looked like the boy she used to know—the one who used to have dreams bigger than the block. Only this time, there was something new. A steadiness. A fire.

She smiled. "You sound different, Jay."

"I *am* different."

For the first time in a long time, Trinity believed him.

Jayden shifted in his seat. "How's Aunt Patrice? I been thinking about her lately. It'd be nice to see her."

Trinity nodded. "She always asks about you. I'll let her know you're thinking about her."

"Yeah," Jayden said, nodding. "Tell her I'm good. Tell her... I'm getting there."

Trinity looked at Jayden and smiled big, "I'll tell her."

And for the first time in years, she left that visit feeling lighter—like maybe, just maybe, her brother was finally finding his way back.

A few days later, Jayden got another visit from Mr. Cookman. This time, the lawyer walked in wearing a grin instead of his usual tight-lipped expression.

"Got some good news for you," Cookman said, setting his briefcase on the table. "We won the appeal. As soon as the paperwork gets processed, you're getting bonded out."

For a moment, Jayden just stared, the words sinking in slow. Freedom. He'd adjusted to life inside, even found peace in ways he never expected, but there was no substitute for fresh air that didn't come through bars. He let out a breath and broke into a smile. "That's great, man. Really great."

Jayden sat forward, a thought suddenly hitting him. "Mr. Cookman, can you reach out to my aunt? See if she can pick me up?"

Cookman nodded. "Yeah, I'll give her a call."

"Appreciate that."

Cookman leaned in slightly, his tone shifting. "You know this is just the first step, right? You're out on bond, but we've still got a fight ahead of us. The state's not backing down."

Jayden met his gaze, steady this time. "I get it. We'll keep it in God's hands."

Cookman studied him for a beat, something unreadable flickering across his face. The man he'd first met a few weeks ago had been defensive, full of excuses, still trying to game the system. Now? There was something different in his eyes—something settled.

"Well," Cookman finally said, gathering his papers,

"Next time I see you, you'll be out of here—a free man."

Jayden nodded, his chest light, his mind clear. "Yeah. I'll be ready."

As he walked back to his cell, the bars didn't feel so heavy. The walls didn't press in the same way. For the first time in a long time, Jayden could see the light at the end of the tunnel—and this time, he wasn't afraid to walk toward it.

The next day, as Jayden sat at the metal table, picking at the bland lunch on his tray, Dre, Joe, and Brooklyn talked around him. They were in the middle of a heated debate about who the greatest NBA player of all time was when a guard approached.

"Thomas, get your things. You're being released."

Jayden froze mid-bite, his fork hovering just above the tray. He looked up, eyes wide.

"For real?"

The guard just nodded, already turning away.

Joe let out a low whistle. "Wow, God moves fast with this guy."

Brooklyn shook his head with a grin. "Man, you got angels working overtime."

Dre leaned forward, resting his elbows on the table. His face was serious, his tone even. "Stay focused on the outside, brother. It's easy to slip back into your old life, old habits, real quick."

Jayden met his eyes, nodding. "I hear you. I'm definitely gonna keep my focus."

Dre studied him for a second, then reached out and clasped his hand, pulling him in for a firm shake. "For real, Jay. Don't let all this be for nothing."

"I won't," Jayden promised.

Joe gave him a nod. "Keep praying. Keep growing."

Brooklyn smirked. "And stay outta trouble, man. I don't wanna see you back in here."

Jayden chuckled. "Trust me, I don't wanna see y'all in here either."

He stood, feeling the weight of the moment settle over him. He had walked into this place lost. He was walking out with purpose.

"I appreciate y'all. For real." He glanced around at them. "I'll stay in touch."

And with that, he turned, following the guard toward the exit, stepping into a future that—for the first time in a long time—felt firmly rooted.

When Jayden stepped into the lobby, the first thing he saw was Aunt Patrice, standing tall, her arms crossed, her smile wide and warm.

"There he is," she said, her voice thick with emotion.

Jayden didn't hesitate. He crossed the space in a few strides and wrapped his arms around her. She smelled like cocoa butter and peppermint, like home.

"Thanks for coming to get me," he said, his voice low.

"Of course, Jayden!" she said, squeezing him tight before stepping back to look at him. "Where else would I be?"

As they walked outside, the late afternoon sun hit him full force. The air smelled fresher, the sky stretched wider. He took a deep breath, filling his lungs in a way he never had before. This was different. This was real freedom.

As they reached the car, Patrice shook her head. "This is the last place I ever thought I'd be picking you up from."

Jayden nodded, but he didn't say anything. What could he say? She wasn't wrong.

They climbed into the car, and as Patrice pulled onto the road, Jayden leaned back in his seat, exhaling. "I'm telling you, Auntie, I got so much clarity in there over the last few weeks. I realized things about life I just wasn't seeing before."

Patrice glanced over at him, nodding. "Yeah, Trinity told me you're looking like a new man. But really, that's the man I always knew you were."

Jayden smiled. "Well, I see it now. And I know what I need to do. I'm going back to New Life Church. And I'm enrolling in school—Non-Profit Management. I wanna do something that actually matters."

Patrice raised her eyebrows. "That's big, Jayden. That's real big. You sure you're going to follow through with that?"

"One hundred percent," he said without hesitation. "I'm done with that other life. God gave me another chance, and I'm not about to waste it."

Patrice nodded, a proud smile stretching across her face. "Well, I got updates for you. New Life's been changing too. We got a new Youth Pastor, and they're carrying on a lot of the work you started before you left."

Jayden's eyes widened. "For real?"

"For real. That church never forgot about you."

That hit him in a way he didn't expect. After all he had done, all the mistakes, they still cared. God still cared.

The 25-minute drive felt like it passed in half the time, and before he knew it, they were parked in front of the Violet Light House. Neither of them moved to get out just yet.

Patrice turned to him, her expression serious now. "You know, it's real easy to slip back into your old ways, especially when the excitement of change wears off. You gotta stay focused, Jayden. Keep pressing forward."

"I hear you," Jayden said, meeting her eyes. "I'm not going back. I got too much to live for now."

Patrice studied him for a long moment before nodding. "Good. Hold onto that."

They sat in silence for a few seconds before she reached over and squeezed his hand.

"I love you, Jayden."

He squeezed back. "I love you too, Auntie."

With that, he stepped out of the car, taking in the familiar sight of the Violet Light House. This time, he wasn't walking in as the same man who left. This time, he was ready.

Jayden had this idea—maybe a naïve one—that because he had changed, everything around him would change too. Like the world had been waiting on him to get himself together, and now that he had, it would fall in line. But the minute he stepped into the VLH, reality hit him like a slap. Some things stay exactly the same.

The first thing he saw was Royal and Essence sprawled out on the couch, a thick blunt passing between them. The air was hazy, the scent unmistakable. They were deep in conversation about African women versus Western women—same old arguments, same old debates.

"Yoooo, look who it is!" Royal hollered, throwing his arms wide like Jayden had just returned from war.

"The man, the myth, the legend!" Essence added, grinning. "They couldn't hold you down, huh?"

Jayden let out a small laugh, shaking his head. "What's up, fellas? Yeah, man, definitely good to be outta that hellhole."

"Oh, snap, we gotta roll you a welcome-back blunt," Royal said, already reaching for the grinder. "Super Bob Marley style, bro. You deserve it."

"Hell yeah," Essence co-signed, his eyes low and lazy. "Gotta get that jailhouse tension up outta your system."

The offer was tempting. Too tempting. Three weeks without a smoke, three weeks of steel beds and bad food, of stale air and locked doors. He felt like he had earned this moment, just one blunt to take the edge off. His mind flickered to all the people he'd just told he was done with this—Aunt Patrice, Trinity, Dre, Joe. He had meant it when he said it. He had felt strong when he said it. But right now? Right now, the old pull was real.

"I appreciate that, fellas, but I'm gonna ease up on the smoking," Jayden said, the words slower than he meant them to be.

Both Royal and Essence gave him a look, their brows raising in unison.

"Uh oh," Essence smirked, exhaling a cloud of smoke. "Did this brother get scared straight?"

Royal grinned. "Don't worry, no popo up in this living room. You safe."

Jayden hesitated, searching for the right words. "It's not that. I'm just tryna keep my mind clear, you know? Stay focused."

Royal and Essence exchanged glances before bursting into laughter.

"Bro, what they do to you in there?" Royal snickered. "Mind control or somethin'? You're the Sour Diesel King in these parts. Don't tell me you not the go-to guy no more."

Jayden swallowed, his jaw tightening. He had expected resistance, but the ridicule? That stung more than he wanted to admit.

"Nah, man," he said, forcing a small smile. "I'm just on a different vibe now."

The laughter died down, but the energy in the room shifted. Jayden could feel it. The unspoken distance growing.

"A'ight, man," Royal said, waving the blunt like a peace offering. "When you ready for this, you know where we at."

Essence chuckled. "Yeah, King J, don't be actin' brand new forever."

Jayden gave them a half-smile, dapped them up, and said, "Yeah, man, I'm wiped. Just tryna get some rest," hoping they'd let it go. Then he turned and headed toward his room.

He could still hear them laughing as he shut the door behind him. Their voices carried through the thin walls, muffled but clear enough—joking, doubting, like they already knew he'd fold sooner or later.

Lying on his bed, he let out a long breath. Something felt off. He couldn't put his finger on it, but a weight settled over him, making it hard to relax.

Maybe it was just being back. Maybe it was the way Royal and Essence looked at him, like they were waiting for him to slip. Whatever it was, it left him uneasy.

Jayden lay on his bed, something gnawing at him. The room looked... off. Not just dusty from being unoccupied, but wrong. His things were shifted, like someone had gone through them with careless hands. His gut clenched.

His money.

He sat up fast, heart thudding, and yanked open the drawer where he'd stashed some cash. Empty. His breath caught. He dropped to his knees and reached under the bed, pulling out the old shoebox. It was still there. But the weight was all wrong.

He flipped open the lid.

Gone.

Jayden's stomach twisted. He sat back on his heels, rubbing his hands over his face. I got robbed.

The first thought that hit him was to call Diamond. At first, he'd been thinking about calling her just to see her, spend some time together. Now, he had questions. He didn't think she'd take his money—at least, he didn't want to believe that—but maybe she knew something.

He grabbed his phone and dialed.

"King J!" Diamond's voice was all excitement. "I didn't even know you were getting out! Oh my God, I'm coming to see you right now."

Jayden wanted to ask her straight up, but he figured it was better to do it in person. "Yeah, cool. See you soon."

Within five minutes, she was at the door. When he opened it, she practically jumped into his arms. "Hey, King J!" she said, leaning in for a kiss.

He kissed her back, but she felt it—his mind was somewhere else.

She pulled back, studying his face. "You okay? It's good to have you back."

"Yeah, it's good to be back." He exhaled, running a hand over his head. "I just—something's stressing me out." He hesitated, then asked, "Was somebody in my room?"

Diamond's whole expression changed.

She sighed, glancing away before meeting his eyes again. "Jayden, I didn't want to tell you while you were locked up, but..." She hesitated, then came right out with it. "The cops came through. They searched everything. Tore this place up."

Jayden's body tensed. "What? When?"

"Few weeks ago," she said carefully. "They took all your weed and your money too."

Jayden's pulse pounded in his ears. "They did what?!" His voice shot up. "And you didn't tell me?" All the peace he had been feeling over the past week immediately left him. His mind spun with anger, frustration, and disbelief. God was the last thing on his thoughts now—replaced by the image of cops rifling through his things, taking what was his.

"I didn't wanna stress you out while you were in there. You already looked miserable."

Jayden's hands clenched into fists. "How the hell can they take my money? It ain't illegal to have cash!" His breath came sharp and fast. "They robbed me."

"I'm sorry, baby," she soothed. "But look, you can get that money back quick. People been waiting on you to get out so they can get that fire again."

Jayden's chest rose and fell as he took it in. She's right. He could make it back fast. His name still held weight. His product was still in demand.

Then he heard his own voice in his head—the promise he'd made. To himself. To God. To his family.

"I'm not looking to do that anymore," he said, barely above a whisper.

Diamond gave him a long, searching look. "Really? But people been asking for you. You got some loyal customers." She tilted her head, watching him closely. "Or... you scared? Think they gonna come for you again?"

Jayden's jaw tensed. He couldn't let her think that. He wasn't scared—at least, that's what he told himself. But he also wasn't about to walk right back into the same mess he'd just crawled out of.

"Nah, it ain't that," he said, keeping his voice even. "I'm just moving different now. Got some things I wanna do, some things I need to do."

Diamond raised an eyebrow. "Like what?"

Jayden exhaled and ran a hand over his head. "Like getting my mind right. Staying clear. I'm just doing some things differently this time, that's all."

She reached into her purse, pulling out a small bag and a pipe. "Here," she said, smiling. "I know you ain't smoked in weeks. This'll help you relax."

Jayden stared at it. And for a moment, he saw himself taking it. Taking a long pull, feeling that familiar peace spread through him, letting it all melt away—his anger, his stress, the weight pressing on his chest.

It'd be so easy.

"I don't know," he mumbled, feeling his will slipping. "I ain't sure I wanna do that."

Diamond slid closer, stroking his arm. "Baby, you need to chill. This will help ease you, get your mind right."

Jayden felt torn, like he was standing at a fork in the road. It felt like he had two voices in his head—one telling him to stay strong, the other tempting him to slip right back in.

He was about to say yes, but then in his mind he saw Aunt Patrice. The way she'd looked at him before he stepped inside VLH. The way she'd squeezed his hand—tight, firm, like she was holding on to something bigger than him.

His jaw tightened.

"I'm good, babe," he said, forcing the words out. "Thanks, but I just need some sleep. I been through a lot."

Diamond studied him for a second, then shrugged. "Okay, baby. Lay down. I'll be here with you."

She curled up next to him, rubbing his arm, but Jayden barely noticed. His mind was too loud.

He stared at the ceiling, his thoughts tangled in knots.

After about thirty minutes he was asleep.

Three hours later, Jayden woke up to the faint sound of pages turning and the scent of burnt herb hanging in the air. Diamond sat in the corner, legs crossed, a book about crystals resting in her lap, a pipe balanced between two fingers. She took a slow drag, her eyes scanning the pages like she was studying for an exam.

Something about the sight irritated him. He wasn't sure why, but it did. Maybe it was the way she was so at peace while his whole world had just cracked open. Maybe it was the fact that he'd barely made it out of jail and here she was, still moving the same way. Maybe it was just the smell.

"Do you always have to get high?" The words slipped out before he could filter them, his voice rough with sleep and frustration.

Diamond's eyes flicked up from her book, her brows knitting together. "Huh?" she muttered, her smile faltering. For a second, she just stared at him, like she was trying to figure out if he was serious. Instead, she changed the subject. "Well, looks like somebody needed some good sleep."

Jayden thought about pressing the issue, but he didn't have the energy to argue. Not right now. "Yeah, I was tired," he muttered instead.

Silence fell between them, but Jayden's mind wouldn't settle. The reality of what happened to his money hit him all over again. He had counted on that cash to float him for the next four months. He'd walked out of jail thinking money was the last thing he needed to worry about. Now, it was the first thing on his mind.

His thoughts started spinning. What were his options? Sell again? Go back to Inner-G's vending hustle? Promote Lion Heart Healing? Get a job?

The idea of selling again hovered at the edges of his mind like a familiar ghost. He knew he could make money fast. He could be back on his feet in days. But that was the old way, the easy way—the way that had landed him behind bars. He'd already promised himself, his family, and God that he wouldn't do that anymore.

"What's on your mind, King J?" Diamond's voice cut through his thoughts. "You look like you're thinking hard."

"Yeah," he exhaled. "Just thinking about how the cops stole my money."

Diamond set her book down. "King J, I know you said you wasn't trying to go back to that life, but... why don't you just sell for a little while? Just to get back on track. You could probably make over $300 by the end of the night."

Jayden's stomach turned. He should've expected her to say that, but it still rubbed him the wrong way. How could she push him to do the very thing that got him locked up? Didn't she care what happened to him?

He didn't reply. Didn't even look at her.

"I know what you need," Diamond said after a beat, pulling something out of her purse. "You need a reading." She held up her tarot cards like they held the answer to all his problems.

Something inside Jayden snapped.

"Yeah, 'cause those did me a whole lot of good last time," he said, his voice dripping with sarcasm.

Diamond frowned. "Excuse me?"

"Your last reading led me straight to jail. You really think those cards give good advice? You really think they speak for the Holy Spirit?"

The words were out before he could stop them. He had just given away his new conviction. It had to come out sooner or later.

Diamond squinted at him, confused. "The Holy Spirit? What are you talking about, King J?"

Jayden hesitated, then squared his shoulders. "God," he said. "I'm talking about God. You really think He speaks through those cards?"

Diamond sat up, suddenly interested. "The Universe uses tarot to tap into universal energies," she said, her voice taking on that patient, mystical tone she used when she thought she was teaching him something. "It helps us access our subconscious, understand our path, and work through our problems."

Jayden shook his head. "What if it doesn't work like that? What if tarot and all this other divination stuff isn't connecting you to 'universal energies' but to something else? Something that pulls you away from God?"

Diamond tilted her head. "Where is all this coming from?"

Jayden leaned forward. "If your cards are so on point, why ain't they telling you to stop getting high all the time and stay sober-minded?"

Diamond's face darkened. "King J, I know jail was rough on you, but don't take your crankiness out on me. I'm just trying to help."

Jayden exhaled hard, shaking his head. He was losing respect for her. For this whole conversation. Maybe she would never understand where he was coming from.

"I'm going for a walk," he said, standing up. "Need to clear my mind."

"Okay," she said, picking her book back up. "Hope that gets you in a better mood."

"Yeah. Me too."

Chapter 22

The Purity Challenge

Outside, the warm night air hit his face, but it didn't do much to ease the frustration weighing on him. This homecoming wasn't anything like he had imagined. For three weeks, he'd been counting down the days, expecting that first breath of freedom to feel like the best moment of his life. Instead, he felt more trapped than ever.

The cops had robbed him blind. Royal and Essence mocking him. Would things ever be cool between them again, now that he wasn't smoking? Diamond was lost in her own world of smoke and superstition. Would she even recognize who he was anymore? He thought about bringing up the Bible, about telling her what he'd been reading, what had been stirring in him. But how would that go? Would she listen? Would she even care?

Then there was Pharaoh. The bitterness in Jayden's chest sat heavy, like a weight pressing against his ribs.

He used to appreciate him. They were boys. Now, he wasn't so sure. He thought about calling him, just to hear what he had to say. But then he decided against it. He didn't feel like dealing with more disappointment.

He thought about talking to Inner-G, just catching up like they used to. But if the Bible came up? He could already hear the cynicism in Inner-G's voice, the way he'd pick it apart, questioning everything Jayden had started to believe. The more he thought about it, the more the admiration he once had for him slipped through his fingers like sand.

No, he needed to talk to someone who understood.

Then he thought of Caleb.

Without hesitating, he pulled out his phone and dialed.

"Jayden!" Caleb's voice was warm and familiar. "Man, I was just thinking about you! What you been up too?"

Jayden hesitated, not knowing where to start. The arrest. The time in jail. Instead, he landed on the one thing that mattered. "I've been good," he said. "Been hitting the scriptures hard."

There was a pause on the other end, almost like he was surprised, then Caleb responded, his voice filled with encouragement. "Oh for real? That's great, man. It's so important to stay in His word and keep that relationship with the Most High."

They talked for two hours—about God, purpose, family, and everything happening at New Life Church. Caleb encouraged him, lifted him up, reminded him of the peace he'd felt all last week. By the time they hung up, Jayden felt more like himself again.

After the conversation ended, Jayden wandered. He walked without direction, his feet leading him to a small park where he sank onto a worn wooden bench, the night folding around him. The air was thick with summer heat, but a chill still crept under his skin. He sat there, staring at nothing, his thoughts circling the same questions, the same uncertainties.

He hadn't expected to feel so out of place in his own home. Shouldn't it have felt like a relief to be back? Instead, he felt like an outsider, like his presence disrupted something that already had a rhythm, but his own rhythm changed.

New Life Church flickered through his mind. Tomorrow was Wednesday. Youth group night.

Should he go? See how things had changed, who was still around? But then Jayson's face popped into his mind, the way he'd looked at him the night he got arrested. The humiliation burned fresh, even now. Jayson was one of the leaders—he'd definitely be there. Was Jayden ready for that? Ready to face the weight of his mistakes in front of people who once looked up to him?

He sighed, rubbing his hands together, listening to his own breath escape into the warm night air.

Maybe he'd sleep on it.

Maybe in the morning, he'd have more answers.

The next day, when Jayden woke up, he felt good—lighter than he had in days. But as soon as his stomach clenched in hunger, a thought hit him he hadn't been expecting.

What am I gonna eat?

Even in jail, he never had to think about food. It wasn't good, but at least it was there. Now, he was free, and somehow, that meant being hungry.

He thought about raiding the fridge, grabbing something unmarked and hoping no one would care. But then the tension with Royal and Essence replayed in his head, and he decided he didn't need more bad vibes in that house.

Diamond? He thought about asking her for some money, but the way their last conversation ended made him think twice.

Then Trinity came to mind.

The smell of breakfast in her kitchen, the warmth of her place, the way she'd show up for him when nobody else did. She had visited him more than anyone—other than his lawyer. Seeing her felt right.

He grabbed his phone and called.

"Hey Jayden," she answered, and he could hear the smile in her voice. "I hear you're a free man."

"Yeah, Trin, I'm out. And definitely not going back!"

"That's what I like to hear."

"What you up to? Would be good to see you."

"I'm just taking care of the little ones. You're free to stop by."

"Cool," Jayden said, already reaching for his keys. "See you in a few."

As he hung up, something in him settled. He wasn't just going over for food, though his growling stomach was plenty excited about that. He was going because he really needed to be around family.

Jayden slipped out the back door, moving fast, like if he lingered too long, his housemates might suck him back into the tension he was trying to escape. Thirty-five minutes later, he stood outside his sister's house, knocking twice before she pulled the door open, a baby propped on her hip.

"Good to see ya, Jay," Trinity said, wrapping him in a one-armed hug. "I don't know if you ate, but I just made pancakes and eggs."

Music. That's what her words sounded like. A whole symphony of comfort. The jail food had been the worst thing he'd ever tasted, a daily reminder that he wasn't free. He and Aunt Patrice had stopped for fast food on the way home, but that wasn't real food. Not like this.

Inside, the place felt different. Warmer, somehow. More like home than it ever had when he stayed there before. Back then, he always felt like a visitor, tiptoeing around, keeping parts of himself hidden. But today, he exhaled. Let himself settle into the peace of it.

Trinity sat across from him while he ate, balancing the baby in her lap. "So how's it feel to be back in the free world?"

Jayden thought about it—the frustrations, the disappointments, the weight of everything he hadn't expected to hit him so hard. He swallowed, then forced a smile. "It's definitely an adjustment."

Not the excitement she was expecting, but she let it slide. "So what's next? What are you gonna do now?"

Jayden scraped the last of his eggs off his plate, chewing over the question. "Well," he said finally, "I definitely gotta get a job. At least I'll pass a drug test now." He smiled, and Trinity laughed. "I'm thinking about checking in on the youth group at New Life tonight. And you know, enjoying a bathroom with a door and hot private showers without a bunch of smelly men around."

Trinity grinned. "I can only imagine. But what made you pick up the Bible again? That's what I really wanna know."

Jayden leaned back, rubbing his chin. He told her about Dre, about Brother Joshua's Bible classes, about Joe, Brooklyn, and Junior. About the way something had clicked inside him when he started really reading the Word.

Trinity listened, nodding. "God shows up anywhere," she said. "Even in jail."

That sat with him. God showing up anywhere.

He hesitated before asking, "You cool if I hang out for a while? I just... don't feel like being at the house."

Trinity gave him a knowing look. "You don't have to ask, Jay. Stay as long as you want."

Trinity looked at Jayden with concern. "Is that house you live in a good atmosphere for you right now?" she asked gently.

Jayden hesitated for a moment, then gave a small nod. "I'll be fine. I'm staying focused," he replied, though the uncertainty lingered beneath his words.

Trinity shook her head, "I hope so," she said softly, her voice carrying a mix of concern and hope as she looked at him.

Around 5:30, John walked in from work, loosening his tie at the door. The minute he spotted Jayden, his face broke into a grin.

"Look who it is," John said.

"Yeah, man, I'm back."

Jayden felt a flicker of embarrassment. Jail. The word sat between them, unspoken but heavy. He pushed past it, kept the energy light. He told John about the experience—the hard mattress, the open toilet, the cold showers, the terrible food. But he also told him about the Bible study, about the men he met inside who made him see things differently.

John nodded, listening. "I'm glad to hear that, man. And you know, you should come down to the community center sometime. Some of the youth would want to hear your story. Especially now that you're getting yourself straight again."

The idea struck something deep in Jayden, like an ember catching fire. It felt right.

"I'd love that," Jayden said. "Just let me know when."

"Cool."

By the time dinner was over, Jayden had made up his mind—he was going to New Life Church. No more second-guessing. No more worrying about Jayson and what he'd seen. He had to do this.

The drive to New Life felt surreal. Six years. He hadn't set foot in that building in six whole years. He thought he'd never be back. And yet, here he was, pulling into the lot, watching clusters of teens and a few adults file inside. His pulse jumped. His fingers clenched around the steering wheel.

Maybe he wasn't ready.

Maybe he should turn around, head back to VLH, figure things out later.

But that didn't feel right either.

He exhaled sharply. "I just gotta do this."

He popped the car door open, stepped out, and walked toward the entrance.

At first, nobody noticed him. Then—

"Jayden?"

He turned. Amiyah stood a few feet away, eyes wide, a slow smile spreading across her face.

"Oh my gosh, it's so good to see you here."

Jayden had to admit—it was good to see her too. A familiar face. A welcoming one.

"Hey, Amiyah," he said, feeling some of the nerves loosen.

"This is wild," she laughed. "Wait till the others see you—the youth leader legend, back in the building! Come on, let me introduce you to Pastor Mike."

She led him to the front of the room, where a medium-built man with a close-cropped haircut and a well-trimmed beard stood in a polo shirt with the New Life emblem on it. He looked up as they approached. Amiyah gestured between them with a smile. "Pastor Mike, this is Jayden. He used to be one of the youth leaders back in the day."

Pastor Mike extended his hand with a welcoming smile. "So you're the famous Jayden. I've heard a lot about you from folks around here. It's good to finally meet you. I hope you'll be joining us for the evening's meeting."

Jayden nodded. "Yeah, I will."

Then—

"Hey, Jayson, look who it is," Amiyah called.

Jayden's stomach tightened. He turned and saw Jayson looking at him, expression unreadable. A flicker of something—hesitation? Uncertainty?

For a second, they just stood there, the memory of Jayden's arrest hanging between them. Then Jayson walked over.

"Hey, Jayden," he said finally, voice even. "I didn't know you were coming. It's good to have you here."

Jayden nodded, some of the tension in his chest unraveling.

Amiyah looped an arm through his and guided him toward the other youth leaders. "We've been talking about staying focused in a world full of distractions," she said. "Third week on the topic—it's been great so far."

As they reached the group, Amiyah's smile widened. "Everyone, this is Jayden," she said, her tone carrying a note of reverence. "Back in the day, he wasn't just part of the youth group—he helped lead it. A lot of what we do now? He helped lay the foundation."

The leaders exchanged impressed glances, a few nodding in recognition.

Jayden took a breath, letting himself settle into the moment.

Maybe this was exactly where he needed to be.

Pastor Mike stood, straightened his polo, and let his eyes sweep over the room before he spoke. "The world is full of false gods," he began, his voice steady, measured. "Anything you put ahead of the Most High is an idol. Could be money, cars, security. Could be food, drugs, people—even your own family." He paused, letting the words settle. "That's why Jesus tells us to 'hate' our mother, father, wife, children, brothers, and sisters—not because we're supposed to despise them, but because our love for God should be so great that, by comparison, everything else fades into the background. Remember, God knows all and sees all"

Jayden sat back, arms folded, chewing on the words. He thought about the idols in his own life. He'd moved heaven and earth to get a weed connect. And once he got a taste of money, nothing else mattered—principles, priorities, people, all slipped through his fingers like loose change. Then his mind drifted to Diamond with her Tarot cards, Inner-G and his crystals, Pharaoh and his excuses. Every single one of them was leaning on something that wasn't God.

Pastor Mike's voice cut through his thoughts. "The love of the world is the norm in popular culture. Any movie with an 'R' rating? Basically telling you upfront—this is filled with smut. Violence, sex, drugs, foul language. Music's no better. Even the news keeps you scared, keeps you trusting in men instead of trusting in God."

Jayden exhaled, feeling a pressure he hadn't expected. How much of this was running unchecked in his own life? If he wanted to stay in God's presence, he had some filtering to do.

After the message, Pastor Mike clapped his hands together. "Alright, let's break into small groups."

Amiyah nudged Jayden. "Come on," she said, gesturing toward her group.

There were seven of them—Amiyah, another leader who looked about early twenties, and five teens. As soon as they all settled in, Amiyah turned to the group. "You guys," she said, her voice buzzing with excitement. "Jayden is the one who started the purity challenge."

The teens' faces lit up. A few of them leaned forward, eyes wide with recognition. "No way," one of them breathed.

"We all signed up," another teen added. "The support system has been everything. We're hit with sexual stuff every day—it's everywhere. Without this, I don't know how I would've stayed on track."

The other leader smiled at Jayden. "I actually graduated the challenge myself," she said. "Met my husband in purity. Didn't fall for the lusts of the world."

Jayden forced a smile, but a weight settled in his chest. They were looking at him like he was a blueprint, but in reality, he had fallen way off the mark. He had lost count of the times he had shared his bed with women who weren't his wife. And then, just as the thought crossed his mind, one of the teens spoke up.

"So, how's it been going for you?"

The words hit him like a punch to the gut. He hesitated, his mind scrambling for an answer. Seven faces stared at him, waiting, expecting. The founder of the challenge—he had to have something to say.

"Well..." Jayden started slowly, buying himself a few extra seconds. "It's been tough. Like Pastor Mike said, the world is full of things trying to pull us away from God. I fell off a little bit." He took a breath, then added, "But I'm recommitting."

As soon as he said it, he second guessed what he just agreed too. Then his mind snapped to Diamond.

They hadn't signed up for this. She was a regular visitor to his bed, and now he had put words into the air—words that, if he meant them, would change everything between them.

Amiyah beamed at him. "Yes, Jayden! It's tough out there, but you're not alone. We've got you."

Jayden forced a smile, nodding along. But inside, his stomach twisted. He had no idea what he had just signed himself up for. Coming to New Life Church tonight had felt like the right thing, but now? Now, everything was shifting in a way he hadn't seen coming.

On the ride home, Jayden gripped the steering wheel, his mind tangled in knots as he drove back to the VLH. The night had been heavy—Pastor Mike's words still rang in his ears, the way those kids at church had looked at him like he was some kind of role model, the commitment he'd spoken into existence without fully meaning to. It was all good, right? But it was fast. Too fast. He had planned to ease his way back to Christ, not get yanked in headfirst.

Halfway home, his phone buzzed. Diamond.

"Hey baby, where you been all day?" Her voice had that soft, teasing lilt he liked.

"I was at my sister's," he said, keeping it vague. "Then I had a meeting."

A church meeting—that part he left out.

She sighed, her tone gentle. "I wanted to apologize... I know I haven't been as understanding about everything you've been going through. I just—I've been missing you. Can I stay with you tonight?"

Jayden swallowed. He already knew what that meant. And here it was, the challenge, coming for him before he even made it back to his room. He could say yes, and technically, nothing had to happen between them. But they both knew what it usually meant. It had been three weeks. The longest he'd gone without intimacy in a long, long time.

"Yeah, you can come by," he said. "I might turn in early,

When Jayden walked into his room, Diamond was already stretched across his bed, waiting. Vanilla candle flickering. Skin glowing like she'd just bathed in some expensive oil. That little pink-and-white nighty she knew would make him weak. It barely covered a quarter of her thigh, left nothing to the imagination.

"Hey love," she purred. "Welcome home."

Chapter 23

Satisfying Hunger

As Diamond lay in his bed, his mind began going in all different directions. He smiled, but inside, his chest felt tight.

"Hey, babe. Good to see you." He needed a second to breathe. "Be right back, I gotta hit the bathroom."

She smiled. "Hurry back."

In the bathroom, Jayden gripped the sink and stared at his reflection. His pulse was already picking up speed. He needed this, right? After three weeks of cold jail cells, was a woman's touch really so bad? Nobody at New Life was about to find out what he did in his own home.

Then, like a lightning strike, Pastor Mike's words hit him: *God knows all and sees all.*

Jayden exhaled. He'd be lying to God if he did this. He could see Amiyah's face in his mind, the way she'd looked at him when he said he was recommitting. She believed him. Maybe, just maybe, he should believe himself too.

When he walked back in the room, Diamond was sitting up now, eyes narrowed. "What took you so long?"

He muttered an apology but didn't explain.

She pulled out her pipe, packed it with weed, and took two slow hits before offering it to him.

Jayden waved it away, now getting irritated. "I told you, I'm not smoking anymore."

Diamond frowned. "You meant forever?"

Jayden nodded.

She sighed and set the pipe down, then reached for him, her fingers tracing slow circles over his arm, his chest. She leaned in. "I know you been through a lot, baby. Let me help you relax."

The touch, the scent of her skin, the way her voice dipped just right—he felt it pulling at him, the old instinct rising. But just as he started to slip, Jayden stood up.

Diamond blinked. "What's wrong?"

Jayden hesitated, then forced the words out. "What about purity?"

She stared. "Huh? What are you talking about, King J?"

The air between them shifted. The heat in the room dimmed, replaced by something thick, tense. Jayden sat back down, trying to gather his thoughts.

"There's some things that are meant for a husband and wife," he said slowly. "I'm not comfortable with everything we've been doing."

Diamond's eyes widened like he had just spoken another language. "Where is this coming from? You been acting different since you got out. "Did something bad happen to you in there?" Diamond's mind went to the disturbing reports she'd heard about what could happen to men in prison, her expression shifting with concern.

Jayden shook his head. "No. Actually, something good happened."

And so he told her. About Dre, Brother Joshua, Joe, Brooklyn, and Junior. About how jail had woken him up. About how he was trying to get back right with God.

Diamond listened, nodding slowly, lips pursed. When he was done, she exhaled. "Look, I think it's good that those men in jail found religion, but I've done my research. I don't believe in that stuff. Plus, I'm spiritual not religious. Religion's just rules, and rules ain't for me."

Jayden studied her. He hadn't expected her to understand, but maybe he had hoped for it. Hoped that something in her would click. But no.

"It's not about religion," he said finally. "It's about relationship. A relationship with God through His son, Jesus Christ."

Diamond gave him a long, unreadable look. Then she scoffed. "Aren't you the same one who used to say the story of Jesus came from older myths? What happened to all that?"

Jayden clenched his jaw. He knew she'd push back. That's who he had been. That's what he had preached. But people could change.

"Yes, I said that," he admitted. "But it's possible to see things differently. The Holy Spirit has shown me something new."

Diamond rolled her eyes. "So what, you're not allowed to have sex anymore? Sounds like a fun religion."

Jayden exhaled. He could feel the conversation spiraling. It was then that Jayden remembered Jesus' teaching about casting pearls before swine. The more he explained, the more she trampled what he said.

"It's not about fun," he said. "It's about freedom. It's about knowing your worth as a child of God. We're a Holy Nation, a Royal Priesthood. But look—you don't have to believe me. I just know I want to spend the rest of my night with the Lord."

Her expression shifted, like he had just slapped her.

"Oh, so that's what we're doing?" she scoffed, snatching up her robe. "I don't know if this is a phase or if you're really changing, but I don't like it. Call me when the real King J comes back."

She stormed out, and Jayden sat there, still feeling the warmth of her body in the air, still smelling the vanilla candle burning low.

But inside, he felt lighter.

Like he had just passed a test.

Amiyah's face flashed in his mind, nodding in approval, giving him a thumbs-up.

Jayden smiled to himself.

Maybe he really was changing.

The next morning, Jayden's phone buzzed, dragging him out of sleep. He squinted at the screen. Pharoah.

"King, what's good with you?"

Jayden exhaled. He wasn't in the mood for this conversation.

"Peace. What's up, bro?"

"I heard you been out a couple days. You don't call nobody?"

"My bad, man. I just been a little busy."

"So what's really going on? I got a text from Diamond. She said you became a Jesus freak in jail. Tell me it ain't so." Pharoah let out a sharp laugh, the kind that cut at Jayden's nerves.

"I'm just tryna live right, bro. Is there something wrong with that?"

"King, you know that's the white man's religion. You a Black king. An African warrior. Don't turn your back on your true identity."

Jayden sighed, rubbing his forehead. This was exactly why he hadn't called. He'd given Diamond a chance to hear him out, but Pharoah? Pharoah wasn't about to listen.

"I'm just moving different now, that's all. I know who I am, and I know I'm a king. But Jesus is the King of Kings."

Pharoah chuckled like Jayden had just said the sky was green. "King J, Diamond told me you ain't tryna bump or grind no more. Like you on some prude stuff. That true? You given up that sweet brown sugar?"

Jayden felt himself checking out of the conversation. "Yeah. I'll get plenty of brown sugar with my wife." He paused, feeling the weight of Pharoah's words hanging in the air, knowing he wasn't interested in entertaining this any longer. "Look, man, I gotta handle some stuff. I'll get up with you later." He said it quickly, hoping to end the conversation without further pushback.

Pharoah scoffed. "Ight, King. Hit me when you wanna link with Buffalo. I know you need that come-up. Diamond told me what happened with your stash."

For a split second, Jayden felt the old itch, the easy money calling his name. He shut it down fast. "I'm good, bro. Peace." He hung up before temptation could get a foothold.

The call left a bad taste in his mouth, like he'd just swallowed something bitter. Pharoah had painted him as a sellout, a religious freak who lost himself in jail. Jayden wasn't no fool—he knew that following Christ would come with opposition, but he hadn't expected to feel so...drained.

And hungry.

His stomach growled, reminding him he was back in the same position as the morning before. No food, no money. Linking with Buffalo would put stacks in his pocket real quick, but at what cost?

Trinity had looked out for him yesterday, but he didn't want to make a habit of showing up at her door with an empty stomach. The only other person he could think of who'd feed him, no questions asked, was his Aunt Patrice. He hadn't been to her house in almost a year. His little sister had moved out six months ago, off doing big things—college graduate, elementary school teacher, her own apartment and everything. But his cousins, Saraiah and Isaiah, they'd still be there.

Uncle Bernard too.

That thought sat heavy on his chest. The last few weeks he lived with them, he and Uncle Bernard barely spoke. The man always looked at him like he was just another lost cause.

But right now, hunger trumped pride.

Jayden pulled out his phone and dialed.

"Hey, baby!" Aunt Patrice's warm voice filled the line. "Good to hear from you. Staying out of trouble, I hope." She chuckled.

"Yes, ma'am. I'm doing good. Just been thinking about y'all. Figured I'd come by and check y'all out."

"Well, your uncle's at work and the kids are at school, but you know my door is always open."

Jayden glanced at the time. It was Thursday. Of course they'd be at school. He felt out of sync.

"That's cool. I'll settle for you," he joked.

She laughed. "Come on by. The kids get home at three. They'd love to see you."

"Ok auntie. See you in about an hour."

Before he left his house, an old habit whispered in his mind. Roll a blunt. Light up.

This time, the craving wasn't just outside temptation—it was coming from within him. His body, his mind, his past life, calling him back. He shook it off. The last thing he wanted was to show up at his aunt's house high.

He showered, threw on some fresh clothes, and headed out.

When he arrived, Aunt Patrice greeted him with open arms. "Come on in, nephew. Make yourself at home. I haven't cooked, but you know the fridge is yours."

Jayden didn't need to be told twice. He made himself a bagel with cream cheese, grabbed a bowl of cereal, and sat down at the kitchen table. His aunt sat across from him, watching like she was reading between the lines of his face.

"I visited New Life last night," he told her between bites. "Met Pastor Mike, joined the group."

Her smile was knowing. "That man is a blessing. He's got a real heart for the youth."

They talked about church, upcoming events, all the things he'd missed. Then, she switched gears.

"Isaiah asks about you often. We didn't tell him about your arrest. I figured that was your business to share." She paused. "Your uncle wanted to. Said it'd teach him a lesson."

Jayden clenched his jaw. Figures. Uncle Bernard never missed an opportunity to make him an example of what not to do.

"We're having a graduation party for him," Patrice continued. "He's heading to Howard University in the fall. We're so proud of him."

Jayden leaned back in his chair. Isaiah—college bound. It didn't surprise him, but it still hit different. To him, Isaiah was still that kid following him around, eyes full of admiration.

"That's good, Auntie. He's a special kid."

Being there, in that house, felt different from kicking it with his friends. It wasn't just familiar—it was safe.

At 3:00 sharp, Isaiah came through the door, his grin wide. "Jayden!"

Jayden pulled him into a hug. "What's up, lil' cuz? How you been?"

"I'm good! Just tryna get through these last few weeks of high school so I can start that college life."

Jayden laughed. "I hear that."

Saraiah came home half an hour later, just as happy to see him. They all sat around talking until Jayden and Isaiah decided to take it outside for some basketball.

As they shot hoops, Jayden kept his tone light but his words heavy. "There's a lot of distractions out here, man. Keep Christ deep in your heart. Don't waver."

Isaiah nodded, eyes serious. "I hear you."

An hour later, Aunt Patrice called from the door. "Jayden! You staying for dinner?"

The thought of facing Uncle Bernard made Jayden hesitate. But the hunger won.

"Yes, ma'am," he said.

His aunt smiled. "Good."

Jayden let out a breath.

Jayden was flipping through one of Patrice's books about living a life for Christ, trying to absorb the words, when he heard the front door open. He looked up just as Uncle Bernard stepped inside, shaking off the weight of the workday. Their eyes met, and Bernard's brow lifted in surprise.

"Jayden," he said, setting his keys on the table. "Didn't know you were stopping by. It's been a long time."

Jayden had been running through different ways to present himself when he finally faced his uncle. He wanted to come off as different—as better. "Yeah, I stopped by New Life Church last night," he said, slipping it in like an offering. "I was just telling Aunt Patrice about it. And I wanted to see everyone, too." He figured throwing in church might smooth things over.

Bernard studied him, his expression unreadable. "So, what's been going on with you? I heard you had a situation."

Jayden knew the jail question would come sooner or later. This was definitely sooner. The old him would've found a way to downplay it, make it seem like no big deal. But he was trying to live differently now. Own up to things. "Yeah, Uncle Bernard," he admitted, keeping his tone steady. "I messed up. But I'm working on getting my life back on track."

Bernard gave a slow nod. "Well, that's good," he said. "I hope so."

Their conversation barely scratched the surface, but neither seemed too eager to dig deeper. Bernard went to change out of his work clothes, and Jayden went back to his book, though his mind kept drifting.

Thirty minutes later, Patrice called everyone for dinner. The aroma of seasoned meat and simmering vegetables wrapped around Jayden, making his stomach tighten with hunger. He took his seat at the table, feeling the tension still lingering between him and Bernard. Patrice must've felt it too, because she jumped in to break the ice.

"So, Bernard," she said, spooning rice onto her plate. "Jayden tells me he's looking to go back to school. He's such a smart young man. I know he'll do well."

Bernard nodded, chewing slowly. "Well, that's good," he said after a moment. "As long as he doesn't sabotage it again."

Jayden felt the jab but let it slide. "I'm focused now," he said simply. "I know what I want to do, and I know what I need to do to get there."

Deciding to steer the conversation elsewhere, he glanced at Isaiah. "Your son's gotten good at basketball. He was giving me a run for my money today."

Bernard smirked, setting his fork down. "Maybe your lungs aren't what they used to be."

Jayden caught the undertone—another dig, this time about his past smoking. The old him would've fired something slick right back. But he'd just read a verse in Proverbs that stuck with him: *A soft answer turns away wrath, but a harsh word stirs up anger.*

He met his uncle's gaze and, instead of pushing back, he smiled. "Yeah, Uncle Bernard, that's probably the case," he said lightly. "But I'm getting my lungs back on track."

Bernard looked momentarily thrown, as if he'd been bracing for a fight that never came. And just like that, the air shifted. The rest of dinner was easy, the conversation light—mostly about Isaiah's upcoming graduation party and what life would be like for him at Howard.

After dinner, Jayden hung back, waiting until Patrice was alone in the kitchen. She was wiping down the counter when he stepped in.

"Hey, Auntie, thanks again for dinner," he said.

"You're welcome, baby. Anytime."

Jayden hesitated, rubbing the back of his neck. "I also wanted to thank you for getting that lawyer. I really appreciate everything you do for me."

Patrice turned to face him fully, sensing something behind his words. "You're welcome, Jayden. Mr.

Cookman and I go way back. He's giving me a real good rate for your case. And trust me, he's a heck of a lawyer."

Jayden exhaled, then finally asked, "You think I could get a few bucks for gas and food until I get back on my feet?"

Patrice blinked, caught off guard. When Jayden was in jail, he had assured Trinity that he was fine financially, and she had relayed the same to Patrice.

"Oh wow, baby. Trinity said you were good with money."

Jayden sighed. No point in sugarcoating it. "I thought I was. But the police raided my room and took everything."

Patrice shook her head. "My goodness." Then, after a pause, she said, "The Bible says, *Wealth gained by dishonesty will be diminished, but he who gathers by labor will increase.*"

Jayden nodded. "Yeah. I get that now. I'm planning to start applying for jobs tomorrow."

Patrice picked up her phone. "I'm going to send you a hundred dollars. That should get you through a few days."

Relief washed over him. "Thank you, Auntie. I appreciate it."

She just smiled. "I know you do, baby."

Jayden said his goodbyes, feeling lighter than when he arrived, and headed back to the VLH.

Chapter 24

A New Assignment

Jayden spent all of Friday searching for jobs, submitting applications online to any place that was hiring. He wasn't being picky—warehouse work, cashier, landscaping—whatever would put money in his pocket. He was done with fast money, done with shortcuts.

Saturday, he dedicated to the Most High. Caleb had been telling him about the Sabbath—how the seventh day was a perpetual covenant, meant to be kept forever, a sacred time to step back from the grind and just be still. Jayden figured if anyone needed a reset, it was him. He hadn't had true quiet, just him and the Lord, in what felt like forever.

By Sunday morning, he was up early, pressing his shirt, making sure his shoes were clean. He was going back to New Life Church. It had been years since he'd seen Pastor Brown—a man he once looked up to as a father figure. He wasn't sure how people would look at him now. But he was ready. Ready to see Caleb, his aunt, his sister. The old youth group crew. He arrived an hour early, hoping to catch the pastor before service.

The moment he stepped inside, he recognized faces from years ago—people who used to see him as the kid with potential, not the one who took a detour into trouble. They greeted him with nods and smiles. Jayden nodded back, then asked for Pastor Brown. They pointed him toward the pastor's office. As he went, he couldn't help but wonder what they were thinking behind those smiles.

When he walked into the office, he found Pastor Brown deep in conversation with Jayson, Amiyah, and Pastor Mike. Amiyah caught sight of him first.

"Jayden!" she said, her face lighting up.

Pastor Brown turned, his eyebrows lifting in surprise. "Well, look who it is. Been a long time, young man. I almost didn't recognize you."

Jayden swallowed the lump in his throat. "Yeah, I took a long way around, but I'm back now. Trying to get right."

The pastor nodded, studying him. "You used to run that youth group like a pro. You've got leadership in your bones. You still interested in running a program?"

Jayden blinked. He hadn't expected that. Leadership? Already? He felt like he was just getting started again. "Well…" He hesitated. "I'm still finding my footing. I might not be ready for that yet."

Pastor Brown smiled knowingly. "You never lose what the God puts in you. What are you interested in these days? I remember you always had your nose in a book."

Jayden thought for a moment. "Health," he said. "A lot of people get sick from things that could be avoided with the right habits. They pray for healing, but don't change how they live."

Pastor Brown leaned back in his chair, his eyes narrowing as if a thought had just clicked into place. "A Wellness Ministry," he blurted out. "That's what we need. A lot of folks in this congregation are struggling— diabetes, high blood pressure, heart issues. You might be onto something."

Amiyah clapped her hands together. "That would be amazing! You'd be perfect for that, Jayden."

Jayden felt something stir inside him. "Okay," he said, a slow smile forming. "I'd consider something like that."

"Let's talk after service," Pastor Brown said. "For now, I need to wrap up this meeting."

As Jayden turned to leave, Amiyah grinned. "Save me a seat, Wellness Minister."

Jayden chuckled and shook his head. "Alright, alright."

When service began, Pastor Brown stood at the pulpit, looking out over the congregation. "I had a sermon planned about repentance," he said. "But this morning, a young man walked into my office and reminded me of something important." He paused, scanning the crowd. "Some of you may remember him—Jayden, a former youth group leader. He's been on a journey, and this morning, he brought up something we don't talk about enough."

Jayden sat up a little straighter.

"We pray for healing every week, but we don't always address why we're sick in the first place. Our bodies are temples, but we fill them with junk—grease, sugar, chemicals. And let's not even get into the fornication still happening." A few chuckles and murmurs rippled through the crowd.

"In the Old Testament, the Temple was a building—an actual structure where the presence of the Most High dwelled. It was sacred, holy, the place where the Israelites gathered to worship, to offer sacrifices, to meet with God. But when Christ came, everything changed. He prophesied that the temple building would be destroyed, and in its place, a new temple would rise—not a building made of stone, but the body itself. The dwelling place of the Holy Spirit is no longer a structure built by human hands; it is within us. We ourselves are now the Temple of Israel."

He let that sink in for a moment, scanning the congregation.

"And yet, how do we treat this temple? We wouldn't drag filth into the Most High's house, but we put it in our bodies without a second thought. We wouldn't defile a holy sanctuary, yet we defile ourselves with things that break us down—poor food choices, lack of discipline, destructive habits. Then we come before the Father asking for healing, when the real healing starts with obedience."

Heads nodded. Some people hollered, "Amen."

"So, starting today, we're launching a Wellness Ministry," Pastor Brown continued. "A ministry that will help us take care of these temples the way we should. And I'm hoping the young man I spoke with will carry this torch."

The congregation erupted into applause, shouts of "Hallelujah!" filling the room. Jayden felt his stomach drop. He was still wrapping his mind around the idea, and now it was official. Amiyah nudged him with a knowing smile. "Looks like you got a job."

After the service, people swarmed the sign-up table, scribbling their names onto the clipboard without hesitation. Jayden spent some time catching up with

Caleb, Trinity, his Aunt Patrice, and her family. They stood outside the church, the sun warming their faces as they talked. Patrice pulled him into a tight hug, her voice thick with emotion as she told him how proud she was. Trinity teased him about his new role, while Caleb nodded approvingly, reminding him that this was just the beginning. They laughed, reminisced, and for the first time in a long time, Jayden felt surrounded by people who truly had his back. But soon, he remembered he had a meeting with Pastor Brown. With a few more handshakes and hugs, he told them he'd catch up later and made his way back inside.

By the time Jayden made it back to Pastor Brown's office, forty-five names filled the list. He barely had time to process it before stepping inside.

Pastor Brown leaned back in his chair, arms folded across his chest, a knowing smile tugging at the corner of his mouth. "They loved your idea," he said, nodding toward the clipboard. "Didn't take much convincing."

Jayden let out a breath, glancing down at the list. "I don't even know if this was really my idea," he admitted. It felt like the whole thing had taken on a life of its own, moving faster than he could catch up.

Pastor Brown chuckled. "You don't think so?" He leaned forward, resting his elbows on his desk. "Who brought it up this morning?"

Jayden shrugged. "I did, but—"

"And who's been studying health, talking about how people need to take care of their bodies?"

"I guess I have..."

Pastor Brown nodded. "You ever think maybe God was setting this up before you even realized it?"

Jayden hesitated. The weight of responsibility pressed against his chest. He had wanted to help people, sure, but leading a whole ministry? That wasn't what he expected as he walked into church today.

"If you're not ready, I understand," Pastor Brown continued. "I can always find someone else to take the lead." His tone was casual, but his eyes held the challenge.

Jayden felt the decision settle deep in his gut. He thought about how hard he had fought to get Lion Heart Healing off the ground, only to struggle for traction. Now, after a five-minute conversation before service, he had a list of forty-five people ready to follow his lead.

He lifted his chin. "I can do this."

Pastor Brown nodded, satisfied. "Good. Let's get to work."

Amiyah grinned. "And I'll help however you need."

As they talked logistics, Jayden's excitement grew.

After the meeting, they walked out, and Amiyah turned to him, eyes serious. "You know, Jayden, I'm not that little girl from youth group anymore. I'm twenty now. In college. Living on my own."

Jayden blinked, caught off guard. He hadn't seen that comment coming. It was true that he was still seeing her as a kid, but now that she said it, he saw what she meant. She wasn't just a girl from youth group anymore—she was a woman. And a beautiful one at that.

She saw the realization flicker across his face and smiled. "Hope to see you Wednesday," she said, pulling him in for a hug before walking off.

Jayden stood there for a moment, trying to process everything. A new ministry. A new path. And maybe, just maybe, a new shift he wasn't expecting.

With that, he headed back to the VLH, a different kind of energy buzzing in his chest.

When Jayden stepped back into the Violet Light House, the air inside felt different—like the energy had been sucked out, like the walls carried the weight of too many lost hours. He had walked in feeling charged, still buzzing from the morning, from the way the pastor had turned their conversation into a movement. Forty-five people signed up. Just like that. But now, standing in the doorway, he felt it—the shift.

In the living room, Essence and Royal were sunk into the couch, a cloud of weed smoke curling around them. Same scene, different day. This time, they were deep in conversation, voices thick and slow, talking about how the system was rigged, how a Black man could never get ahead because the world was built against him.

Royal caught sight of him first, holding up the blunt like an offering. "King J, just in time."

Jayden shook his head. "Nah, I'm good."

Essence smirked, exhaling a lazy cloud. "That's King Sober now," he said, nudging Royal as they both chuckled.

Jayden dapped them up, keeping it cool. "Yeah, that's me. Anyway, I got some things to handle. I'll catch up with y'all."

Royal leaned back, eyes half-lidded. "Okay, King J. We still waiting on that good Sour Diesel you used to come through with."

Jayden nodded, not bothering with a response, and headed straight for his room. The moment he shut the door, he let out a breath.

He stretched out on his bed, staring at the ceiling, replaying the last few hours. The way Pastor Brown had stood before the congregation, shifting the entire sermon because of their talk. The way people lined up to put their names on that list. The weight of stepping into something bigger than himself. It felt real. It felt right.

Then came the knock.

He sat up, unsure who it could be, but the knock carried a weight that made him hesitate before turning the handle.

Inner-G.

Chapter 25

Five Day Notice

Inner-G stood in the doorway, arms crossed, eyes sharp like he'd been waiting for this moment. "Wow. Had to come find the long-lost king myself."

Jayden let out a dry laugh. "Come on, man. It ain't even like that."

Inner-G stepped inside, his energy thick, filling up the space. "I ain't heard from you in weeks."

Jayden exhaled. "Yeah, I got locked up."

Inner-G nodded, slow. "Yeah, I heard. Also heard you been back almost a week. You hiding out or something? I ain't the police brother."

Jayden frowned. He knew Inner-G wasn't the police, but this was starting to feel like an interrogation.

"Nah, man," Jayden said, keeping his tone even. "Just been getting my head right."

Inner-G tilted his head, watching him too closely. "Been hearing things. People saying you on some white man religion stuff now. They colonize you in jail?"

Jayden felt his jaw tighten. He knew this was coming. He just hadn't expected it this soon. "Nah," he said. "Just been learning some different things."

"Oh yeah?" Inner-G leaned against the wall, arms still crossed. "What kind of 'different things' you learning?"

Jayden sighed, trying to piece together the right words. He knew how Inner-G felt about the Bible, about anything to do with Jesus. There was no changing that.

"Well," Jayden started, careful. "I been learning about the Holy Spirit. How it moves. How it works."

Inner-G let out a sharp laugh, shaking his head. "Oh, the Holy Spirit?" His smile turned razor-edged. "The same Holy Spirit that kept your mama alive?"

Jayden's breath caught.

He hadn't seen that coming.

The room turned still, heavy.

For all the time he'd known Inner-G, all the talks they'd had, he had never—not once—seen this side of him. It felt low. Vile.

Jayden's voice came out quiet, controlled. "What does my mother have to do with anything?"

Inner-G shrugged, too casual. "Just saying. You know how those people are. Talk all holy, but they live filthy."

Jayden thought about New Life Church, about the people he'd seen today—how different they felt from what Inner-G was trying to paint. He thought about the Wellness Ministry, the way folks signed up, ready to change.

"Well," Jayden said, keeping his voice even, "maybe I can help them with that."

Inner-G scoffed. "King, all I can say is—they vibrating on a lower frequency. Some people just don't want to be enlightened. And if that's what you're trying to do? You wasting your time."

Jayden let the words sit for a moment. Vibrating. Frequency. He thought about how full he had felt at church—how dead the air felt in this house. It was obvious to him now which place had the higher vibration.

"I'm heading up a Wellness Ministry," Jayden said finally. "Got forty-five people signed up. I do think I can make a difference."

Inner-G let out another sharp laugh, but this time it didn't reach his eyes. "King, don't lose your crown to a slave religion. Manifest your greatness."

Jayden nodded once. "Yeah. That's exactly what I plan to do."

Inner-G studied him for a long moment, his face hardening. "I put a lot of time into you. Saw a lot of potential." He exhaled through his nose. "I don't know what happened to you in jail, but I agree with Diamond—we need the real King J back."

He turned to leave, pausing in the doorway. "We having a crystal energy alignment ceremony later this evening. Come check it out. You need that."

No handshake. Barely even a goodbye.

And just like that, he was gone.

Jayden let out a slow breath, rolling his shoulders. The energy in the room still felt heavy, but underneath it all, deep inside himself, something else was still burning. That excitement. That certainty. He wasn't going back. He wasn't the same.

And no matter what Inner-G or anyone else thought, he knew—he was on the right path.

That evening, Jayden could hear the murmurs and rhythmic hum of the crystal energy alignment ceremony drifting down the hall, but he stayed put. He knew skipping out would widen the already growing gap between him and his housemates, but he wasn't about to sit in on something that didn't align with where he was now. The energy in the VLH felt off—like he'd stepped into the wrong frequency and everyone else was vibing to a beat he could no longer hear. Instead, he slipped out the back door, letting the night swallow him whole as he set off for a walk, hoping the fresh air would clear his head.

The next morning, a knock rattled his door, yanking him from a restless sleep. Jayden sat up, rubbing his eyes. He wasn't expecting anybody. When he opened the door, there stood Wize, arms crossed, face unreadable. In all the time Jayden had been at the VLH, Wize had never come to his room. Whatever this was, it wasn't a social call.

"Grand rising, King J. What's good?" Wize said, his tone smooth but measured.

Jayden nodded, masking his suspicion. "Peace, Wize. Everything's good. What's good with you?"

"You missed a powerful energy alignment last night," Wize said. "Thought you were gonna come through."

Jayden shrugged. "Had some things to take care of."

Wize let a slow smirk tug at the corner of his mouth, like he saw straight through that excuse but wasn't going to press. "I hear you," he said. "Anyway, hate to bother you like this, but rent's due. When you planning to handle that?"

Jayden blinked, caught off guard. Rent? Now they were pressing him about rent? When he first moved in, they gave him space, said they understood he was getting back on his feet. He'd been here long enough to know this wasn't about money.

"Oh, yeah, I got you," Jayden said carefully. "Cops raided my room, took everything. My whole stash. I'm looking for a job now, but I'll have it soon."

Wize studied him, eyes narrowing just enough to make Jayden feel like he was being weighed and measured. "Really? King J getting a job? That's new." He let the words settle, then added, "I'll give you 'til Friday."

Jayden gave a slow nod. "Cool. I got you."

And just like that, Wize was gone.

Jayden sat there for a long minute, staring at the spot where Wize had stood. He had five days to come up with seven hundred dollars. Even if he got hired today, a paycheck was weeks away. Still, he wasn't about to sit around and wait for a miracle. He grabbed his laptop and started firing off applications, determined to make something happen.

Later that day, his phone rang. Pastor Brown.

Jayden straightened up before answering. "Hello?"

"Jayden, son, I've been thinking about this Wellness Ministry, and I'm excited about what's happening. I want to move forward. Can you meet with the group tomorrow evening?"

Jayden felt a charge run through him. "Yeah, absolutely."

"Good. Come prepared with some information."

"No problem," Jayden said. If there was one thing he knew, it was health and wellness.

As soon as the call ended, he went to work, organizing his notes. He decided to start with processed foods—the way they snuck poison into everyday meals, the dangers of high fructose corn syrup, sodium overload, artificial additives, trans fats. People didn't realize how much garbage they were eating, how it drained their energy, made them sick, stole years off their lives. The more he planned, the more charged he felt.

The folks at New Life were good people; they just needed a shift in priorities. A part of him wished Inner-G and Diamond weren't so set against Christianity. They had knowledge, insights that could have been useful if they weren't so busy shutting the door on anything that even smelled like religion. But he knew that was a dead-end road. This, the Wellness Ministry, was his path now. Whether he walked it alone or not, he was moving forward.

The next day, Jayden's phone buzzed with a call from an unknown number. He frowned at the screen, letting it ring. Probably spam. Or worse—a bill collector. Three weeks in jail had put him behind on everything. No income, no cushion, just a mess of overdue notices piling up.

A voicemail notification popped up. He sighed and pressed play.

"This message is for Jayden. This is Robert from Clean-Cut Landscaping. We received your application and were wondering if you could come down for an interview. If you're interested, please call us back."

Jayden sat up. Landscaping? He barely remembered applying, but it didn't matter. The moment he heard the callback number, he was already dialing.

Robert picked up on the first ring. "You available to come in today?"

"Yes, sir," Jayden said, maybe a little too fast, but he didn't care. "I can be there in an hour."

An hour later, Jayden sat in a small office that smelled like fresh-cut grass and motor oil. Framed pictures of neatly manicured lawns lined the walls, rows of green so perfect they looked fake. Across from him sat an older, light-skinned man, maybe early forties, stocky build, a few gold teeth flashing when he talked.

"Thanks for coming in on short notice," Robert said, scanning Jayden's application. "I see you got warehouse experience but no landscaping. That right?"

"Yes, sir," Jayden nodded. "But I can learn fast."

Robert tapped his pen against the desk, then glanced back at the paperwork. "I also noticed you left the section blank about prior arrests. We gotta have that on file."

Jayden felt heat crawl up his neck. He knew this part was coming. Still, it hit like a punch to the gut. Would his past keep him from even getting a shot? That was the game, wasn't it? Keep a man from making money the right way, then wonder why he turns to the wrong way.

Jayden took a breath. "Yes, sir. I got one arrest."

Robert leaned back, nodding, but his expression didn't change. Then, a small smile broke across his face. "Appreciate your honesty. That don't knock you outta the running. You're looking at a man who did fifteen years."

Jayden's eyes widened. "For real?"

"For real," Robert said, his voice calm, steady. "When I got out, I knew I had two choices—go back or go forward. Started this company from scratch, built it up. Stayed on the right track." He paused, looking Jayden in the eye. "There's something I like about you. If you can show up on time, put in the work, and take this job seriously, I'll give you a shot."

Jayden sat up straighter. "Yes, sir. I will."

"Good," Robert said, sliding a paper across the desk. "Since you got no experience, I'm starting you at fourteen an hour. We'll check back in a few months, see about a raise."

Fourteen an hour. It wasn't much, but it was something. A chance. That's all he needed.

"I'll take it," Jayden said without hesitation.

"Alright then." Robert stuck out his hand, and Jayden gripped it firmly.

"Be here tomorrow morning, seven sharp," Robert said. "We'll get you started."

Jayden walked out of that office feeling lighter, his steps a little quicker. He had a job. A real one. Clean-Cut Landscaping might not be his dream, but it was a way forward. And that? That was enough.

As the evening approached, Jayden felt a restless energy bubbling inside him. Nervous. Excited. Tonight was the first meeting of the Wellness Ministry, and he wanted it to go right. He told Amiyah he'd meet her at 6:30 to go over the agenda, but when he pulled up to the church, she was already outside, arms crossed, shifting from foot to foot as she waited for Pastor Brown to unlock the door.

"Been thinking about this all day," she said, eyes bright.

Jayden nodded, exhaling. "Me too."

She grinned. "This is gonna be great. I'll take notes, keep things moving."

"Appreciate you," Jayden said, and he meant it.

Pastor Brown arrived a few minutes later, greeting them with a firm handshake. "Looking forward to what you have for us tonight," he said.

By seven, folks started trickling in—slow at first, but by 7:30, more than thirty people filled the room. Jayden took a deep breath and stepped forward. He introduced himself, then launched into the topic, breaking down how processed foods chip away at health, how reading ingredient labels was a form of self-defense. Heads nodded. People leaned in, listening.

But then he got to the hard part. "When we eat low-quality food, it diminishes our quality of life," he said. "Over time, it can even lead to premature death."

A murmur rolled through the room.

A woman in the back raised her hand. "Doesn't the Lord determine when people die?"

A few amens followed.

"As long as we pray over the food, God will bless it," another woman added.

Jayden hadn't expected this pushback. The circles he used to run in never questioned that eating healthy was a key to longevity. But this was different.

He gathered his thoughts. "Yes," he said slowly. "God determines our time. But we can speed up the process."

A man frowned. "We can speed up God's decision?"

Jayden saw Pastor Brown nodding, encouraging him to keep going.

"We know God gave us free will," Jayden said. "God has a plan for us, but we don't always follow it. If someone goes out, gets drunk, and dies in a car accident, was that God's will? Did God will them to drink and drive? Or was that their choice?"

The room went quiet.

"When we eat foods that harm our bodies," Jayden continued, "we're taking the slow road to our own demise. It's no different than that drunk driver—except it happens gradually."

More murmurs. Some approving, some skeptical.

"But doesn't scripture say all foods are clean if received with thanksgiving?" a man asked.

Jayden didn't hesitate. "That verse has to be taken in context. The Israelites already knew the dietary laws in Deuteronomy, so Paul didn't need to clarify that. What he was saying was that strict diets—like only eating vegetables—aren't necessary for righteousness. But that doesn't mean God's original laws about food don't matter."

"But aren't we under grace?" a woman challenged. "Why worry about laws? Jesus did away with all that."

Jayden was ready. "Jesus didn't do away with the law. Just the law of sacrifice—because He became the sacrifice for our sins. But He said Himself in Matthew 5:17—He didn't come to destroy the law, but to fulfill it. He even warned that whoever breaks the least commandment and teaches others to do so will be least in the kingdom of heaven. Paul backed this up in Romans 3:31—'Do we then make void the law through faith? God forbid: we establish the law.'"

People sat up. Some nodded. Some whispered to their neighbors.

A man in the back raised his hand. "So you think God will punish us if we don't eat right?"

Jayden shook his head. "We punish ourselves. With our choices. On Sunday, Pastor Brown told us—we are the temple of God. First Corinthians 3:17 says, 'If any man defile the temple of God, him shall God destroy.' When we destroy our bodies, we seal our fate."

A few people nodded. Others shook their heads, unwilling to budge.

One woman crossed her arms. "Well, I'm still gonna eat my BBQ ribs," she said with a laugh.

Laughter rippled through the room. But then, a man in the front spoke up. "Nah, he's right. We gotta do better. Look around—so many of us sick. We gotta stop playing with our lives."

A few scattered amens. A low rumble of agreement.

By the end of the night, people weren't just questioning Jayden—they were asking him for guidance. What should they eat? What brands should they look for? How could they start? The meeting was supposed to end at nine, but folks lingered, hungry for more, stretching it until nearly 9:45.

Pastor Brown finally stepped in. "Before we close, let's take up an offering for the ministry," he said.

Afterward, as Jayden and Amiyah packed up, Pastor Brown clapped him on the back. "You did good tonight, son. Real good."

Amiyah grinned. "They were engaged the whole time. I think you got yourself a real ministry here."

Jayden nodded, a slow smile spreading across his face. "Yeah," he said. "I think so too."

As he drove back to the VLH, he felt something deep in his chest. Not just happiness. Not just relief. Something purer. Stronger.

It was a high. But not the kind he used to chase. This? This was real.

Jayden spent the rest of the week grinding at the landscaping job, his body sore but his mind sharp, locked in on that paycheck. Robert told him he'd get paid for the three days on Friday. That was a relief—sooner than he expected—but it still wasn't enough to cover the $700 rent. After taxes, he'd be walking away with a little over $300. Not even half.

When he got home that evening, his stomach knotted up. He wasn't sure what to tell Wize. The man had looked real serious when he said, *Friday, no later.*

Jayden considered an option—hustle, maybe try to flip something quick—but he pushed that thought away. He wasn't that dude anymore. He had to do this right.

All Jayden could think was, *I'm about to be homeless.*

He paced his room, running his hands over his face. This wasn't supposed to happen. Not after everything. Not after he'd been working, doing right, trying to walk the straight path. He needed more time—just one more week, and he'd have another paycheck, enough to cover the rent.

He decided to go talk to Wize. Be straight with him. Wize had to understand—this wasn't Jayden being irresponsible. Life had just thrown him a punch, and he was still trying to get up.

Jayden went upstairs and knocked. Wize opened the door, face blank, unreadable.

"Peace, brother," Jayden said, holding out the money. "I got some of the rent. I apologize; it's been a rough few weeks. I'll have the rest for you next week, for sure."

Wize didn't even look at the cash. Didn't move to take it.

"You got *some* of it?" He crossed his arms. "King, we need *all* of it. You think Joe, the owner, takes partial payments? If you don't got it today, pack your stuff up.

We got somebody ready to move in that can pay the full amount.”

Jayden felt his stomach drop. He hadn’t expected that.

They could have spotted him the rest if they wanted to. He knew that. And if this was just about money, they would have. But it wasn’t. This was about something deeper.

“Aight, bro,” Jayden said, slipping the cash back into his pocket. “I’ll get the rest.”

Wize didn’t nod. Didn’t shake his hand. Just turned and shut the door.

Jayden went back to his room, heart pounding. *How am I supposed to come up with almost $400 by the end of the day?*

He tried not to go there, but the questions started creeping in. *God, where you at?* He had been trusting, believing, moving forward. Now he was about to be out on the street. *God, you know I need a place to stay. How you just gonna let me hang like this?*

Silence. Jayden didn’t hear anything from God.

Reality sank in. *I gotta pack my stuff.*

He had money to rent a room for a few nights. If he found something cheap, he could possibly stretch it until payday. He grabbed his laptop, started searching. Found a no-frills motel, $50 a night. It would have to do.

Jayden began packing, his movements slow, mechanical. This wasn't how the week was supposed to end. Just a few days ago, he'd been feeling good, like his life was finally lining up. And now? Now he was just another man with a few possessions but nowhere to go.

Jayden packed his car to the brim, cramming in clothes, shoes, and everything he owned. Boxes stacked on the seats, bags filled every gap. As he shut the door, the weight of it all settled on his chest. It felt final. He turned as he heard the front door creak open behind him.

Panther stepped out, slow and steady, like he'd been waiting for the right moment. He crossed the porch with purpose, bare feet hitting the wooden steps like soft drums. His locs were tied back, and his eyes carried that quiet fire Jayden had come to recognize— an old soul kind of knowing.

He walked up and gave Jayden a firm pound, then held it a moment longer. "I been hearing how they talk about you," he said, voice low, words weighted with meaning. "Little whispers, sideways glances, all that coward talk folks do behind your back. But you? You stood tall.

Didn't bend, didn't try to fit in where your spirit don't belong. That's rare. That's warrior work."

Jayden nodded, jaw tightening, a mix of gratitude and grief swimming behind his eyes. "I appreciate you, bro. For real. I'll definitely stay in touch."

Panther looked him over one last time, then gave a half smile. "You always got a comrade in me, brother. Wherever you land."

They shared a final salute—solid, grounded, the kind of gesture that said more than words ever could.

Before he left, Jayden went back upstairs and knocked on Wize's door one last time. When Wize opened it, Jayden held his head high.

"I couldn't come up with the rest. I'm leaving."

Wize looked him up and down, arms still folded. Then, that smirk—slow, knowing.

"I guess your God couldn't help you with this one."

Jayden clenched his jaw. He knew then—this was never about the money. Wize had been waiting for this moment.

Jayden met his gaze, steady. "My God will provide."

Wize let out a low chuckle. "You stopped manifesting and started believing in some imaginary God. Look where it got you." He shrugged. "I'll let everybody know you're out."

Jayden didn't say another word. Didn't give Wize the satisfaction of a response. He just turned and walked away.

Headed for the motel.

Headed for whatever came next.

Chapter 26

Divine Redirection

Jayden lay stiff on the hard motel mattress, staring at the ceiling, his mind tangled in frustration. How could God let this happen? If He saw everything, if He knew Jayden was trying—really trying—shouldn't He step in? Shouldn't He make a way? Why was God silent to my plea? The room felt cold, empty in a way that had nothing to do with temperature.

He reached for his Bible, flipping it open with shaky hands. His eyes landed on Philippians 4:19: *"And my God will supply every need of yours according to his riches in glory in Christ Jesus."* He exhaled sharply. *I sure hope so.*

His mind drifted to Wize, that smug look, the unspoken *I told you so.* And the others—Diamond, Royal, Essence, Inner-G—they'd all be talking, shaking their heads. *Look at him now. Mr. Holy Man. Put all that faith in God, and where did it get him?* The thought gnawed at him, made his chest tight. He wanted to prove them wrong, to show them his God was real. But tonight, with his life packed into a car and his body stretched across a scratchy motel blanket, he wasn't sure how to do that.

The questions circled, doubt creeping in like a slow-moving fog. Eventually, exhaustion pulled him under, but even in sleep, the weight of it all lingered.

Jayden woke up feeling something he hadn't expected—peace. Not relief, not excitement, just a deep, unshaken calm. He had already decided he'd spend the entire Saturday resting, soaking in the Sabbath, reading his Bible. The motel check-out was at 10:00 a.m., so he went ahead and booked another night. Another $50 gone. At this rate, he knew his money would run out by Wednesday, maybe Thursday. Still, despite everything—being uprooted, being broke—he felt steady, like something unseen was holding him up.

Sunday morning, Jayden extended his stay one more night before heading out to New Life Church. He was looking forward to seeing the people from the Wellness Ministry. After last week's meeting, so many had come up to him, thanking him, saying they'd be back. That meant something.

He arrived fifteen minutes early and spotted Pastor Brown near the front. As soon as their eyes met, the pastor motioned him over.

"Meet me in my office after service," Pastor Brown said.

Jayden nodded.

When service began, Pastor Brown did his usual warm welcome, then opened his Bible. His voice rang out strong:

"Blessed is the man who remains steadfast under trial, for when he has stood the test he will receive the crown of life, which God has promised to those who love him."

Jayden sat up. Just a few words in, and the message had already gripped him. The past week had tested him in ways he never imagined, and doubt had slithered into his mind more than once. But he'd already decided—he wasn't making the same mistake again. He wouldn't turn his back on God just because things got hard. That was how he got lost in the first place.

Pastor Brown's voice rang out over the congregation. "Sometimes, God has a strange way of working. It can feel like we're left out in the cold. We cry out, but Yahweh stays silent. It's in these times that our faith is tested the most. But if we endure, as the disciple James said, we receive the crown of life. And if we don't?" He let the words hang in the air before shaking his head. "Well, that's when another level of misfortune sets in.

We don't serve a God of instant gratification, a God of wishes granted on demand. We serve a God who teaches us through long suffering, who builds in us perseverance, patience, and faith."

Jayden leaned forward, elbows on his knees, hanging onto every word. It was like Pastor Brown had stepped into his motel room the night before and read the thoughts off his pillow.

The pastor closed his Bible and looked out over the congregation. "Jesus said, *'You will be hated by all men for my name's sake, but he that endures to the end will be saved.'* He didn't say those who start off on fire for the Lord but grow cold when trials come will be saved. He said those who *endure.* So that's the word I'm leaving with you today—*endure until the end.*"

A wave of hallelujahs and amens swept through the church. Claps, shouts, hands raised in the air.

But Jayden just sat still, letting it sink in, letting it settle deep. Because this wasn't just a sermon. This was God talking straight to him.

After service, Jayden lingered, catching up with his people—his Aunt Patrice and her family, Amiyah, Caleb, Trinity. They asked how he was doing, how the Wellness Ministry was going, and for a moment, he let himself soak in their warmth. But soon, he excused himself and made his way to Pastor Brown's office.

"Jayden!" Pastor Brown greeted him with a broad smile, waving him in. "Come on in, son. How are you?"

"I'm good, Pastor. That was a powerful message. I needed to hear that today," Jayden said, still feeling the weight of the sermon in his chest.

"Glad to hear that. The Word has a way of meeting us right where we are," Pastor Brown said, nodding. "I wanted to take a moment to congratulate you on a successful first meeting with the Wellness Ministry. I've been getting messages all week—folks saying how much they got out of it, how they're looking forward to the next one."

Jayden smiled, grateful. "That's good to hear. I'll definitely be back with more."

Pastor Brown slid an envelope across the desk. "This is from the collection we took during the meeting. I want you to have it."

Jayden hesitated, then picked up the envelope and peeked inside. His eyes widened—$436. His mind reeled. He hadn't expected that. Not even close.

Pastor Brown chuckled at Jayden's stunned expression. "Yes, son. When you do the Lord's work without expectations, He will bless you."

Jayden swallowed hard, nodding. "Thank you, Pastor. This is going to help me a lot right now." He didn't go into details about losing his place, just vaguely mentioned he was going through some things.

Pastor Brown leaned back in his chair, watching him. "God will supply every need of yours according to His riches in glory in Christ Jesus."

Jayden stiffened. That was the exact verse he had read the night before at the motel. A chill ran through him. If there had been any doubt, it was gone now—God was at work.

As he drove back to the motel, gratitude filled him, but questions still lingered. If he'd gotten this money two days earlier, he could've kept his place. Why now? Why not when he was pleading with God, desperate to stay at the Violet Light House?

He gripped the steering wheel, his jaw tightening. He could still hear Wize's voice, smug and dismissive—"*I guess your God couldn't help you with this one.*" And in that moment, it had felt true. It had felt like God had left him out there, watching as he packed up his life and drove off to a shabby motel.

He exhaled hard, rolling down the window as if the rush of air might clear his mind. His family always said, "*God is always on time.*" But was He? Because this felt two days late.

He drummed his fingers on the wheel, his emotions twisting in knots. *Is this a test?* Was God waiting to see if he would still trust Him even when things didn't go his way?

Why does it have to be like this? Jayden thought bitterly. *Why does following You feel like always walking blindfolded, hoping I don't trip?*

His mind went back to Pastor Brown's sermon. *"We don't serve a God of instant gratification and granting wishes. We serve a God who teaches us to endure long suffering while building patience and faith."*

Jayden replayed those words in his head, rolling them over like stones in his palm. Was that really how God worked? Letting people struggle just to build their patience? That didn't sit right with him. He wasn't looking for an easy way out—he was doing the work, trying to live right. So why did it feel like God waited until he lost everything before stepping in? Would this so-called lesson have been any less effective if the money had come two days earlier?

He pulled into the motel parking lot and shut off the engine, gripping the keys in his hand. He was grateful— he really was. He had a roof over his head, money in his pocket, a new opportunity right in front of him. But deep down, he couldn't shake the feeling that he was missing something. That maybe he didn't understand God as well as he thought he did.

Back at the motel, Jayden sat on the bed and pulled out his laptop. It was time to look for a permanent place. He had steady income now—he could afford a studio. His search turned up several options, most ranging between $850 and $1,200 per month. Two stood out, both just outside the Arts District. One was $950 a month, the other $1,000. The second one caught his eye—it was running a special: first month free and only $500 to move in. That was a deal he couldn't pass up. He applied for both and waited.

Minutes after submitting the second application, a message popped up: *Pre-approved. An agent will follow up shortly.*

Jayden barely had time to process before his phone rang. A leasing manager from the second apartment introduced herself. "We got your application. If you're free today, you can come take a tour. I'll be in the office until five."

Jayden didn't hesitate. "I'll be there."

He hopped in his car and drove straight over. The building was clean, the unit spacious enough. The leasing agent showed him around, listing amenities, but Jayden barely heard her. The moment he stepped inside, he knew—this was it.

"If you're interested, we have a unit available," she said.

"Yes, ma'am," Jayden blurted, almost shouting.

Within thirty minutes, he had signed the paperwork, handed over the $500 deposit, and walked out with the keys to his new apartment.

"Wow." Jayden sat in his car for a moment, gripping the key in his palm. He couldn't believe how smooth it had all gone.

He spent the next hour moving his things in, trip after trip from his car to his new apartment. With every box he unloaded, it sank in deeper—he wasn't homeless anymore. God had provided.

By Tuesday evening, Jayden was running on fumes. The sun had been relentless all day, beating down on him while he landscaped, his shirt clinging to his back, dirt settling deep under his fingernails. He wanted nothing more than to collapse onto his bed, maybe let the TV drone on in the background while he let the exhaustion take him. But there was no time for that—tonight was the second Wellness Ministry meeting, and people were expecting him.

Sighing, he grabbed a clean towel and hopped into the shower, letting the warm water wash the day off him. As the dirt swirled down the drain, so did some of the tension, but the fatigue lingered. He pushed through it. He had a lesson to deliver.

He flipped through his notes one last time before heading out. Tonight's lesson? Fresh air, sunshine, and exercise. The irony wasn't lost on him. He'd had more than his fill of all three today. As he pulled into the church parking lot, he saw a steady flow of people walking inside, more than last week. He barely made it through the doors before people he hardly knew started coming up to him, saying how much they were looking forward to the session. The weight of their expectations pressed down on him. He hadn't signed up to be a preacher, but here he was, leading a ministry, answering questions, guiding people. How had his life shifted so drastically in just a few months?

He spotted Pastor Brown up front, deep in conversation with Amiyah and two other members. Jayden made his way over, and the pastor greeted him warmly.

"There's definitely a lot of interest," Pastor Brown said, motioning toward the growing crowd.

Jayden nodded, scanning the faces in the room. His aunt, his sister Trinity, John, and Caleb had just arrived, finding seats near the middle. At exactly 7:15 PM, Pastor Brown stepped forward, raising a hand for quiet.

"Greetings, everyone, in the name of the Father, the Son, and the Holy Spirit. Welcome back to our second Wellness Ministry meeting," he said, his voice rich and full of authority. "I see we've already grown since last week."

Jayden took a deep breath and looked out. By his count, there were at least fifty people—almost double last week. The pastor turned to him with a smile. "I won't hold you all up. I know you're not here to hear me preach. Let's welcome our wellness minister—Pastor Jayden."

Jayden felt his stomach twist at the title. Pastor Jayden. It felt surreal, like hearing someone else's name. Just a few months ago, he'd been doubting, running, questioning. Now he was standing in front of a congregation, leading a ministry. Pastor Brown had assured him he'd continue discipling him, preparing him for the role, but still—it was overwhelming.

He stepped forward, greeted the crowd, and launched into his lesson. "I want to talk today about the importance of fresh air, sunshine, and exercise."

A few scattered "Amen's" filled the room, but he also caught a few confused looks. He kept going, explaining how most people spent their lives indoors, breathing stale air, glued to screens, moving less and less. He talked about how sunlight helped the body produce vitamin D, how fresh air improved lung health, how outdoor time reduced stress and boosted the immune system. He broke it down in ways they could understand, made it practical.

Then, a hand went up.

He hesitated. He'd planned to hold questions until the end, but leaving her sitting there with her hand raised felt wrong. "Yes, ma'am?" he said.

She stood. "Is any of this in the Bible?"

Jayden exhaled slowly. He should've seen that coming. This was church, after all. He could feel the room shifting, people waiting to see how he'd answer. But even as the question settled in the air, the response came to him, almost like it had been waiting for this moment.

"Ma'am, you have to remember—people spent most of their time outdoors in Biblical days. This issue we have today, staying inside all the time? That's new. Just like you won't find airplanes in the Bible, you won't find warnings about sitting inside all day. It wasn't a problem back then. Jesus wasn't hopping in a car and walking into buildings from the parking lot. He walked, miles at a time, from one town to another. So did the people following him. And carrying water from wells? That's exercise. Anyone ever carried a full bucket of water? It's heavy. The people in Biblical times got plenty of fresh air, sunshine, and exercise just from living."

A murmur spread through the room. Heads nodded. A few scattered "Amen's" followed. Jayden glanced at Pastor Brown, who smiled, encouraging him to keep going.

"The Bible tells us not to eat pork or shrimp," Jayden continued, "but it doesn't say anything about crack cocaine. Why? Because crack didn't exist back then. If the Bible was written today, it would definitely warn against it. Some things we have to let the Holy Spirit teach us. And in Luke 24:15, it says, 'Jesus Himself, having drawn near, was walking along with them.' Jesus walked. Not drove, not hopped in a Lyft—he walked. We talk about walking spiritually with Jesus, but we can't forget to walk literally, too. Get active."

This time, the reaction was bigger—smiles, nods, murmurs of agreement. A few skeptical faces still lingered, but Jayden could feel the shift. He had their attention. More importantly, he had planted a seed. And that was enough.

As the meeting wrapped up, Pastor Brown called for another offering to support the ministry. People lingered, circling Jayden, clapping him on the back, shaking his hand.

"Man, you keep expanding my mind every time, brother," one man told him, his eyes bright with excitement.

Pastor Brown gave Jayden a firm pat on the back. "Well done, son."

Amiyah beamed at him. "You don't even realize the impact you're making. People keep telling me they're changing their eating habits—all because of you!"

Jayden chuckled, shaking his head. It was still surreal.

His Aunt Patrice and Trinity pulled him into a hug. "You look like a natural up there," Patrice said, pride shining in her eyes.

Then Caleb stepped forward. "Pastor Jayden," he said with a grin, his voice full of admiration. It was almost the same look he used to give Jayden back when they were kids in the youth group.

For the next thirty minutes, Jayden stood among them, talking, laughing, answering more questions. Slowly, the crowd thinned, leaving only Pastor Brown, Amiyah, Caleb, Trinity, and John. The room felt warm, full of familiarity and quiet joy.

Jayden decided it was the perfect time to share his news. "Well, y'all, I got a new apartment," he said, grinning.

A chorus of surprise followed. Trinity's eyes widened. "Wow, really? Thank God! I was praying He'd bless you with a new place," Trinity said with a grin. "I never liked that house you were living in. Too much negativity, too many people stuck in cycles they don't want to break."

Jayden nodded, but Trinity's words stuck with him. *I was praying God would give you a new living situation.*

A revelation settled over him, deep and unshakable.

Looking back, everything aligned too perfectly to be random—the eviction, the unexpected check, the apartment deal. And then it struck him even harder—God hadn't just provided; He had *redirected* him.

Jayden had fought to stay at Violet Light House, convinced it was where he belonged. But was it? The negativity, the sideways glances, the quiet doubt from people who didn't share his faith. If the money had come two days earlier, he would've paid rent and stayed stuck. But God had something *better*. He had *orchestrated* a way out.

He exhaled, a weight lifting from his chest. "Yeah," he said, his voice steady. "God is definitely at work."

He let that truth sit with him for a moment before flashing another grin. "I want y'all to come by after service Sunday. Housewarming at my place."

Laughter and excitement bubbled up around him.

"Oh, we'll be there," Amiyah said.

"No doubt," Caleb added.

Jayden looked around at the faces of the people who had stood by him, who believed in him. He wasn't just starting over—he was stepping into something new, something bigger than himself.

As Jayden walked Amiyah to her car, she beamed at him. "I'm so glad you're back at New Life," she said. "You have no idea how much of an impact you've made in just a few weeks—just like you did with the youth group back in the day."

Jayden smiled, grateful for her words. "And I appreciate you," he said. "None of this would've happened without your support."

Amiyah hesitated for a moment, then let out a soft laugh. "You know, I used to have the biggest crush on you," she admitted. "I imagined us getting married, having this big wedding—the whole thing."

Jayden chuckled, but something in her words struck deeper than he expected. He looked at her, really looked at her. A woman of faith, solid values, kindness, beautiful brown skin with natural braids, and unwavering support- what more could a man ask for? She challenged him and wasn't always agreeable, but he knew she always had his best interest at heart. Holding her gaze, he grinned. "He who finds a wife finds a good thing," he said, winking.

Amiyah blinked, caught off guard. She wasn't expecting that.

Jayden surprised even himself with his next words. "I mean it," he said, his voice steady but his heart racing. "I didn't realize this before, but standing here with you, hearing what you just said, something clicked. It feels right. Like maybe this is something God's been aligning all along, and I just wasn't paying attention. I'd like us to spend more time together, really get to know each other, and see where this could go—toward something real. Prayerfully to the vision you had when you were younger"

For a moment, Amiyah just stood there, processing his words. Then, slowly, her lips curved into the biggest smile. "I'd like that," she finally said.

They ended up standing in the parking lot for three more hours, talking about everything and nothing, as if time had no hold on them at all.

Chapter 27

Pre-Trial Conference

Three Months Later

Jayden had finally told Pastor Brown, Amiyah, Caleb, and a few others he was close to about his arrest. He didn't see the point in keeping it a secret—he was still facing charges, and prison time was a real possibility. They prayed over him, laid hands on him, but the truth of what Dre had told him back in jail never left his mind: Sometimes, you gotta pay for the things you did before you gave your life to the Lord.

He met with his attorney, Mr. Cookman, several times. Cookman assured him that, because it was his first offense, he probably wouldn't get the maximum eight-year sentence. But they would have to fight hard to keep him from doing any time at all. They planned to push for a plea deal at the pre-trial conference.

Meanwhile, his life on the outside kept moving. He and Amiyah had grown close—closer than he thought possible. He wanted to propose, to build something real with her, but he didn't want to start a marriage from a prison cell. He told her as much. If he got years, she didn't have to wait for him. But Amiyah had squared her shoulders, looked him dead in the eye, and said, *"I'll wait."*

Still, as the trial date loomed, anxiety clawed at him. He had no problem taking responsibility—he wasn't running from his past—but the thought of going back behind bars, being stripped of this new life he'd built, gnawed at him. During the day, he worked his landscaping job under the hot sun, pouring sweat into the soil. On Tuesday nights, he led the Wellness Ministry, which had grown to over a hundred people. Wednesdays, he sat in on youth meetings, sharing his story with kids who still had time to make different choices. His off days were filled with Amiyah, Caleb, Trinity, John, or his Aunt Patrice's home-cooked meals. For the first time in a long time, things felt *right*. But his past still threatened to snatch it all away.

The night before his pre-trial, the weight of it pressed heavy. He prayed, but doubt crept in. *The What ifs?* Amiyah stayed with him late, doing her best to keep his mind at ease. Before she left, she took his hands in hers, closed her eyes, and prayed:

*"Father God, we come before You today, standing on Your promises, trusting in Your word, and believing in Your justice. Lord, You know every detail of Jayden's heart, his journey, and the struggles that brought him here. You are a God of redemption, a God who turns ashes into beauty, who makes crooked paths straight. Right now, Lord, I ask that You go before him into that courtroom. Be his defender, his shield, his strong tower. Let the truth be revealed, and let Your favor rest upon him.

Lord, remind Jayden that no matter what happens today, he is not walking in there alone. You are with him. Your hand is on his life, and Your plan is greater than any ruling made by man. Give him peace that surpasses understanding. Let him walk in confidence, not in fear, knowing that his future is in Your hands.

We declare victory, Lord—not just in this trial, but in Jayden's life. You have already started a good work in him, and we trust You to bring it to completion. We thank You in advance for the doors You are opening, the lessons You are teaching, and the testimony that will come from this moment.

In Jesus' mighty name, Amen."*

As she spoke, something in Jayden shifted. He felt it— peace, real peace—rolling over him like a wave. He wasn't in control. He never had been. And maybe that was okay.

The next morning, he woke up steady. No panic, no dread. Just resolve. He met Mr. Cookman outside the courthouse, went through security, the metal detectors, the long hallway, all of it. The lawyer reminded him to be personable, to smile, to let them *see* who he'd become. Jayden nodded. He could do that—because it wasn't an act.

Inside the courtroom, he scanned the faces. The prosecutor sat stiff in his sharp brown suit, his slicked-back hair too neat, his eyes too cold. He was all business, no concern for Jayden as a man. The bailiffs stood like stone, reminding Jayden too much of jail guards—watching, waiting for someone to step out of line. He wasn't planning to. But he knew with men like them, it didn't take much.

Then, the judge entered. Jayden's eyes narrowed. Something about him seemed *familiar*—the clean-cut look, the receding hairline, the slightly rounded belly. *Where do I know him from?*

The prosecutor started in, his voice sharp, listing Jayden's past mistakes like they defined him. *A deviant, a repeat offender in the making.*

Then, Mr. Cookman stood, his tone calm but firm. He spoke of Jayden's transformation—his ministry, his work, his clean drug tests, the lives he was impacting.

And the whole time, the judge kept looking at Jayden. Not just *at* him—*through* him. Jayden couldn't place the expression.

Finally, the judge leaned forward and spoke.

"Young man, I've seen many faces in this courtroom, but I didn't realize yours was on my docket until I walked in today. Over the past four weeks, I've come to know you in a completely different setting—not as a defendant, but as a leader. I've been attending the Wellness Ministry at New Life, and I must say, I've been inspired by what you're doing.

"I've seen firsthand the work you're doing. You're guiding people toward better health—physically, mentally, and spiritually. I, myself, have taken some of your advice. I've been making changes—less sodium, more water, walking every morning. You said it could lower blood pressure naturally, and you know what? It's working."

"When I first saw your name here, I had to stop and think. Justice isn't just about punishment; it's about recognizing change, supporting redemption, and ensuring that a man who is actively changing lives—

including his own—has the opportunity to keep moving forward."

"Mr. Thomas, you've motivated people. You've given them hope. You've shown them change is possible. And I believe in second chances. So, I'm not going to stand in the way of the work you're doing. You will complete your community service—but what you've built at New Life will count toward it. Because, in truth, you're already serving your community in ways a court order never could."

"But hear me on this—you must remain consistent. You must continue walking this path. If you do, this court will consider your debt to society paid in full. But if you stray, if you find yourself back in front of me for any wrongdoing, there will be no leniency next time."

"Stay free in Christ, Jayden. That's the kind of freedom no courtroom can grant or take away. Case closed."

The gavel hit.

Jayden sat still, his brain catching up. *Did that just happen?*

He turned to Mr. Cookman, confused.

The lawyer leaned in, a small smile playing at his lips. *"Son, you have angels watching over you. The judge just cleared you."*

A slow grin spread across Jayden's face. He reached for Cookman's hand, shaking it tight.

The Lord truly *was* good.

Follow-Up

A year after Jayden walked out of that courtroom a free man, he stood at the altar, watching Amiyah walk toward him, her veil floating like a whisper, her eyes locked on his. They had weathered storms together, but now, they were stepping into the light. Amiyah had honored her commitment and graduated the Purity Challenge, and Jayden had followed through on his own purity recommitment, walking in discipline and faith for the full year of their engagement. Their journey was just beginning, built on love, faith, and the kind of strength that only comes from walking through the fire and coming out refined.

For a while, Jayden stuck with his landscaping job—hands in the earth, sweat on his brow, the kind of work that kept a man grounded. But the call on his life was bigger. The Wellness Ministry kept growing—fifty, then a hundred, then three hundred people showing up every Tuesday night, hungry for change, for healing, for the kind of wisdom that didn't just extend their years but made them *worth* living. So he stepped out on faith, left the job behind, and took on the ministry full-time.

Then came the book. *Wellness in the Body of Christ: Living a Healthy Christian Lifestyle*. He never thought of himself as an author, but the words flowed like testimony, like truth that had been waiting to be told. The book flew off shelves, became a bestseller, found its way into homes, churches, and hospital waiting rooms. Major online retailers still sell it to this day.

Success brought him to stages around the world, preaching what he had lived—how faith and health walk hand in hand, how addiction loses its grip when people have the tools to break free. He spoke in churches, schools, rehab centers, prisons—anywhere they would listen. And they did.

Then one day, another door opened—one he never expected. His father.

They started talking, slowly at first. Two men, bound by blood, divided by time. But the more they spoke, the more Jayden saw the reflection. His father's past was his own. The same streets. The same choices. The same brokenness. But also, now, the same redemption. His father had given his life to Christ too, and for the first time, Jayden didn't just see him as the man who had been absent—he saw him as a man who had fought demons of his own.

Forgiveness wasn't a single moment. It was a series of conversations, of understanding, of choosing to let go of the weight he had carried since he was a boy. And in doing so, Jayden freed himself, too.

His life had been a story of second chances. And he had made the most of every one.

About the Author

Karajah Yashar is a counselor, educator, and publisher with a deep passion for culture, spirituality, and storytelling. A graduate of Rutgers University with a degree in Anthropology, he has worked with institutions such as the University of Central Florida, Rutgers University, and The Transition House, where he served as a Substance Abuse Counselor for incarcerated men.

In 2016, Karajah founded *Passed-Over-Press* (Formerly Blackstone Publishing), a literary house based in Orlando, Florida, dedicated to publishing works on spirituality and cultural heritage. Over the years, he has overseen the publication of hundreds of books that explore the richness of God's people and heritage.

With *The Violet Light House*, his debut fiction novel, Karajah brings his anthropological insight and real-world experience into a compelling narrative that delves into themes of self-discovery, spirituality, and redemption.